Borto Milan was b...... York, and raised in .... since then he has m........ to reside in or pass through forty-eight of the fifty American states. He has always found something energizing about being on the road, and motorcycles, traveling and writing remain his addictions.

He has been writing since he was aged thirteen – short stories, plays, novels, poetry – and his first published book, *Her Monster* (under the name Jeff Collignon), was described by Scott Bradfield in *The New York Times* as 'dark, funny, compelling and filled with a canny sense of the monstrous ... a moving and unforgettable first novel'.

The author has been settled in Naples, Florida, for five years now (something he considers a bit of a record).

Also by Borto Milan

In the Drift

Riding
Towards Home

Borto Milan

Copyright © 1995 Borto Milan

The right of Borto Milan to be identified as the Author of
the Work has been asserted by him in accordance with the
Copyright, Designs and Patents Act 1988.

First published in Great Britain in 1995
by HEADLINE BOOK PUBLISHING

First published in paperback in 1996
by HEADLINE BOOK PUBLISHING

A HEADLINE FEATURE paperback

10 9 8 7 6 5 4 3 2 1

All rights reserved. No part of this publication may be
reproduced, stored in a retrieval system, or transmitted,
in any form or by any means without the prior written
permission of the publisher, nor be otherwise circulated
in any form of binding or cover other than that in which
it is published and without a similar condition being
imposed on the subsequent purchaser.

All characters in this publication are fictitious
and any resemblance to real persons, living or dead,
is purely coincidental.

ISBN 0 7472 4787 0

Typeset by Keyboard Services, Luton, Beds

Printed and bound in Great Britain by
Mackays of Chatham PLC, Chatham, Kent

HEADLINE BOOK PUBLISHING
A division of Hodder Headline PLC
338 Euston Road
London NW1 3BH

O one, o none, o no one, o you:
Where did the way lead when it led nowhere?

Paul Celan

'There Was Earth', *Die Niemandrose*, 1963

One

The fear didn't hit Ricky until he was led into a holding cell and strip-searched. Up until that moment, Ricky still felt that everything would be all right.

It was when he was ordered to strip and grab his ankles that he suddenly realized just how serious his situation had become.

'What about my phone-call?' Ricky asked, as the desk sergeant threw him a pair of faded green overalls.

Ricky quickly grabbed them to cover his nakedness.

'You already made it.'

'There wasn't any answer.'

'That's not my problem.' The sergeant shrugged, watching as Ricky pulled on the overalls.

'But I—'

'C'mon,' the policeman interrupted impatiently, nodding towards the door.

Ricky stepped out into the hallway and started to turn towards the main office of the police station.

'No. The other way,' the sergeant grunted, reaching out and grabbing Ricky's shoulder. He held on to the boy's arm and directed him to the locked door at the end of the hall.

The metallic grate of the key in the lock echoed off the cinder-block walls.

The door swung open, and the sergeant waved him inside.

The first thing that Ricky noticed was the smell. It was a combination of urine, sweat and ammonia.

'Down at the end.' The sergeant pushed him.

Ricky stumbled, then, regaining his balance, turned to the other man.

'But what about my phone-call?' Ricky pleaded. 'I get to make at least one, don't I?'

'Quit breaking my balls, kid. You had your chance.'

'But no one was there.'

'You can try again tomorrow.'

'But what about tonight?'

'Well.' The sergeant smiled. 'Tonight you get to be the guest of the Bell County Sheriff's department. Now move your ass, kid.'

Reluctantly, Ricky turned and shuffled down the short hallway.

Bracketing each side of the hall were three cells. Five of them were empty. The sixth was occupied by three men. Ricky became the fourth.

The cell was no more than twenty feet deep by fifteen feet wide. A pair of bunks ran the length of each side of the cell. Centered against the far wall was a tiny stainless-steel sink. Set to the side of the sink, and a little below it, was a seatless porcelain toilet.

The two men sitting together on the bottom bunk examined Ricky intently as he was pushed into the cell. The

2

man on the upper bunk, across from them, appeared to be sleeping.

'My phone-call,' Ricky gasped softly, as the jailer closed and locked the cell door.

The man snorted, then turned and walked away.

Ricky held on to the bars, listening to the man's footsteps until they disappeared behind the closing door of the cell block.

'Hey, kid, what you in for?'

Ricky turned to see the two men looking up at him. There was an intensity to their gaze that made him uneasy.

'Nothing.' He shrugged, then stepped over and sat on the lower bunk across from them.

'That's my bunk, kid. Get your hunky little ass off of it,' one of the men said, leveling his gaze at the boy.

Ricky quickly stood up.

The man smiled. 'You best wait until you been asked, before you be spreading your ass on my bed, boy.'

'I'm sorry,' Ricky apologized.

The man snorted disdainfully, then, after one last appraising glance, turned back to his friend.

Ricky walked to the end of the bunks and cautiously climbed up, trying not to bother the two men below.

He stared up at the concrete ceiling, listening to the soft murmur of the two men below and the steady drip of water from one of the other toilets in the cell block.

A little before sunset the door to the hallway opened, and a trusty wheeled a food cart down to the cell.

Ricky waited until the two men below him had been served before he climbed down.

'Who's the newboy?' The trusty smiled. He handed Ricky his tray and glanced over at the two men sitting across from each other on the lower bunks. 'And how come I don't get me any fresh blood?'

'Fuck you, Tommy,' one of the men casually answered.

'Eat shit,' Tommy retorted, then glanced over at the upper bunk 'Hey, you, Mr Hell's Angel?'

'What?' the man on the top bunk responded hoarsely, without moving or opening his eyes.

'You eating tonight, or are you still dieting?'

The biker ignored him.

'Well, fuck you, then,' Tommy muttered. He turned and started to wheel his cart back down the hall. At the corner of the cell he paused to peer through the bars at Ricky.

'You sleep good tonight, newboy.' He grinned maliciously, then, snickering, disappeared from sight.

Ricky shuffled across his bunk, until he leaned back against the cement wall. He balanced his tray on his knees and tried to stop the trembling in his hands and legs.

A short while later, an older trusty came by to collect the trays. It was as Ricky was handing his tray through the bars that one of the men reached over and ran his hand down Ricky's back to his hip.

Ricky jerked away, smashing his tray against the door and dropping his cup to the ground.

Bending over to pick it up, he heard one of the men behind him laugh. The other whistled softly.

As he handed him the cup, Ricky caught the trusty's eye.

The older man quickly looked away and shuffled down the hall.

'Hey, boy. Lights out in about fifteen minutes,' one of the men called up to him softly.

Ricky felt a cold bead of perspiration run along his ribs.

'You get spooky up there, boy, you just come on down here and Leroy and me'll take real good care of you.'

Ricky closed his eyes tightly, trying to still the rush of adrenalin flooding through him. It left him breathless and trembling.

Twenty minutes later the lights flashed, then a moment later flicked off.

The only illumination came from an overhead light at the far end of the hall. The shaft of light, fractured by the cell bars, spread grotesque shadows across the interior of Ricky's cell.

He heard the sound of movement below him. Willing himself not to look, terrified by what this sound might mean, Ricky locked his eyes on the ceiling.

'Hey, boy, how you doing?'

One of the men was standing beside his bunk, looking over at him.

'You okay up here all by yourself?' he asked softly. His hand crept over the edge of the bunk and touched Ricky's arm.

'First night's kind of weird, isn't it, boy?'

The man's hand rested lightly on Ricky's biceps. His fingers began to gently massage Ricky's arm.

'Sometimes it helps if you got friends,' the other man said, rising to stand beside his partner.

'Everybody needs friends inside.'

'Hey, c'mon, guys, just leave me alone, huh?' Ricky said, trying to shift out of the other man's grip.

The man's hand locked firmly around Ricky's arm.

'What's wrong, boy. You don't like us?'

'I don't think he does, Rudy.'

'Well that's fucking gratitude for you, Leroy. Here we are trying to help the boy, and look at how he acts.'

'He doesn't know what it's like inside, how important it is to have friends.'

'That right, boy? You don't know about friends. About how you got to be nice to your friends?'

'Cut it out,' Ricky growled, jerking his arm from the other man's grip. He shifted across his bunk until he came up against the wall.

'That's no way to act, boy,' Rudy said, shaking his head sadly.

'No way to act at all,' Leroy added.

'Maybe we need to show you what we mean,' Rudy said, gripping the side of the bunk.

Ricky's gaze dropped to the man's hands. Even in the dim light he could see the whitened knuckles and the throb of veins popping out in the other man's forearms. He glanced around desperately.

'You just leave me alone. I don't want any trouble.'

Rudy laughed. 'Hey, boy, we ain't looking for trouble. Are we, Leroy?'

'No, boy. That's not what we're looking for at all.' His eyes locked hungrily on Ricky.

'How old are you, boy? Sixteen, maybe seventeen?'

'Just leave me alone, or I'm going to call somebody.'

'Hell, boy, you can call all you want, but no one's going to be listening to you. Ain't no one here but Leroy and me, and that fat-assed deputy sitting out there, sleeping. So you just go ahead and yell as much as you want.'

Leroy suddenly reached over and grabbed the front of Ricky's overalls. He twisted and jerked at the fabric. It ripped away from Ricky's chest.

'Look at this, Rudy. Boy doesn't have a hair on him. Wonder if he's like that all over.'

Ricky struck out at the hand clinging to the front of his overalls.

Leroy snorted disgustedly and threw him back against the wall.

Ricky's head smashed into the cinder block. For a moment the dull thud of pain dimmed his vision. When it cleared, he saw Rudy's arm dart out and grab his leg.

'Cut it out,' Ricky yelled.

Leroy giggled and grabbed his arm.

Together the two men lifted him from the bunk and dragged him down to the floor.

'C'mon, you fucking punk, let's see what you got,' Rudy grunted, ripping at the boy's overalls.

Ricky felt himself being lifted and turned over on to his stomach, until he was pinned across the lower bunk.

Leroy ripped off the boy's overalls.

'Hardly a hair on him,' he heard Leroy whisper.

He swung out wildly with his fist and feet, but his movements were muffled by the two men's bodies.

He felt their hands on his back, sliding lower, until they gripped the cheeks of his ass.

He heard Leroy giggle, then heard the rustle of fabric as one of the men began to undress.

Ricky screamed and thrashed around on the bunk. His foot lashed out, catching one of the men in the stomach. He heard the man grunt, and he quickly kicked out again.

'You fucking punk,' one of them growled, then slammed a fist into his side.

The blow stunned him.

'Time I'm done with you, you fucking pussy, you're going to be begging me to stick it in. Get him over on his stomach again, Leroy,' Rudy ordered.

Frantically, Ricky tried to twist away, but they easily turned him and re-positioned him over the lower bunk. He felt a draft of cold air along his nakedness, then felt Rudy's hand on his body.

He threw his head back and screamed.

'No one to hear you, boy,' Rudy whispered excitedly.

Ricky could feel his breath against the back of his neck.

'Spread that cherry.' Leroy giggled.

Ricky felt their hands clawing at his body, raising and spreading his legs.

Screaming for help, he tried desperately to twist out of their grasp.

Leroy thumped him on the back.

He felt one of the men step between his upraised legs, felt the rasp of a hairy leg against his own.

'Oh, God, please help me,' Ricky sobbed.

He heard Leroy's giggle, heard the hoarse wheeze of Rudy's excited breath, and clenched his teeth – suddenly realizing that there was no one to help and nowhere to hide.

Two

Two weeks after he'd buried his brother in Florida, Ryan got as far as Houston before he pulled over to the side of the interstate.

He parked his cycle on the shoulder, then swung his leg up over the gas tank and leaned back to smoke a cigarette.

Twenty minutes later he was joined by a state trooper.

'You got a problem?' the trooper asked, after cautiously approaching the biker.

'No.' Ryan shook his head, noticing the unclipped holster.

'Then I'd suggest you move on.'

Ryan nodded, then flicked his cigarette off to the side and started up the bike. He wheeled back on to the highway and kicked up through the gears. In his rear-view mirror he watched the trooper following behind.

Ryan turned off at the first exit. He gassed up at a Mobil station, then stopped at a pay phone on the way back to his bike.

He dialed the number from memory.

'Cycle World?'

'It's me.'

11

'Hey, man, when you coming back?'

'Soon. Everything all right?'

'Yeah, everything's cool,' Fish answered. Then, after an awkward moment, added, 'You okay, bro?'

'Yeah, I'm fine.'

'I'm sorry about your—'

Ryan didn't let him finish. 'That's all right,' he interrupted. 'I think I'm going to ride for a while.'

'That's cool, man. Do whatever. I'm holding your place down. I kind of like this Mr Businessman shit.'

'All right. You take it easy, Fish. I'll be talking to you.'

'Ride hard, man.'

Ryan climbed on his bike and rode out towards the interstate. He stopped at the first intersection, staring up thoughtfully at the two entrance ramps.

A moment later he blew by the arterial to 10 west. He kicked up into fourth, and, leaning into the cycle, ran the curve leading him back the way he'd come.

A little outside of New Orleans, Ryan cut north on 65. He let the rhythm of the bike and the passing countryside take him. The steady throb of the engine muffled his thoughts, and kept him firmly locked in the present.

A few miles north of Montgomery, Ryan stopped and got a motel room for the night.

Sitting in the small room, in front of the scarred desk against the wall, he suddenly caught sight of his reflection in the mirror. He quickly rose to his feet and turned towards the door. He carried the mental image of his bloodshot eyes across the parking lot.

12

He found a package liquor store three blocks from his motel.

He returned to his room and opened the bottle of tequila.

He drank steadily, trying to avoid the bloodshot gaze that seemed to seek him out from the flat plane of the mirror.

By the time Ryan hit Chattanooga, he couldn't hide from it any longer. He pulled over at a rest stop and climbed on to one of the park benches. He sprawled out across the top of it and stared up at the sky. It was cloudlessly blue. The only obstruction was from the overhang of an oak tree.

Ryan lit a cigarette and closed his eyes. Within that darkness, he found her waiting for him.

Zella.

'Well, we have to go back sometime,' she said.

'Why?' Ryan grinned.

'Because.'

'Because why?'

'Because it's where I was born. Don't you want to see where I grew up?' she asked, examining him closely.

'I don't need to.'

'Why not?' Zella stepped over to him.

'It's not important.' Ryan caught and held her gaze. He reached out to cup the side of her face. 'You're all that's important.'

Zella smiled and reached out to him.

13

Ryan stepped into the circle of her arms and held her tightly.

'I want you to see it sometime. Please. It's important to me,' Zella whispered, and Ryan clung to her, and promised they would ride there in the spring.

Ryan opened his eyes and looked up at the tree overhead. A leaf, yellowed and frayed by autumn, detached itself from a branch and slowly drifted to the ground.

Ryan climbed back on his bike and hit the interstate. He rode hard, focusing himself completely on the road, pushing away everything ahead and behind him.

Ten miles from Harlan, Ryan abruptly wheeled the bike to the side of the road. He climbed off and lit a cigarette. He smoked, looking around at the rising countryside.

Crushing his cigarette beneath his boot, he turned back to his cycle and climbed on. He reached for the key, then paused and stared blankly at the road ahead of him.

Harlan was fifteen minutes away.

He started the bike, then, without allowing himself to think about it, circled around and headed back the way he'd come.

Coming up to a long bank of curves before Middlesboro, Ryan accelerated and threw himself and the bike into them.

His back wheel skidded out and he almost lost it on the first section. But he kept his hand locked on the throttle and weaved forward, ignoring the treacherous dirt shoulders and oncoming traffic.

At the final curve, Ryan gunned it. He shifted the bike

until it was almost parallel to the pavement, and unraveled the road ahead, screaming at the top of his lungs.

The squad car was parked by the side of the road at the entrance to town. With a burst of sirens and lights, it darted on to the highway and rapidly crept up behind him.

Feeling the hard edge of the adrenalin burning off, Ryan pulled over to the side and watched the policeman approach him.

'Speeding.' The judge paused to glare at Ryan. 'Thirty miles over the posted limit, reckless driving, and vehicular endangerment. Do you have any comment?'

Ryan stared back at him silently.

After a curt nod, the judge went on. 'That's a three-hundred-dollar fine or thirty days in jail.' He tapped the desk with his gavel. 'You can pay the court clerk on your way out.'

'I'll take the thirty days,' Ryan said quietly.

The judge glanced up at him sharply.

Ryan met his gaze.

'You realize, don't you, Mr Ryan, that I've been somewhat lenient with your fine? I understand your financial condition and have adjusted my sentencing in accordance to that finding.'

'I appreciate that.'

'Then why, Mr Ryan, if I might ask, are you being so obstinate? I'm well aware that you can afford the fine.'

'I need the rest.' Ryan shrugged, holding the judge's gaze.

'Bailiff, take Mr Ryan into custody. We don't want to

keep him awake any longer than we have to,' the judge continued, gesturing distastefully at the man before his bench.

For the first week, Ryan had the cell all to himself. He would lie on his bunk, with his eyes closed, and let the memories unravel before him.

Zella and his brother Neal were his almost constant companions.

Ryan went with the drift of memory, never questioning it, never wondering about the oddity that these two people, who'd played such important roles in his life, were both dead.

The second week of his incarceration, he was joined by two men. After a number of futile attempts at conversing with their cell mate, they quickly learned to ignore him.

At first Ryan found them distracting, but he soon discovered a way of going deeper into himself that took him far away from his present predicament. It took him to a depth of memory that made him slightly uneasy. It was too real, and it was populated with only the ghosts of his past.

There was no present and no future in this place that Ryan had discovered within himself.

By the third week of his sentence, Ryan was barely cognizant of anything that was going on around him. There was a small, almost silent part of him that he occasionally heard entreating him to return, but he ignored it, and stayed within the warm glow of Zella and his brother.

* * *

It was the voices that finally began to draw him back. He tried to ignore them, tried to go deeper within himself but they kept intruding in the drift of memories that surrounded him.

He pushed away at the voices, desperately clawing his way back into memory, until he found himself once again in the small motel in San Cristobal, New Mexico.

The metallic tick of his cycle as it cooled down outside the motel door. Still feeling the steady throb of the engine, the vibrations in his arms and legs.

Zella sprawled across the bed. Her hair still damp from the shower.

Ryan, stepping out of the bathroom, toweling his chest, pausing as he spotted her lying across the bed.

The line of her legs, curving up to her thighs and hips. The dark shadow of hair between her legs. The gentle rise and fall of her breasts.

Smiling, raising her arms.

Ryan moving across the room and lying beside her, feeling the warm press of her body against his. The clean scent of her flesh, the texture of her skin against his lips . . .

The angry rush of voices shattered the image.

Ryan closed his eyes more tightly, and pushed the intrusive sounds away.

Neal steps out from the mangroves. His face is stained with tears and he carries the imprint of a blow across his cheek. Behind him their father angrily stalks along the path. In his hand he carries a switch of bamboo which he flicks in front of him. The sharp cracking of the branch disturbs the torpid air.

Neal running up to him and cowering behind him.

The drunken rage solidifying and focusing in his father's eyes.

'Leave him alone.'

'Get the fuck out of my way, boy.'

'Eddie, please.' Neal whimpering behind him.

Ryan stepping out to silently confront his father.

His father's arm flashing out and catching Ryan across the face.

Ryan falling to the dirt, feeling the metallic taste of blood flooding his mouth.

The sound of the switch rising and falling.

Neal screaming.

His father's drunken laughter.

Screaming . . .

Ryan jerked forward and opened his eyes to the shadows of his cell.

The scream continued to echo around him.

'Neal,' Ryan whispered, then quickly swiveled to the side of his bunk.

On the lower bunk opposite him, the two men had a boy pinned across the bed. One of the men was standing between the boy's spread legs and lowering his overalls. The other was laughing and holding the struggling boy in place.

'Take a deep breath, punk. Here I come,' the man between the boy's legs sneered, and he shuffled forward.

The other giggled excitedly.

'Back off,' Ryan grunted hoarsely. His voice came out rusty from disuse.

Startled, both men twisted around to stare up at him. The boy kicked out and scrambled free.

'Leave him alone,' Ryan said quietly.

One of the men glanced over at the boy crouched fearfully against the wall, trying to cover himself with his shredded overalls.

He then turned back to Ryan and smiled.

'Plenty to go around, friend.'

Ryan stared back at him silently.

The other man sat down on the edge of the bunk and reached over for the boy's leg.

The kid lashed out at him with his foot.

The man laughed and trapped the boy's ankle in his grip.

'I said to leave him alone,' Ryan repeated, gripping the side of his bunk.

'You ain't got no call to tell us what to do,' said the man standing in the aisle, glaring up at Ryan.

'Let it go.'

'Hey, Rudy, I think he just wants the little pussy for himself.'

'Well,' Rudy drawled. 'He ain't going to get him. He's ours,' he said, never taking his eyes off of Ryan.

Leroy laughed, and yanked Ricky towards the edge of the bunk.

'You got a problem with this, you just close your eyes and go back to sleep,' Rudy taunted, then turned.

'Now, hold him down there, Leroy,' Rudy said, crouching over and stepping between the struggling boy's legs.

19

'Don't,' Ryan said softly.

Both men ignored him.

Bracing himself against the edge of the bunk, Ryan kicked out. His foot hit Rudy in the back of the head, toppling him over the two other figures.

By the time he'd recovered, Ryan had dropped down to the aisle between the bunks.

'Kid, get over here.' Ryan gestured behind him.

Ricky quickly scrambled out from beneath the two men to the opposite bunk behind Ryan.

'Get up on top,' Ryan told him, without turning.

Ricky leaped to the top bunk, and cowered against the wall.

'You asking for some trouble, friend.'

'No, I'm not. I'm just trying to get some sleep.'

'Well, you don't get out of our way, you're going to be doing more than just sleeping.'

Ryan met both men's gazes, then abruptly glanced away.

When he bought his eyes back up to them, he relaxed and smiled sheepishly.

'Hey, man, sorry. I was just...' Before he finished his sentence, he threw a fist into Rudy's stomach. The blow doubled him over. Before his friend could react, Ryan lashed out again and caught the other man on the side of the jaw.

Leroy fell back against the wall.

Ryan moved in on Rudy. Using his fist, he battered the man until he crouched over and fell to his knees in the middle of the aisle.

Ryan kicked him in the face, then whirled on Leroy.

'You want some, motherfucker?'

'I don't want no trouble,' Leroy said quickly, backing away until he came up against the wall.

Ryan glared at him, then turned and sat down on the edge of the lower bunk.

Rudy groaned.

Leroy started to shuffle forward to help his friend.

'Leave him,' Ryan spat out, then fell back across the bunk.

He closed his eyes – then quickly opened them when he felt the threat of a memory waiting for him.

He listened to the ragged sound of Rudy's breath coming from somewhere in between the bunks.

Above him, he heard a muffled sob from the kid.

Neal, Ryan thought, then shook himself away from the image.

He stared up at the underside of the upper bunk, and settled back to wait for the night to pass.

Three

Thomas Howard waited until he and his daughter Jane finished their dinner before he retired to his office to play back his messages.

It was understood, by almost everyone that mattered, that Mr Howard was not to be disturbed from six to seven p.m. any evening of the week. This was his dinner hour. If any business arose at that particular time, no matter what the degree of importance, it was to be postponed until 7:01 at the very earliest.

Thomas reasoned that if it was an urgent message, its urgency would not be affected by a sixty-minute wait, and if it wasn't urgent, then the phone-call should never have been made in the first place.

Howard made himself comfortable behind his desk, before he flicked on his answering machine.

'Dad, please answer. I need help.' It was the recorded voice of Thomas's son. 'I've been arrested in Middlesboro, Kentucky and I need bail money. Please, Dad, they're going to put me in jail,' Ricky pleaded.

A moment later Thomas heard the sound of the phone being replaced.

Thomas picked up the receiver and dialed information. Before the representative came on the line, Thomas hung up the phone and leaned back thoughtfully.

'Was it anything important?' Jane asked. She stood at the entrance way to her father's office. She wouldn't step inside unless invited.

'No, just a salesman.' Howard shook his head dismissively. He stood up and stepped around the desk.

'Would you like a brandy, Dad?'

'No.' Thomas smiled. 'Not tonight, I have to see Christian.'

'Has he changed his mind?'

'No, this is about something else,' Thomas said casually, turning away.

Jane followed him to the front door. She reached out to help him on with his coat.

'I'm sure the meeting will run late,' he informed her, then reached for the door. He paused, then glanced back at her. 'If there are any calls for me, just let my machine pick them up.'

Jane nodded, then stepped to the doorway and watched her father walk down the drive to his car.

She waited until he'd pulled out to the road before she closed the door. She leaned against it; then, with a decisive shake of her head, she quickly climbed the stairs to her room.

She sat on the edge of her bed to make the call.

'He's gone,' she said without preamble, once she heard the receiver at the other end being lifted.

'How long?'

'At least a couple of hours,' Jane responded, absently running a hand along the line of her thigh.

'Okay,' the voice answered.

Jane replaced the receiver, and glanced across the room at the large oak dresser facing her bed. She pushed back a dark strand of hair, then rose and stepped over to her closet.

She changed, then walked downstairs and entered her father's office.

Fifteen minutes later, she heard the doorbell. She rose and paused before the mirror. She now wore a long, black silk robe. The transparent material made the dark outline of each areola clearly evident. She turned from the mirror and hurried down the stairs.

'You look wonderful,' he said admiringly, then stepped into the house and took Jane into his arms.

Jane allowed herself to be held. 'We don't have much time.'

'I thought you said a couple of hours.' He pulled back to look at her.

'We don't want to get caught, do we?' Jane said softly, examining him closely.

'God, no,' he responded vehemently, then put his arm around her shoulders and led her towards the stairs.

He had no trouble finding his way to her room.

As he began to position himself above her, Jane closed her eyes. When he entered her, and she felt his shoulder wedge itself beneath her chin, Jane opened her eyes and stared up at the ceiling.

'Oh, God, you're so beautiful,' he gasped, as he began to move within her.

Jane let her body begin to move in rhythm with his. She did this automatically. Her gaze strayed to the mirror on the bureau. She could see the pale clenched mounds of his buttocks rising and thrusting against her. The sight was so ludicrous that she almost laughed out loud.

She bit back her laughter and adroitly shifted beneath him, bringing him to climax. She watched his face as he threw his head back and moaned. There was a focus to his features that she had never seen before. It mystified her how something so completely physical could appear to be so mentally motivated.

He rolled off of her. His hand reached out to momentarily touch her breast.

'I better get out of here before he gets back,' he said, planting a quick kiss on her cheek.

Jane propped herself up on an elbow, and watched him dress.

'I'll call you,' he promised – then, throwing her a kiss at the doorway, hurried out of the room and down the stairs.

Jane waited until she heard the front door close before she flopped back across the bed.

She stared up blankly at the ceiling, feeling the cold smear of his seed leak across the back of her thighs.

'Am I the last?' Christian asked.

Thomas Howard only smiled in response.

'Oh, I guess that's impolitic of me to ask that question, isn't it?' he continued.

'Don't be coy, Christian. We both know which way you're going to throw your support. The only question is what it's going to cost me,' Thomas said, glancing out at the dark waters of Lake Michigan.

They had decided to meet at the Yacht Club. At this time of the evening, and year, it was notoriously slow.

'How does this place survive?' Christian glanced around the almost empty room. His gaze stopped on a couple sitting at the bar.

'Out of the beneficence of its members,' Thomas responded, following Christian's gaze.

'Beneficence?'

'Yes, it's my *word* for the day.'

Christian nodded, then reached for his brandy. He twirled it thoughtfully in his hand before he glanced up at Howard. 'What are you offering for my support?'

Thomas smiled, then shook his head. 'No, Christian, the question is: what do you want?'

Christian nodded to the other man, as if acknowledging a point scored.

'Well, to be perfectly honest with you, Thomas, I don't know if you can offer me what I want.'

Thomas waited for Christian to lift his glass before he said, 'What about re-election?'

Christian quickly jerked his glass away.

Thomas was pleased at his reaction.

'What the hell are you talking about? You have no control over the voting in my district.'

'You might be surprised, Christian, at just how much control I *do* have.'

27

Christian examined the other man intently.

'What do you want, Christian? I'm assuming that was the reason for this meeting.'

'Let's go outside to talk about this,' Christian said abruptly. He quickly finished his brandy and stood up.

Thomas signed the bill, then followed the other man out the door.

They walked out to the veranda overlooking the lake. It was still early enough in autumn so that the wind coming off Lake Michigan only chilled rather than froze.

Christian leaned against the railing and looked out at the dark line of boats bobbing in the water.

'I want complete approval for all the construction bids,' Christian said softly, without turning.

Thomas looked out at the lake. He peered at the swaying line of yachts, trying to find the shadow of his own boat.

'You want the project to go through as is?'

'Yes.'

Thomas smiled.

Christian turned to him.

'Caldwell Construction?'

'Yes.' Christian nodded defiantly. 'Anything wrong with that?' he challenged.

'No.' Thomas sighed. 'Nothing wrong with that at all. What else is family for but to help each other.'

Christian glanced away.

'Okay, I can do that. But in turn I want your full support on the mall.'

'And if the mall fails?' Christian asked coyly.

'Then.' Thomas paused, transferring his gaze from the

28

water back to Christian. 'I think your brother-in-law will have to find a job that pays a little less.'

Thomas entered his office to check his messages. He was mildly surprised to find that there hadn't been any. He'd expected another call from Ricky.

Before turning off the light in his office, he paused, wondering if he should have responded to the boy's plea.

Deciding then that the boy needed a little strengthening, he flicked off the light and climbed the stairs to his room.

'Dad?'

'Yes?' Thomas opened the door to Jane's room and leaned against the doorframe.

She sat propped up against the headboard, with a book in her lap.

'How'd it go with Christian?'

'Fine,' Thomas nodded, then glanced around her room. He brought his gaze back to his daughter.

'How was *your* night?' he asked carefully.

'Okay.' Jane nodded, raising her eyes to his.

'That's good,' Thomas said softly, then backed out of her room and retreated down the hallway to his bedroom.

Four

At twelve thirty, Ricky stood before the city clerk and carefully counted out the money. After he'd paid the fine, he was left with only a hundred dollars from the thousand that had been sent to him.

The clerk gave him a receipt and informed him that it would take at least thirty minutes to process.

Ricky nodded and turned away. He stepped out through the front doors and sat down on the concrete steps. Hunched forward, with his arms wrapped around his sides, Ricky looked out at the town of Middlesboro.

The town was aligned along each side of State Highway 25. Fast-food franchises, hardware stores, automotive repair shops and one huge shopping mall seemed to be the predominant make-up of the town.

Ricky watched two policemen start up the steps. They both glanced his way as they passed.

Ricky quickly looked away from their penetrating gazes.

He was still somewhat stunned by the events of the previous night. He had never expected anything like that, and even now, hours after it had happened, had trouble believing that it had actually taken place.

Ricky shuddered, suddenly realizing what would have happened to him if that man hadn't helped him.

He quickly rose to his feet and walked down to the sidewalk. He began pacing up and down the block. The movement seemed to calm him.

Ryan stepped through the front doors. He paused at the entrance and looked out at the town before him. He spotted the kid, hunched forward, walking away from him.

He watched the kid walk to the end of the block, then quickly turn and start back towards the city jail.

The kid's eyes were glued to the pavement in front of him.

'Hey,' Ryan called to him.

Startled, the kid abruptly twisted around and glanced up at him.

'Thanks,' Ryan said softly, struck again by the boy's resemblance to Neal.

Ryan stepped down beside him.

'You okay?'

The kid nodded, unable to meet Ryan's gaze.

'You didn't have to do that,' Ryan said, nodding towards the building behind him. 'I only had a couple more days to go.'

'I wanted to . . .' the kid paused, shuddered, 'to thank you.'

Ryan shrugged, then glanced up and down the street. 'I wonder if there's a coffee shop around here.'

'Over there.' The kid pointed down the block to a Denny's restaurant.

'You interested?' Ryan asked, already starting to move down the sidewalk.

Without bothering to respond, the kid began to follow him.

They sat in a booth overlooking the parking lot. Ryan waited until they had their coffee before he asked, 'Where you from?'

'Waukegan.' The kid lifted his coffee cup. The cup trembled in his hand. He used his other hand to steady it.

'Hey, it's over, kid. You got to let it go.'

'I can't,' Ricky gasped, then glanced out the window.

'How old are you?'

'Seventeen.'

'What'd they pop you for?'

'Expired driver's license.'

Ryan leaned back to look at him. 'You fuck with any of these people around here?'

Jarred by his choice of words, Ricky twisted around to face him.

'I mean, did you give anyone a hard time?' Ryan gently amended.

Ricky shook his head, then, a moment later asked, 'Why?'

'You're seventeen. You shouldn't've been put in there with those guys.'

'Why did they do that to me?' Ricky whispered intently, leaning across the table.

'I don't know.' Ryan shrugged. He reached into his pocket and pulled out a pack of cigarettes. He pulled one

33

out, then, after a meaningful glance to the kid, threw the pack on the table between them.

Ricky looked down and discovered that he was tapping nervously on the table top with both hands. He grabbed a cigarette and lit up. The smoke bit into his lungs and throat.

'Small towns.' Ryan shrugged dismissively. 'They do anything they want.'

'Nobody said anything about it this morning. They all just pretended like nothing happened.'

'Hell, kid, nothing *did* happen,' Ryan said, trapping the boy's gaze.

'But it could've ... those guys could've...' Ricky paused.

'But they didn't, and that's all that counts.' Ryan picked up his cup. He held it with both hands and looked across the rim. 'Even if it had, there's a lot worse that can happen.'

'Bullshit,' Ricky said vehemently.

Ryan glanced out the window. A battered pick-up truck pulled into the lot and parked in front of them. Two men, both wearing cowboy hats, climbed out and sauntered towards the restaurant.

'Who are you?'

'Ricky. Ricky Howard.'

'I'm Ryan.' Ryan held out his hand.

The kid reached over and took it.

Neal, standing beside him, reaching up to take his hand. Ryan feeling the small grip of his brother's hand in his as he led him down the hallway to his classroom. His first day of school. His little brother standing beside him, looking up at him...

'You okay?'

'What?' Ryan shook his head and saw the kid, Ricky, staring worriedly at him across the table.

'You just looked out of it there for a minute.'

'Bad flash.' Ryan sighed, then finished off his coffee. 'What're you going to do now?'

'I don't know.' Ricky shrugged.

'Maybe you should think about going home.'

'Yeah.' Ricky nodded, then asked, 'Where are you from?'

'West coast, mostly. I was coming up from Florida when they grabbed me.'

'That's where I was, too.'

Ryan stubbed out his cigarette.

'I was down in Miami visiting my grandmother. She moved down there about four years ago. She used to live up in Illinois with us but, after my grandfather died, she said she wanted to move someplace warm. It's really nice down there,' Ricky said nervously, running the words together, finding a certain solace in the sound of them.

'How you going to get home?'

'I still have the rental car for another couple of days. I'll just...' He paused, looking across the table at Ryan.

Ryan nodded meaningfully. 'Yeah, maybe you better come up with a better idea.'

'What's it cost to fly from here to Chicago? Do you have any idea?'

'No.' Ryan shook his head, smiling softly.

'You're going west?'

'Yes.'

Ricky nodded thoughtfully.

'I should get moving,' Ryan said, pushing his cup away and rising to his feet.

Ricky quickly finished his coffee and stood up beside him.

Once outside the restaurant, Ryan started walking back towards the jailhouse. Ricky followed beside him.

'I'm back there,' Ryan said, pausing at the corner of the building and pointing to the parking lot behind.

'Listen, I want to thank you again...'

'It's no big thing.' Ryan shrugged. He started towards the alley leading to the city lot, then stopped.

The kid still stood on the sidewalk, watching him.

Sighing, Ryan turned. 'You going to be all right?'

'Yeah, I'm going to be fine. I'll just call a couple of the airlines and see what it costs to fly home.'

Ryan reached the corner of the alley before he stopped again.

This time the kid waved when he looked back.

'I'll hang out until you get set up,' Ryan said, as he approached the kid again.

'You don't have to. I'm okay now.'

'It's no problem.'

'You sure?'

'Yeah, I'm sure.' Ryan gestured to a phone-booth across the street.

He leaned against the corner of the booth while Ricky called the airlines.

'It's okay.' Ricky smiled, stepping out of the booth. 'They've got a flight up to Chicago at two forty-five.'

'Then you're all set.'

'Yeah.' Ricky nodded happily. 'They have a shuttle leaving from the travel agency.'

Ryan pulled a cigarette. He offered the pack to the kid, then fired up his own before handing Ricky the matches. He watched the kid awkwardly light up.

'Well, I'll get going then.'

'Okay. Thanks again, Mr Ryan.'

'Just Ryan, all right?'

'Sure.' Ricky stuck out his hand.

Ryan took it, then shook his head, turned and started across the street.

At the corner of the alley he glanced back to see the kid walking along the sidewalk towards the far end of town.

Ryan found his cycle parked at the rear of the lot. He crouched down, running his hands over the fittings, checking for any looseness. He climbed on, then pulled a map from the zippered back of the seat. He traced his route westward, then replaced the map and hit the ignition.

The bike kicked in on his first attempt. Ryan cocked his head to the side, listening attentively to the sound of the engine.

He leaned forward to adjust the idle, then kicked into gear and slowly wheeled out of the lot.

He paused at the intersection of State Road 25. According to the map, he needed to go south to pick up 40 west.

Shaking his head in annoyance, Ryan turned northward. He figured he'd ride out a few miles, just to make sure.

Passing the last of the business district, Ryan kicked up into fourth and scanned the road ahead.

Five minutes later he made out the slight figure standing on the shoulder of the road with his thumb out.

Ryan passed him, then pulled over to the side. In his rear-view mirror he watched the figure approach him uncertainly.

'It's you,' the kid said, smiling enthusiastically.

'I thought you were going to fly.'

'I don't have enough money.' Ricky shrugged sheepishly.

'How much you need?'

'I couldn't do that.' Ricky shook his head, stepping back.

'Hitch-hiking's illegal in Kentucky,' Ryan pointed out.

'What?'

'They could pop you again, kid. And I don't think you want another shot at city hospitality.'

Ryan glanced over at the boy. 'How much you need?'

'I can't take your money.'

'You're not taking it. I'm offering it.'

'No, I won't do that.' Ricky shook his head adamantly.

Ryan sighed.

'Listen, I'll be fine. Don't worry about it,' the kid said, backing away.

Ryan watched the boy start down the highway. A truck came up behind him, but the kid continued to walk without turning.

Ryan kicked into gear and slowly drove up beside him.

'What, are you going to *walk* home?'

'No, I'm just going to get outside the city limits, and then I'll start hitching.'

'It's illegal in the whole state, kid, not just the city.'

Ricky hunched his shoulders forward. 'Well, then I'll just keep walking until I get out of the state.'

'You're looking at a good two hundred miles.'

'I'll be fine,' Ricky said, then turned and walked away.

Ryan hit the kill switch and pulled out a cigarette. He lit up, looking thoughtfully at the road ahead and the slight figure of the kid beside it.

Eventually flicking his cigarette off to the side, he started up the bike and raced up beside him.

'Get on,' he growled.

'You don't have to—'

'Just shut up and get on.' Ryan gestured impatiently behind.

Ricky glanced at his face, then climbed on the back of the motorcycle.

'Go with the bike, kid. Don't fight it,' Ryan directed, kicking into first and pulling out on to the highway.

He ran up through the gears and leveled at sixty-five. He felt the throb of the engine running through his hands and feet, and let the sound and feel of it wipe everything else away.

Five

Alongside of the western shore of Lake Michigan, midway between Chicago and Milwaukee, sits Waukegan. Its waterfront location had made it a prime industrial area during the late Fifties. By the end of the Sixties, Waukegan could claim that it had more industry per square foot than any other city in America.

Throughout the next decade, the townspeople had watched as factory after factory had closed down and moved southward. By the mid-Eighties, all that was left of the industrial boom was the nuclear plant, located two miles from the downtown area on the lakeshore.

In 1989 Charles Presley ran for mayor on a platform of rejuvenating the city. This promise was heard by the voting public with a certain jaded cynicism. They had been burned before, and were therefore not quite so quick to believe. But Presley brought a vigor and power to his words that had been lacking in the last two elections.

He won the mayor's seat with an unprecedented majority. His first official declaration was an announcement that the downtown area would now be closed to traffic. He

41

proposed to turn the whole downtown section into an open-air shopping mall.

Within a year of taking office, Mayor Presley's efforts to rejuvenate the downtown district began to finally halt the inexorable movement of small businesses westward into the county.

Having completed his work on the town proper, Presley began to move outward. He brought in a developer from Washington DC, who began to redesign the lake front. Within two years the Yacht Club opened its doors to customers from as far away as Milwaukee and Chicago.

Mayor Presley had revived the town. He had all but stopped the westward movement of businesses into the far reaches of the county. He had given the city a chance to compete in a different arena, and almost everyone in town worshiped him.

The few who didn't were those who had seen their profits begin to evaporate with the mayor's increased local emphasis. Developers, who in the Seventies had heavily invested in city land to the west, now saw their investments rapidly plummet.

A few men – those with a little more foresight and funding than their peers – had managed to emerge from the Eighties land-rich. The problem that they now faced was finding a way to turn these investments into an even more profitable venture.

One of these ventures was the shopping mall proposed by Thomas Howard. It was to be built at the furthest western border of the town's city limits. The planned structure was to be the largest in the country, encompassing a full twenty-two acres of land. It would offer over two million square feet of shopping and living space. It would be a completely self-contained environment.

This proposed structure had polarized the community as well as the city council. Mayor Presley himself was obdurately opposed to such a development. In his estimation, the construction of such a mall would simply recreate the problems that had almost buried the city when he had first taken office.

A public petition for zoning variances to build the mall had quickly been circulated. The petition soon garnished enough signatures to force a public vote. An election was slated the first week in November, three weeks away.

Mayor Presley now found his efforts completely focused on the upcoming election. This new focus became so all-encompassing that he began to overlook the day-to-day running of the city, which, in turn, only gave the opposition more ammunition to use against him.

And they used this new ammunition gleefully.

'Where do we stand now?' the mayor asked wearily.

'Michaels is with us.'

The mayor waited for a moment, then abruptly turned. 'That's all?' he asked in disbelief.

'Charlie, you're worrying too much.' The councilman smiled reassuringly. 'It's still three weeks to the elections and we've got a majority of the council behind us.'

'With me as the deciding vote,' Presley glumly added.

'Yes, but we don't know yet which way Lewis and Constantine are going to go.'

'Constantine!' The mayor snorted disgustedly. 'I don't think there's any doubt which camp he's in.'

'Well, even if he doesn't come over, with Michaels and me, and your vote, we'll be fine. Our endorsements will be more than enough to carry a majority.'

'I don't know.' Mayor Presley shook his head and stepped over to his office window. His office was on the fourteenth floor of the City Building. He could see whitecaps shifting across the face of Lake Michigan.

'Charlie?'

The mayor turned.

'You don't have to worry about this. We've got the vote in our pockets. I think what you need to do now is to begin applying yourself to some of these other projects that you've started.'

'Like what: the day-care regulations?' the mayor said sarcastically.

'Yes, exactly like that. You're letting this mall thing take over your whole administration.' The city councilman held up a hand, halting the mayor's protests. 'I agree with you, it is important. It's vital. But at the same time, Charlie, you've still got a lot of people out there counting on you, and you can't let them down.'

'You're right.' The mayor sighed. He stepped away from the window and sat down at his desk. He leaned back and looked across the room at his friend and fellow council-member. 'Thanks.' He smiled. 'Sometimes I just need a kick in the ass to remind me what I'm doing here.'

'Any time you need a kick, you just give me a call.'

Christian Huntington grinned, then, nodding, turned and left the mayor's office.

The mayor picked up a report for the new drug program he'd been trying to get off the ground on the south side of town. He forced himself to read the report, struggling to make sense out of the words. His thoughts kept straying to the upcoming vote, and the impact it would have on the city.

'Shit,' he muttered in frustration, then rose and returned to the window.

He glanced down at Main Street, noticing the steady flow of pedestrians moving along the sidewalks, peering into windows and restaurants. He remembered how the town had been when he had first taken office: the almost empty streets, populated with only lurching drunks and the aimless wanderings of the homeless. At that time the signs dotting Main Street had all been garish neon advertisements for beer and fast food.

The mayor crouched forward and stared down at the clean streets, now bustling with activity. As he leaned against the window, feeling the cold press of the glass against his forehead, he futilely tried to understand the logic behind this proposed development of a mall ten miles from the urban centre. He knew, without a doubt, that the construction of this mall would negate all the effort and work he'd put into the town over the last seven years. It wouldn't happen overnight, but gradually there would be a slow shift of people once again moving westward, leaving the downtown to fend for itself. Soon those shops below would begin to close, and the lack of any viable tenants would frighten their owners into renting them to the first applicant. Within months the town would revert to what it had once been.

And this time, Mayor Presley thought sadly, there would be no stopping its decline.

Ernie Sawyer had twenty-eight years in, and at fifty-eight figured he might just take an early retirement at sixty. It would afford him full medical benefits, plus forty percent of his present salary. The medical benefits, Ernie figured wryly, might be useful. The forty percent wasn't worth shit. But this wasn't something that Ernie was particularly worried about. He'd covered that aspect of his retirement quite well on his own.

Ernie was parked alongside of Powell Park in a newer model Toyota. The car and driver had both been confiscated on a drug charge two months ago. The driver had ended up downstate for a minimum of eight, while his car had been allocated for official police use, which suited Ernie just fine. He preferred the easy maneuverability of the imports to the high-powered domestic automobiles the city always seemed to purchase.

Ernie glanced down at his watch, then back at the park.

He had another ten minutes before he was supposed to meet his man. He lit a cigarette, coughed, spat out the window, then leaned back in his seat and contemplated further the thought of an early retirement. He figured he'd then get a boat and maybe take it down to the west coast of Florida. He'd heard great things about that side of the state. A man with a fair-size boat, he'd been told more than once, had his choice of female companions – a possibility that Ernie found immensely entertaining.

At seven o'clock, Ernie saw his man glide from the shadows of the band shell in the center of the park.

Ernie climbed out of the Toyota, then hitched his suit coat across the holster buckled to the side of his belt. He flicked his cigarette into the road, then walked down the slight embankment into the shadows of the park.

'You're early,' Ernie commented.

'No. You're late,' the other man said pointedly, glancing at his watch.

Ernie grunted in annoyance. Two minutes, in Ernie's opinion, wasn't even worth mentioning.

'What's the deal?'

'We have some problems,' the man said, carefully enunciating each word.

Ernie could see the gleam of his eyes through the darkness. This image made him uncomfortable. He stepped closer to the man, until they were both hidden beneath the shadow of the band shell.

'I figured that was the case, or else you'd never have set up a meet.'

'That's very astute of you, Detective Sawyer.'

'Thanks,' Ernie replied dryly. He fumbled in his breast pocket.

The other man's eyes followed his every move.

When Ernie pulled out his cigarettes, the other man visibly relaxed.

'So what's the big problem?' Ernie asked, after he'd lit

his cigarette. He blinked. The sudden flare of the match had momentarily blinded him.

'It's quite simple, really, Mr Sawyer,' the man said, quietly stepping to Ernie's side.

Ernie, still struggling with his blurred vision, didn't notice the man's movements. It was his voice that suddenly startled him. It came from right beside him.

'You,' the man whispered.

Ernie wheeled around to face his companion. His right hand automatically reached for his revolver. He had it out of the holster before he regained his composure.

'Jesus,' Ernie said, shaking his head. 'You scared the—'

The man reached out and grabbed Ernie's right hand. Effortlessly he lifted the hand towards Ernie's face.

'What the fuck are you doing?' Ernie shouted, struggling uselessly against the other man's grip.

Smiling disdainfully, the man easily raised Ernie's revolver until it was pointed directly at the policeman's head.

'Bye-bye,' he whispered happily, then, with a sudden jerk, twisted Ernie's arm and closed his fingers around the detective's hand.

The single shot exploded in Ernie's face, jerking his head back and knocking him to the ground.

The man quickly knelt beside him and pulled an envelope from his back pocket. He slid it into the breast pocket of Ernie's suit coat, and rose to his feet. He brushed off his knees, then quickly turned and glided back into the shadows.

Ten minutes later, the man from the park stepped into a bar

on Grand Avenue. He ordered a beer, then walked to the back of the room and picked up the phone. He made two calls.

For the first call, he pulled the phone-book out from the tray and looked up the number.

The second call he dialed from memory.

He leaned against the wall and surveyed the bar, as he waited for the phone to be picked up.

'Yes?'

'It's done,' he reported curtly, without identifying himself.

'Everything?'

'Yes. I just got off the phone with the newspaper.'

'No problems?'

'None at all.' The man grinned.

'That remains to be seen,' the voice at the other end commented. Then he hung up.

Shaking his head in amusement, the man from the park replaced the phone, and walked back to his beer. He drank it slowly, idly admiring the long legs of the barmaid.

When she gestured towards his empty glass, the man reluctantly shook his head, and left the bar. It wouldn't do to be remembered here.

He walked back to his car, then drove down Grand Avenue. As he passed the park, he caught the flash of a camera going off near the band shell.

A mile later, hearing an oncoming siren, he pulled over to the side and watched a police car race down the highway, heading towards the park.

Smiling contentedly, the man pulled back on to the road and drove home.

Six

Sixty miles from Lexington, they got rained off the highway.

Crouching beneath the overhang of a bridge, Ryan pulled the collar of his jacket more tightly around his neck.

Ricky sat beside him, looking down at the motorcycle now sheltered beneath the cement structure.

'How long you think it's going to last?' Ricky asked, glancing out at the thick gray clouds to the north of them.

'A while.' Ryan shrugged and pulled out his cigarettes.

He lit up, then, catching Ricky's glance, handed him the pack.

'You're picking up a habit, kid,' Ryan commented, watching as the boy drew his legs up to his chest and wrapped his arms around his knees.

Ricky grinned at him and hit his cigarette. He leaned back and tried to blow a smoke ring. A draft of cold air quickly destroyed his efforts.

Ryan shifted further up the cement incline.

Ricky mimicked his movement.

The rain poured down on the bridge. Underneath the

shelter, small rivers had begun to form on each side of the concrete incline. The water ran down in an inverted triangular shape with Ricky and Ryan at the base of the configuration. Trucks and cars thundered through and above the underpass.

'It's loud, isn't it?' Ricky commented.

Ryan nodded.

'You always do this when it rains?'

'Depends.'

After a moment, Ricky realized that Ryan wasn't going to offer any more.

'Depends on what?' he asked.

'On where I am.' Ryan looked over at the boy. 'If there's time to get inside, I'll make a run for it.'

'Could you ride in this?' Ricky nodded towards the downpour outside their cold shelter.

'Yeah, if I had to.'

'Isn't it dangerous?'

Ryan glanced over at the boy.

'Well, it is, isn't it?' Ricky said uncomfortably.

'Everything's dangerous, kid. It's just how you do it that matters.' Ryan abruptly turned and looked to the south.

'What, what is it?'

Ryan kept peering out at the veil of rain obscuring the highway.

A moment later the sound of an engine could be heard.

Ricky squinted at the highway behind, trying to see what had caught Ryan's interest.

A moment later he made out the dim outline of a motorcycle headed down the road. He watched as the bike suddenly slowed and pulled on to the shoulder beneath the bridge. It stopped behind Ryan's cycle. It was only then that Ricky noticed the rider.

'It's a woman,' he said softly.

'Good eyes, kid,' Ryan complimented wryly, nodding a greeting to the figure below.

The woman returned his nod with an appraising glance.

'There's room,' Ryan called down to her, waving to his side.

She swung her leg over her bike and stepped over the guard-rail. She wore weathered black leathers, fringed at the wrists and pockets.

Ricky watched intently as she started up the incline. 'You know her?' he whispered.

'Just smoke your cigarette, kid,' Ryan suggested. 'How you doing?' he said, turning to face the woman.

'Wetter than snot back there.' The woman nodded towards the highway. She stood above Ryan, looking down at him carefully. After a moment she turned her gaze on Ricky.

'Cute little guy. What's he, your son or something?'

'Or something,' Ryan responded dryly, catching her taunting smile.

'He's my friend,' Ricky quickly interjected.

'Yeah, well, we all got to have friends, don't we. Shove over, there, would you,' she said to both of them.

Ricky waited until he saw Ryan move before he did the same.

The woman plopped herself down between them and grabbed her knees.

'It's colder than shit under here,' she gasped. 'Don't be strangers now. Come warm mama up a little bit.' She glanced at each of them.

Again Ricky waited to see what Ryan would do.

Ryan slid over beside her.

Ricky did the same.

'Ahh, that's better. But you,' she turned and pinched Ricky's thigh, 'have got the hottest little legs I think I've ever felt.' She grinned wickedly.

Ricky blushed and quickly stared out at the highway. His blush only deepened when he heard Ryan's amused snort.

'Where you coming from?'

'Florida.'

'What about your son here? He from Florida, too?'

'We hooked up in Kentucky.'

The woman nodded absently as she unzipped her jacket. She reached in and came out with a pack of cigarettes. She offered them around.

As she lit her cigarette, Ricky looked over at her. She was wearing only a T-shirt beneath her jacket. The white cotton fabric was damp, and clung tightly to her breasts.

Ricky quickly glanced away as she turned to him, holding out her lighter.

He crouched forward to catch the light, trying unsuccessfully to avoid staring at her breasts.

'You done looking there, hon, or you want stuff a dollar down my front.'

Blushing furiously, Ricky quickly turned away. He shuffled a few inches away from her.

'Don't be shy now, baby.' She reached over and pulled him back against her side.

'Where you coming from?' Ryan asked, leaning back on an elbow.

'I was down in Charleston for a while. Before that I was in Atlanta.'

'How's Charleston?'

'It's cool,' she said, swiveling around to look at Ryan. 'Where were you in Florida?'

'Naples.' He explained, 'It's down at the western tip.'

'Anything going on down there?'

'Nothing.' Ryan shook his head and stared out bleakly at the rain.

'What about you, hon? Where were you?'

'I was in Miami.' Ricky turned back towards her.

'Visiting grandma and grandpa.' She grinned.

'How did . . . ?' Ricky started, then abruptly stopped.

'Everybody's grandma and grandpa's in Florida. That's where they all go to die. It just like those elephants in Africa all go to that hidden canyon.'

'What hidden canyon?' Ricky asked curiously.

'The one in Tarzan, kid,' Ryan answered wearily.

'It's true,' the woman contended. 'Friend of mine was over there and saw it. Said it was filled with the biggest bones he'd ever seen.'

Ryan watched as a semi-trailer barreled through the underpass, spraying water over each of their bikes.

'He even brought home one of the bones – a little elephant's toe.'

Ricky glanced incredulously over at Ryan.

Ryan shrugged.

'I'm Flame,' the woman said, turning back to Ryan.

'That's Ricky. I'm Ryan.'

'Didn't you use to ride with the Angels?' the woman asked, eyeing him speculatively.

'Long time ago.'

'You rode with Hell's Angels?' Ricky exclaimed.

Ryan turned away from Ricky's excited stare.

'I've heard of you,' the woman said thoughtfully. 'My old man, Cain – he knows you.'

'Out of Tucson?'

'Yeah, right. He used to ride with the Gypsies.'

'Last I heard, Cain had some trouble down around Kingman.'

Flame snorted disgustedly. 'Three to five years' worth of trouble.' She paused to hit her cigarette, then spat the smoke out angrily. 'Whole fucking thing was bogus.'

'When's he due?' Ryan asked, noticing Ricky's wide-eyed glance.

'End of this year.' Flame stared out at the downpour. 'That's kind of where I was headed now,' she added softly. She turned to Ryan. 'I kind of figured it might be nice I was there when he walked out.'

Ryan nodded in agreement.

'You guys hungry? I got some stuff down there,' Flame said abruptly, pushing to her feet. She brushed off her leathers, then scrambled down the incline to her bike.

'You rode with the Hell's Angels?' Ricky whispered in disbelief.

'Let it go, kid. It's no big thing.'

'Jesus.' Ricky shook his head admiringly.

'Kid.' Ryan turned to him. 'It's not who you ride with. It's how you ride.'

Flame returned, carrying a twelve-pack of Hostess Twinkies and a six-pack of Bud.

They sat there, drinking beer and eating Twinkies, for the rest of the afternoon.

'You guys be cool,' Flame said, climbing on to her cycle.

'You tell Cain I remember him.'

'I'll do that, Ryan.' Flame turned to look at Ricky. She winked at him lasciviously, then cackled loudly when she saw him blush.

She kicked into gear, wheeled out to the highway and sped away.

Ignoring the boy's constant questions, Ryan climbed on to his bike and gestured behind him. He waited until Ricky had settled comfortably before he pulled out to the highway.

Within moments, he steadied off at seventy and let the road flow behind him.

The sound of the cylinders moved within him, until he felt their rhythm become an integral part of his body. He let the sound and vibration pull him back.

'It's nothing, man,' Tombstone said, standing at the edge of their campfire, looking off into the dark curtain of the desert.

Ryan glanced over at him.

Tombstone turned and crouched before the fire. He picked up a dried piñon branch and shoved it into the flames. 'It's all bullshit, man.' He shook his head wearily. 'You ride, thinking maybe that's the way it should be, just you and the road and nothing else.'

Tombstone pulled the branch out of the fire. The tip of it glowed brightly through the darkness.

'Freedom, man, it just ain't possible. It's a fucking movie made by Spielberg. Only freedom there is' – *Tombstone paused, waiting for Ryan's eyes* – *'is fucking death,' Tombstone said, then took the burning tip of the branch and laid it across his forearm.*

With the scent of burning flesh in his nostrils, Ryan watched on impassively as Tombstone burned the letter F into his arm.

Two weeks later, Ryan pulled over to the side and parked. He glanced over at the highway as the army of cycles roared past him. At the end, trailing slightly behind the others, was Tombstone. He raised his fist in the air, and grinned fiercely at Ryan as he rode by.

Three months later, Ryan heard Tombstone had been busted on a murder rap in Fort Lauderdale. He'd been convicted and sentenced to life without parole.

'Hey, Ryan, we going to stop somewhere or drive all night?'

'Ride, kid. Ride – not drive,' Ryan corrected, glancing over his shoulder.

'Well, are we going to ride all night, or what?'

Ryan suddenly noticed the lengthening shadows shifting across the road. He felt the chill of the coming night burrowing beneath his collar.

'Let's get past Lexington,' Ryan shouted back to him.

He felt the kid nod, then he crouched over and hit the throttle. The bike surged forward, eating up the dark road ahead of them.

Seven

Thomas Howard received the call at seven forty-five. He was seated in his office when the phone rang. He let his machine take the incoming call. It was only after he recognized the voice on the other end that he picked up the receiver.

'Hello, Donald, what can I do for you?'

'Well, Thomas, to be perfectly honest, I think it's more a case of what I can do for you,' replied Donald Alder, acting editor of the *Waukegan News*.

'And what might that be?'

'Earlier this evening the body of a police detective was discovered in Powell Park. The man's name was Ernie Sawyer. At this point they're calling it a suicide.'

'Why should I be interested in this . . .' Thomas paused, then said carefully, 'morbific occurrence?'

'Morbific, huh?'

'Yes, it means causing or producing—'

'I know what it means, Thomas,' Donald said impatiently.

'Then you understood my question.'

'Yes.' The other man sighed. 'I understood the question.'

'Then I think you should answer it.' Thomas could

almost feel the other man's anger traveling through the thin wires of the phone. The sensation amused him.

'There are a few things about his death that don't add up,' Donald said tightly.

'Such as?'

'Such as the anonymous phone-call we received about the location of his body.'

'*You* received?' Thomas quickly asked.

'Yes,' Donald responded. Surprised, as always, by Thomas's incisive ability to digest information.

'The newspaper was called first?'

'Yes, we had a man out there before the police arrived.'

'What else?'

'What makes you think there's something else?' Donald asked innocently.

'You wouldn't have called otherwise.'

'There was a letter found on the detective's body. It was the usual "*I can't live like this*" stuff, but the interesting part of this particular plea was *why* he couldn't go on living.'

'And why was that?'

'Because he claimed that, over the last four years, he had been fronting for Mayor Presley in a scam to buy up as much downtown property as possible,' Donald said, then listened to the silence at the other end.

'Did he go into details?'

'Some,' Donald replied casually, sensing the shift of the conversation, enjoying the sense of having the upper hand. He knew that would only be temporary, but he was determined to enjoy it for as long as possible.

'Are you going to tell me the rest of it?' Thomas finally asked, breaking the silence.

'I'm going to do better than that, Thomas. I'm going to send you a copy of the letter.'

'You have the original?' Thomas asked incredulously.

'No. There's no way we could have pulled that off. But my man had enough sense to realize what he had stumbled over. He copied the letter before the police arrived on the scene. I'll fax it over to you.'

'I would certainly appreciate that.'

'I thought you might.'

'Are they sure it was a suicide?'

'That's what they're releasing to the press.'

'What do *you* think?'

'If it was suicide, it was very neat. The anonymous call came into our office five minutes before the second call to the police. It gave us more than enough time to get a man on the scene.'

'And enough time to read the letter,' Thomas completed thoughtfully.

'Yes, that too.'

'How are the police handling it?'

'They've acknowledged that a suicide note was found on the scene, but they're not releasing its contents.'

'And how are *you* going to handle it?'

'It's news,' Donald said nonchalantly. 'And news always has a way of being reported.'

Thomas smiled.

'So I'll fax it over to you.'

'I would appreciate that.'

'And I'll be hearing from you soon, won't I, Thomas?'

'Yes, Donald. I would think we'll be talking tomorrow about our future financial considerations.'

Thomas hung up the phone and stepped over to the fax machine.

The hum of the machine announced the oncoming arrival of the letter.

'*To whom it may concern...*' was the first sentence that appeared.

Thomas's smile grew as he read the rest of the fax.

It was only after he'd read the letter a second time that he leaned back and began to consider its full import.

Thomas reached for the phone. He grimaced when he heard the sound of an answering machine. He waited for the beep.

'Will, please get back to me as quickly as possible,' he said into the recording device, without bothering to identify himself.

Thomas hung up the phone and thoughtfully poured himself a brandy. He again picked up the letter and re-read it, then leaned back, waiting impatiently for Will to return his call.

In 1982, six years before Charles Presley took office, the Waukegan Police Force voted to go on strike.

Of the one hundred and thirty-four policeman on the force, eighty-two called in sick on the designated afternoon with what came to be known as the Blue Flu.

The mayor at that time was renowned for his intractable inability to negotiate. He felt that the art of negotiation was simply stating what he wanted, and then waiting for the other side to capitulate. In accordance with this philosophy, the mayor publicly announced that any policeman calling in sick the next day would be fired.

Fourteen policeman called in sick that morning. All fourteen were summarily fired. The terms of their dismissal negated all of their accumulated benefits.

Will Leland was one of them. After eight years on the force, Leland had reluctantly decided to support the strike. His support was more a measure of solidarity than any strong belief in the ultimate aims of the inchoate union.

On the first evening of the strike, Will had met with the other eighty-four policemen at a local bar. They had all drunkenly vowed to stand firm until the mayor conceded to their demands. The next morning the majority of them had changed their minds, without bothering to inform Will.

Suddenly finding himself unemployed, and pointedly avoided by all those who had returned to work, Will lost it. Embittered and despondent over his firing and the apostasy of his fellow officers, Will found a measure of comfort in drinking.

For almost thirteen months Will looked for answers in the bottom of a bottle. By the end of that year, he slowly came to realize that there weren't any answers. There were only more questions.

It took him almost another full year to pull himself back together. He began attending classes at a local junior college, and frequenting the smoky rooms of AA meetings.

Two and a half years after his dismissal, Will had his real-estate license and a reasonably good chance at putting his life back together.

He took a job with a local real-estate agency, and soon found himself in charge of rental properties. Over the next three years Will proved to be very effective at his new occupation. His effectiveness did not go unnoticed by his employers. He was amply rewarded financially.

Despite his success, Will still missed his work on the police force. There was a sense of excitement and challenge about it that his present occupation couldn't compare to.

He'd often thought about trying to return to the force, maybe in another city or state. But whenever his thoughts turned to the possibility of police work, he still found a corresponding sense of bitterness over his treatment at the hands of the city and those who controlled it.

While he missed police work, he vowed to never return to it unless he could do so on his own terms.

When Thomas Howard had first approached him, Will had quickly accepted his offer. This had as much to do with the type of work Howard desired as it did with Howard himself.

Will, along with almost all the other policemen on the force, had been an avid admirer of Howard. Thomas at that time had been the State's Attorney, and had a well-deserved reputation for tenacity in his pursuit of indictments. It was said that once Howard took up a case, the verdict was a foregone conclusion. The only factor in question was the amount of prison time the indicted would serve.

Will's first job for Thomas was a security check on a potential customer. He had little trouble with his inquiries.

Over the intervening five years, Will had carefully repaired his relationships with most of the men still on the force. Friendship and guilt were the motivating factors in Will's frequent requests to them for help.

Will knew this and used it.

His relationship with Thomas Howard continued, and gradually changed over the years. He slowly began to handle all of the security problems encountered by Howard Ltd. The legality of some of these problems, Will realized, was questionable at best. But he found the excitement of the job and the financial remuneration much too attractive to refuse.

Will discovered the message on his machine at eight twenty-five. He dialed the number, smiling in anticipation as he thought of Thomas Howard and the lucrative jobs he sometimes commissioned.

'Mr Howard?'

'Yes, Will. I've been waiting for your call.'

'What can I do for you, sir?'

'Ernie Sawyer,' Thomas said, without preamble. 'He was a detective with the city police.'

'Was?'

'Yes, was.' Thomas smiled, pleased at Will's question. 'His body was discovered this evening in Powell Park – an apparent suicide. I would like you to look into it for me. Try to find out how seriously it's being handled, and what information the police have on the subject.'

'I take it, sir, that there are some questions about the suicide?'

'Possibly. That's what I want you to find out for me.'

'Have you done anything on your own?'

'No, it's important that I distance myself as far as possible from this investigation.'

'Okay, Mr Howard, I can start on it immediately.'

'Keep me apprised of any developments.'

'I'll do that, sir.'

'Thank you, Will.'

Will hung up the phone, then hit the stop button on his answering machine. He had a complete recording of the conversation. He replaced the tape with a fresh one, then carried the old one into his bedroom.

In the bottom right-hand corner of his closet, he lifted a carefully crafted section of the floorboard. Inside the small compartment was a shoebox. Will pulled out the box and opened it. It was filled with tapes from his answering machine.

Will took the new tape and carefully recorded the date and time, then scribbled Thomas Howard's name across the front of it. He put it in the box, then replaced it in its hiding place.

The ubiquitous advent of answering machines often amused Will. He wondered if people had any idea how easily their conversations could now be recorded.

Will grabbed a bottle of O'Douls on his way to the

phone. He carried both the phone and the non-alcoholic beverage to the couch.

He sat down and dialed. As he listened to it ring at the other end, he grinned, beginning to see a possible way he could make it all work out to his benefit.

Eight

Jane returned from the ladies' room to find a fresh drink placed before her seat at the bar. She glanced up at the bartender.

'Crayton,' Bob answered, responding to her inquisitive glance. He gestured across the crowded room.

Jane turned and caught Bill Crayton's ready gaze.

She smiled, nodding her thanks, then slid on to the barstool and picked up her drink.

It was nine thirty. Jane had been in the lounge for the last hour and a half.

She'd left the offices of Howard Ltd at six, and decided to stop at the Burgundy Room for a glass of wine.

The Burgundy Room was situated two blocks east of the courthouse, and was the local hang-out for many of the lawyers and judges that practiced in the city proper. The combination lounge and restaurant offered generous drinks and a modest menu.

Jane had sipped her first glass of wine slowly, listening to the soft murmur of voices around her. Then the thought of going home to the silence of the house had incited her to order a second. As she drank this one, she'd found herself absently surveying the menu.

She'd finished her drink, then ordered another and carried it with her into the restaurant portion of the building. She'd taken a window table in the back and ordered dinner. She'd pulled her book from her purse and read while she ate.

Over coffee, she'd suddenly become aware of the voices around her. She'd glanced up from her book, surprised by the sight of the now crowded room.

She'd replaced her book in her purse, then ordered a brandy and carried it with her into the lounge, deciding she would allow herself one last nightcap.

She'd taken a seat at the bar and surveyed the predominantly male clientele. Through her father's business, and his years with the State's Attorney's office, most of the men were familiar to her. Many of them had been out to the house. She'd acknowledged their greetings, then turned to face the bar.

The back bar was lined with bottles. Behind the bottles was a rectangular mirror. Jane caught sight of her reflection through the multi-colored bottles. She pushed back a strand of dark hair and picked up her drink.

'How you doing, Jane?' Crayton said, stepping up beside her.

'Fine.'

'I haven't seen you down here in a while.'

'I've been busy,' Jane said curtly, without turning to look at him.

Crayton glanced around, then leaned over her shoulder. 'I was going to call, but...' He shrugged.

'But what?' Jane turned to him.

'Well, you know.' Crayton glanced away.

'Your wife?' Jane smiled tightly.

'C'mon, Jane. You knew I was married.'

'Yes, I did.' Jane turned and held her own reflective gaze.

'Let me buy you a drink.'

'You already did.'

'Well' – Bill grinned – 'then let me buy you another.'

'Is Sylvia out of town?' Jane asked pointedly.

'Matter of fact she is.'

'Bill.' Jane turned to face him. 'Thank you for the drink and the offer, but I would really rather be alone, if you don't mind.'

'Sure, no problem,' Crayton said quickly, backing away from her.

Jane swiveled back to the bar, catching sight of his swift retreat in the mirror. She knew his easy exit had more to do with who her father was than anything she had said.

Jane sipped her drink, beginning to feel the first effects of the alcohol.

She leaned back in her chair and studied her reflection. She felt a sense of dislocation from the image before her, as if the image were not hers but someone else's. The person in the mirror seemed strong and in control.

Jane raised her glass and silently toasted this woman.

Bob, the barman, appeared, nodding towards her empty glass.

Jane debated, then shook her head. She picked up her purse and carefully made her way through the crowd towards the door. She felt the men's eyes follow her as she passed them.

She walked down Main Street, peering into the shop windows. Her reflection peered back at her from the dark glass, and it seemed to mock her with its easy display of strength.

Jane drove down to the waterfront. She parked and walked out on the concrete breakwater. At the end, in front of the small lighthouse, a young couple stood with their arms wrapped around each other.

Jane paused to watch them.

They suddenly became aware of her and quickly stepped apart. Holding hands, they passed her, avoiding her glance.

Jane leaned against the lighthouse and stared out at the dark water. The waves lapped softly at the concrete pilings.

Jane closed her eyes and rested her head against the structure's cold plating.

She remembered her mother, remembered the warmth of her arms and her voice, and remembered the sudden coldness that had seemed to seep throughout the house once her mother had gone.

'I knew you'd be here.'

Startled, Jane opened her eyes and turned.

Bill Crayton stood a few feet from her.

Jane stared at him.

'It's where you always come, isn't it?' He shrugged, then stepped over to her.

'Are you okay, Jane?' He reached out to touch her shoulder.

'I'm fine,' Jane said, then quickly glanced away, wondering how many times she could tell this lie, and trying to remember the last time she'd been able to believe it.

'You sure?'

'Yes.'

'It's nice out here,' Bill said a moment later. He turned and looked towards the shore. 'I put the boat back in last week.' He turned again to look at Jane.

'You remember the boat?'

'Yes.'

'I miss that,' he said quietly, trying to capture her gaze.

Jane took a deep breath. She felt it catch in her throat.

'What do you want, Bill?'

'You,' Bill whispered.

'And Sylvia?'

'What about her?' Bill said, bracing his arms against the lighthouse, trapping her inside of them.

'She's your wife.'

'So?' He shrugged, leaning forward.

Jane tilted her head and met his lips. She felt his hands close around her sides, then begin to slide down to her hips.

His grip tightened, pulling her against him. His hand rose and closed around her breast.

She shut her eyes tightly as his hand began to feverishly burrow beneath her clothing.

'Love me,' she whispered softly, and knew that he hadn't heard – and knew also that she hadn't wanted him to hear.

* * *

'I have to go.' Jane abruptly rose from the berth and began to pick up her clothes. She felt Bill's eyes examining her.

She sat on the edge of the bed to put on her shoes.

At the door she turned to look at him. He was sprawled on his back with his arms crossed behind his head, smiling at her.

'Drive carefully,' he said.

As she turned away, she saw him reach for the television remote.

Standing on the dock, she heard the piercing sound of a police siren coming from the television set below deck.

The outside porch light was on when she got home.

She quietly let herself into the house and stopped in the kitchen. She poured herself a glass of orange juice and drank it, leaning against the sink. The silence of the house magnified her every sound.

She climbed the stairs to her room.

'That you, Jane?'

'Yes, Dad.'

'It's late.'

'I know,' she said to his closed door.

'Were you working?'

'Yes, Dad. I was working,' Jane said wearily.

'Goodnight, Jane.'

''Night, Dad.'

Only after she'd closed the door to her room did she feel safe.

* * *

'What the fuck is going on?' Mayor Presley asked, as he stalked across his living-room.

Christian sat on the couch, watching him.

'What?' the mayor demanded, pausing to look at his friend.

'I don't know, Charlie. I don't know what the hell it's all about.'

'Goddamnit.' Presley began to pace again. 'This thing's going to be all over the papers tomorrow.'

'I thought you had that covered.'

The mayor paused to glare at Christian. 'Alder does whatever he wants, and what he wants now is that goddamn mall.' The mayor slammed his hand against the wall. 'Jesus, what the hell is going on?'

'What do *you* think's going on?' Christian asked quietly.

'I think that goddamn Howard is behind all of this.'

'You think he killed the detective?' Christian said incredulously.

'No, I don't think he's that desperate.' Presley stopped in front of Christian. 'But I think he had something to do with that letter.'

'How?'

'I don't know,' the mayor said thoughtfully, then a moment later added, 'Maybe he was working with Sawyer all along, and somehow he convinced him that I was behind it.'

'That's pretty far-fetched, Charlie.'

'And what happened isn't?' Presley demanded.

'I see your point.' Christian nodded. 'But I can't see how

77

Howard could have carried that off. After all, Sawyer was a detective. I'm sure he didn't take anything at face value.'

'You're probably right.' The mayor took a deep breath, then sat down across from Christian.

'Who do you have working on it?'

'Ellroy.'

'He's good.'

'Yes, and he's also someone I can trust, which seems to be becoming a pretty scarce commodity these days.'

'Don't sell yourself short, Charlie. You've still got the backing of a lot of people.'

'Well, I'm sure the hell going to need it when this thing hits tomorrow.'

'What have you done so far to control it?'

'The usual: a statement denying any knowledge and complicity on my part. For whatever good that's going to do me,' he added disgustedly.

'Charlie.' Christian rose and crossed the room to the other man. He gripped the mayor's shoulder. 'You have a lot of people in your corner. The only ones who are going to believe this are the ones that want to believe it – and you've already lost them anyway.'

'Christ, Christian, I wish I could believe that, but I think this thing is going to muddy up the whole referendum. The issue isn't going to be about the mall anymore. It's going to turn into a vote of confidence about my administration.'

'Well, I don't think you have anything to worry about there. The people in this town know damn well whose side you're on.'

'Thanks.'

'Hey, don't mention it.' Christian smiled.

The mayor rose to his feet. 'I've got to get down to the office.' He shrugged into his suit coat.

'Why? It's almost two o'clock in the morning. Why don't you get some rest?'

'No, this thing goes wrong, and I'm going to have plenty of time to rest *after* the election.'

'What can you possibly do now?'

The mayor paused at the door. 'I don't know, Christian, but if there is anything to be done, I want to be available and ready to do it.' He nodded to his friend. 'Lock up when you leave.'

Christian stepped over to the window and watched the mayor pull out of the drive.

He turned away and stepped over to the liquor cabinet standing against the wall. He poured himself a scotch and carried it over to the couch. There he sat, sipping the smoothly aged liquor, and smiled thoughtfully at the empty room.

Nine

Ryan sprawled across one of the double beds in a Motel Six, a few miles west of Shelbyville. The sound of the shower came from the bathroom. He leaned over to stub out his cigarette, then fell back across the bed. He stared up at the white stucco ceiling, and let it draw him back.

Zella, lying on the hospital gurney. The bright fluorescent lights leaching her face of color.

The almost painful grip of her hand in his.

The battered yellow doors of the surgery before them.

Leaning over to kiss her, watching her suddenly rear back in horror, unable to remember him.

The tumor had already taken that portion of her brain.

The hours of waiting in the hallway. The passage of time measured by the cigarette butts in the ashtray.

The weary resignation on the doctor's face as he stepped through the surgery doors.

The sight of the brown oblong casket disappearing into the belly of the plane.

The cold and seemingly endless emptiness of the house.

Zella.

81

'Your turn.' Ricky grinned, standing at the edge of the other bed, toweling himself off.

Ryan grunted, then rose and stepped into the bathroom. He gripped each edge of the sink and stared at his reflection. The bloodshot gaze that looked back at him forced him to quickly turn away.

'Food,' Ryan growled, once he'd showered and dressed.

Ricky scrambled to get his coat. 'It's cold,' Ricky observed, stepping outside.

Ryan grunted and started across the parking lot.

'Where we going?' Ricky asked, matching his stride.

Ryan nodded towards the Waffle House across the lot.

'I've never eaten at one of those before. Are they any good?'

Ryan turned to examine him. When he was sure the kid was serious, he snorted in disbelief.

'What?' Ricky asked.

'Nothing.' Ryan shrugged. Then, as they approached the door, he offered, 'Just don't order the Beef Wellington. They never get it right.'

They sat in a booth overlooking the parking lot. Ryan ordered the steak and eggs and coffee. He lit a cigarette as he and the waitress waited for Ricky to make up his mind.

'Just get the steak and eggs,' Ryan finally said, impatiently.

'I don't think I want meat,' Ricky responded, glancing across the table.

'Why don't you try one of the omelettes,' the waitress suggested hopefully.

'Well, I don't really feel like eggs.' Ricky went back to his examination of the menu.

'Could you get my coffee while he's trying to decide? Seems like it's going to take him a while.'

'Sure.' The waitress retreated behind the counter.

Ricky gave him a hurt look.

Ryan shook his head and leaned back against the booth. He and Ricky were the only customers. One of the waitresses stepped from behind the counter towards the jukebox.

As their waitress brought over Ryan's coffee, 'Achy Breaky Heart' blared out of the speakers.

'Christ,' Ryan muttered disgustedly.

'What's wrong?'

'You decide yet?'

'Yeah.' Ricky smiled. He glanced over at the waitress as she placed Ryan's coffee before him. 'I think I would like the steak and eggs.'

Ryan muttered softly under his breath, as Ricky carefully explained how he wanted his steak and eggs done.

As the waitress walked away, he caught Ryan's glance.

'If you don't tell people what you want and how you want it, you never get what you want,' Ricky said primly.

'Where the hell did you hear that?'

'My father.' Ricky shrugged.

'Your father always gets what he wants?' Ryan asked, pulling the ashtray over and stubbing out his cigarette.

'Always.' Ricky reached for Ryan's cigarettes and pulled one out.

'Why?'

'What do you mean?'

'I mean how come your father always gets what he wants?' Ryan paused, looking thoughtfully over at the kid. 'I don't think I know anyone who *always* gets what they want. Usually it's only what they deserve.'

'My father used to be the State's Attorney,' Ricky said importantly.

'So?' Ryan shrugged.

'So he's a pretty powerful man in Waukegan.'

'Where the hell is Waukegan? I don't think I've ever heard of it,' Ryan said, studying the boy carefully.

'It's about fifty miles north of Chicago, and a little sou—' Ricky suddenly stopped and looked across the table.

Ryan grinned back at him.

After a moment, Ricky returned his smile and nodded. 'Okay, it *is* a small town,' he grudgingly admitted. 'But still, he's done real well for himself.'

Ryan shrugged and reached for his coffee.

'...and, after she died, it was pretty much Jane who raised me.'

Ryan leaned back, pushed away his plate, and stretched.

Ricky took his napkin from his lap and neatly folded it, then placed it beside his empty plate.

'She works with your father, then?'

'Yes, she's pretty much his right hand – or, at least, that's what he calls her.'

'And you're going to be his left hand?'

Ricky glanced over and caught Ryan's smile.

'No.' He grinned. 'I don't think so.'

'You don't want to go into the business?' Ryan caught the waitress's eye and motioned to his coffee cup.

'Not really.' Ricky glanced away.

'What do you want to do?'

'I don't know.' The boy shrugged, then looked up gratefully as the waitress appeared.

Ryan leaned back, watching her clear away their plates and refill their coffee cups. He lit a cigarette, then slid the pack over to Ricky. He waited until the kid lit up, before asking, 'You don't have any idea?'

'About what?' Ricky said innocently.

'About what you want to do when you get out of school.'

'I'm already out. The last two years I took summer courses. I just graduated last September.'

'That's great, kid, but *now* what are you going to do?'

'I guess I'll probably work with my father for a while.'

'No college?'

'Not right off. Maybe later.' Ricky shifted uncomfortably, avoiding Ryan's eye.

Ryan waited until he'd caught the boy's gaze. 'What do you want to do, Ricky?' he asked quietly.

'Nothing.' Ricky shrugged.

'What?' Ryan asked again, unwilling to let it go.

'I'd like to go to medical school,' Ricky said a moment later, raising his eyes to Ryan's.

'Dad doesn't want you to, huh?'

'No.'

Ryan shrugged. 'What happened to *unless you tell people what you want and how you want it, you don't get it?*'

85

Ricky picked up his coffee, avoiding both Ryan's eye and his question.

'What do you think?' Ryan said, pausing outside the restaurant and nodding down the highway.

Ricky turned and saw a brightly lit bar set a little back from the road, about four blocks away from them.

'I don't think they'd let me in.'

'You want to find out?' Ryan asked.

'Yeah, why not?' Ricky grinned excitedly.

Ryan nodded and started walking.

Fifty yards from the bar they could hear the plaintive strains of a country-music song pealing out through the closed doors.

At the entrance, Ricky paused.

Ryan clapped him on the back, then reached around and opened the door.

They stepped into a dark hallway. The hallway opened into a large, smoke-filled room. At the far end of the room a four-piece band stood highlighted beneath an array of colored lights. Opposite the band was a long mahogany bar. Tables dotted the space between the bar and the band. The tables stopped a few yards short of the band, allowing for a small rectangular dance floor.

The tables were all occupied, as was most of the bar. Ryan spotted two empty stools at the far end, and nudged Ricky towards them.

'Two Buds,' Ryan ordered.

The bartender paused, eyeing Ricky carefully. He glanced over at Ryan.

'We're just going to have the one, and then we're out of here,' Ryan said, holding the bartender's gaze.

The man nodded reluctantly, then turned away. A moment later he placed two Bud long-necks in front of them.

Ryan picked up his beer, smiling at Ricky's excited grin. He drank, then turned and looked over at the band. The dance floor was tightly packed with men wearing cowboy hats and with women in fringed dresses and white cowboy boots.

'This is great,' Ricky said enthusiastically.

'Yeah, it sure is,' Ryan commented dryly.

Ricky turned to lean back against the bar, emulating Ryan, and looked out at the crowd.

The band finished their song and segued into another. The dance floor quickly regrouped and began to line-dance. The tables emptied as couples hurried out to join in.

'You know how to do that?' Ricky nodded to the synchronized dancers.

'No.' Ryan shook his head. 'Not my style. What about you?' he added.

Ricky giggled and raised his beer.

Ryan noticed that it was almost empty. He glanced down at his own practically full bottle, then shrugged and pulled out his cigarettes.

After watching the kid fumble three matches, Ryan commented, 'You don't drink too much, do you kid?'

'I drink a lot,' Ricky maintained, leaning forward, finally managing to bring the tip of his cigarette to the flame.

'Yeah.' Ryan nodded. 'I can see that you're a real drinking man.'

'I like scotch best of all,' Ricky confided. 'That's a man's drink.'

'That what your father drinks?'

'How'd you know that?'

'Shot in the dark.' Ryan turned as the band ended their song with a drum-roll. The lead singer then announced a short break and, a moment later, canned music drifted in over the speaker system.

Ryan turned to face the bar.

Ricky did the same. He took a last sip at his empty bottle, then placed it on the bar in front of him, and glanced over expectantly at Ryan.

Ryan shook his head. 'You're on Cokes now, kid. One's enough for the night.'

'I can handle it.'

'I can see that,' Ryan acknowledged.

'You don't think I can?'

'Yeah, I think you're fine. We just don't want to get the bartender in trouble,' Ryan told him.

'Oh yeah, right.' Ricky nodded.

Ryan waved the bartender over and ordered a Coke for Ricky.

'On the house,' the bartender said, placing the glass on the bar.

'Thanks,' Ryan nodded to him.

'It's all right.' The bartender glanced down the bar, then leaned forward. 'Where you guys headed?'

'Waukegan,' Ricky responded.

'Where?'

'Illinois,' Ryan told him.

'Cold up there now?'

'That's what I hear.' Ryan raised his beer.

'You riding, huh?' The bartender nodded at Ryan's leather jacket.

'Yeah.'

'What're you on?'

'Suzuki.' Ryan sighed.

'Gook bike?'

'Yeah.'

'Shit, those rice-burners, man.' The bartender shook his head disdainfully.

'The thing's a horse,' Ryan shrugged. 'It's too good to let go.'

'You'd never catch me on one of them.' The bartender straightened. 'If it ain't a hog, it shouldn't be on the road.'

'It's a damn good motorcycle,' Ricky said suddenly.

Both Ryan and the bartender turned to look at him.

'Well, it is,' Ricky stubbornly defended, glancing over at Ryan for approval.

'It's a good ride,' Ryan agreed.

Ricky glared across the bar at the bartender.

'Hey, kid, take it easy, huh.'

'Well you shouldn't be putting down my friend's motorcycle.'

'Ricky—' Ryan tried to interrupt.

'Kid, I'm doing you a favor by just letting you in here.' The bartender paused, leveling his gaze at Ricky. 'Now don't be an asshole.'

'I'm not the one who's being an asshole,' Ricky countered angrily.

The bartender whipped around and grabbed Ricky's shirt front. He jerked him against the bar.

'You calling me an asshole?'

'Let's chill out here,' Ryan said quietly, aware of the sudden silence in the bar.

'I asked you a question, punk?' the bartender spat out.

Ricky suddenly stiffened at the word punk. He reached up and tried to pull the man's hand from his shirt.

The bartender grinned and twisted his fist into Ricky's chest.

'Let him go,' Ryan said softly.

The bartender glanced over at him.

'You got a problem, Billy?'

Ryan looked over and saw a man standing a few feet to his side. The man wore a T-shirt with the bar's logo printed across the front of it. His heavily muscled arms jutted out from each sleeve.

Ryan backed away from the bar, until he had both the bouncer and the bartender in sight.

'There's no problem here. We were just leaving,' Ryan said, turning to the bartender. 'Let him go, Billy.'

The bartender glanced over at Ryan.

'We don't want this to get out of hand, do we?' Ryan said softly, holding the other man's gaze.

'Get out of here,' the bartender said disgustedly, shoving Ricky away.

Ricky stumbled, then regained his balance and glared across the bar at the other man.

'Leave it alone,' Ryan said sharply, sensing Ricky's impending outburst.

Startled, Ricky glanced over at him.

Ryan took him by the arm and gently nudged him towards the doorway. He felt, more than heard, the bouncer following them.

At the entrance to the hallway, Ricky tried to twist out of Ryan's grasp.

'Ricky, leave it be,' Ryan ordered, moving the boy into the hallway and toward the front door.

'Why didn't you do something?' Ricky demanded, once they'd stepped outside.

'Like what?' He reached for his cigarettes and offered one to Ricky.

'Hit him?' Ricky spat out, pulling a cigarette and waiting for Ryan to pass him the matches.

'And then what?'

'What do you mean "and then what"?'

Ryan shrugged. 'What happens after I hit him.' He started down the highway towards their motel.

'Well then you could have—'

'Could have what?' Ryan interrupted, pausing to look back. 'Could have spent the night in jail, got the shit kicked out of me. What? What the fuck do you think was going to happen in there?'

Ricky stepped back from Ryan's outburst.

'Kid,' Ryan said, shaking his head wearily. 'First thing you got to learn is when to pick your moves. And standing on somebody's turf, winging a fist at his head, is just fucking stupid.'

91

'Yeah, and what's the second thing?' Ricky asked.

'The second thing.' Ryan stopped to level his gaze at the boy. 'Is that you were way off base.'

'That's bullshit,' Ricky sputtered.

Ryan ignored him and continued to walk along the highway.

At the door to the motel room, he waited for Ricky to catch up, then opened the door.

'The guy insulted your motorcycle,' Ricky said, fumbling with the key.

'Did he?'

'Yeah, he called it a rice-burner.' Ricky finally fitted the key into the lock and opened the door.

'It *is* a rice-burner.' Ryan stepped into the room.

'But...'

'But what?' Ryan sprawled across his bed, and looked over at the boy.

Ricky stumbled over to his bed and sat on the edge of it. 'I don't know.' He paused, then shrugged. 'It just seemed like you should've done something.'

'There wasn't anything to do. Guy was just talking. He wasn't looking to jump anybody.'

Ricky fell across the bed and curled up on his side. He looked over at Ryan. 'You think you could've taken him.'

Ryan snorted derisively and crossed his hands behind his head. He stared up at the ceiling.

The next time he glanced over at Ricky, the boy was asleep.

Ryan pulled off the kid's shoes, then covered him with the bedspread. He paused, standing over the boy, then

92

turned off the light and climbed on to his bed. A moment later a match flared in the darkness.

Ryan smoked, letting the drift of memories wash over him. He cautiously allowed them to play out before him, having discovered in the jail cell how deeply potent they had become.

'Is Daddy sick?' Neal asked.

Ryan glanced across the room. He could just make out the pale features of his brother's face across the dark shadows of their bedroom.

'What do you mean?' a twelve-year-old Ryan asked, then listened to the silence.

'How come he's so mean all the time?' Neal finally said.

Ryan propped himself up on an elbow and looked across the room.

'How come Mom doesn't do anything? How come she lets him keep hurting us?' Neal asked.

Ryan heard his brother's sob, then moved across the room to him.

'It's okay. He's just tired,' Ryan said softly, touching his brother's shoulder.

Neal winced.

'What's wrong?'

'Nothing.' Neal turned his head away.

'What is it?' Ryan asked, gently touching his brother's shoulder again.

Neal moaned.

Ryan turned on the light, then crouched beside his brother's bed and carefully pulled away Neal's T-shirt.

Across his shoulder was a darkening bruise.

93

'Did Dad do this?' Ryan asked, catching his brother's gaze.

'I fell,' Neal cried, shoving his face into the pillow.

'Neal,' Ryan whispered softly, then climbed into bed beside him.

Neal quickly turned and threw his arms around Ryan's chest. He hugged him tightly.

'Don't let him hurt me any more. Please, Eddie, don't let him do that to me,' Neal sobbed.

Ryan held him until he fell asleep. Only then did he turn away from his eight-year-old brother's bed and leave the room.

He tiptoed down the hallway to the door of his parents' room, then paused and listened. He opened the door and peeked inside.

His mother was curled up along one side of the bed. The other side was empty.

Ryan quietly made his way down the stairs. He found his father sprawled across the couch; an almost empty bottle of Jack Daniels dangled from his fingers.

Ryan sat on the cold floor in front of the couch and stared at his father's face, trying to find something in it he recognized. His eyes kept straying to his father's gnarled, work-worn hands, imagining them clenched into fists, rising and striking out at his brother.

His father suddenly coughed and jerked forward.

Ryan sat impassively in front of the couch, staring up at him.

His father blinked and ran a hand across his eyes. He suddenly became aware of Ryan seated before him.

'What the fuck do you want?' his father snarled.

Ryan forced himself to meet the angry glare.

'Well – what?' his father demanded, raising the bottle and finishing it off. He threw the empty behind the couch and leaned forward.

'Get me a beer, would you, kid.'

Ryan remained motionless before him.

'What the fuck's wrong with you,' his father suddenly shouted, pushing himself to his feet. He swayed for a moment, then reached out for the arm of the couch to regain his balance.

'Get me a fucking beer. Now!' the man shouted.

Ryan stared back at him.

'You little faggot,' his father snorted, then started to turn away.

'Leave Neal alone,' Ryan said softly.

His father whirled around to glare at him. 'What the fuck you say to me?' He squinted down at his son.

'Leave him alone,' Ryan said again, struggling unsuccessfully to control his quivering voice.

His father reared back and laughed. 'Or what?' he demanded, crouching forward to smirk at Ryan. 'Just what the fuck do you think you're going to do about it?'

'Please, just—'

'You fucking mealy-mouthed little prick.' His father lashed out with his foot.

The blow caught Ryan on the shoulder and tumbled him across the room. He quickly curled up on his side, as the man staggered over and kicked him again.

A moment later he heard the sound of the refrigerator

door opening. Hugging his ribs, Ryan quickly stumbled to his feet, and up the stairs to his room.

He listened to the sounds of his brother sleeping, then staggered over to his bed. He bit the edge of his pillow to muffle his sobs, and vowed that he would never let anyone hurt Neal again.

Two weeks later, Ryan came home from school to find Neal hiding in the mangroves behind the stilt-house, gingerly cradling his arm.

It had been broken in two places.

Neal wore a cast for the next three months.

Ricky suddenly shifted, and muttered softly in his sleep.

Startled, Ryan jerked forward and stared across the dark room.

'Neal?' Ryan whispered, then quickly rose to his feet and stepped over to the other bed.

He stared down at the kid, then, shaking his head wearily, retreated back to his bed.

Propped up against the headboard, Ryan lit another cigarette and stared blankly at the flickering images of the TV set before him.

Ten

'Don, how are you?'

'Just fine, Charlie. How about yourself?'

'I've been better,' the mayor admitted, swiveling around to look out the window of his office. An east wind angrily capped the waves washing across the lake.

'I can certainly understand that, Charlie. You seem to have something of a situation here.' Don Alder smiled at the receiver.

'Yes, that's what I wanted to talk to you about.'

'Well, you know, Charlie – anything I can do to help, you just tell me.'

'I'm glad you feel that way, Don, because there *is* something I was wondering about.'

'And what's that?'

'I was wondering when you might get around to printing my statement.'

'Charlie, by the time we got your statement, it was much too late to get it into today's edition.' Alder grinned. 'But I can promise you: first thing tomorrow morning we'll have your rebuttal right there on the front page.'

'I would certainly appreciate that, Don.'

'Charlie, you know me. Whatever I can do to help, all you have to do is ask.'

The mayor turned back to his desk and glanced at the front page of the *Waukegan News*.

MAYOR IMPLICATED IN LOCAL DETECTIVE'S DEATH is what the headline read.

Presley snorted in disgust.

'You say something, Charlie?'

'No, just admiring your headline.'

'Should sell a lot of papers.'

'Yes, I imagine it will.'

'It's a big story, Charlie.' Alder glanced up as his secretary tentatively knocked on his office door. He angrily waved her away, then turned his attention back to the telephone. This was a call he'd been expecting with great anticipation.

'Anything else I can do for you, Charlie?'

'No, Don, I think you've done more than enough.'

'Well, you take care, Mr Mayor.'

'I'll do that,' the mayor responded, then hung up the phone.

'Asshole,' Presley muttered, glaring at the telephone. He shook his head in disgust, then transferred his gaze to the man sitting across from him.

'What do you have so far?' he asked.

'Nothing,' Detective Ellroy responded. Then, catching the mayor's glance, explained. 'We haven't had time to do anything but a preliminary investigation.'

'Which means what?'

'We canvassed the park area. Nobody heard or saw

anything. And we checked out his house, and came up with nothing. This morning I'm going to get a warrant from Peters, and I'll take a look at his financial records.'

'Have you found anything that would give any credence to his allegations?'

'Nothing yet, but then I haven't had time to get into the financial end of it,' Ellroy said, wearily running a hand through his thinning hair.

'I appreciate this, Tom. I realize you're putting in some extra hours on this.'

Ellroy responded with a tired smile.

'I won't forget it, Tom, believe me.'

'I should get back to it.' Ellroy pushed himself to his feet. He rubbed the small of his back, then turned towards the door.

'You'll let me know if anything comes up?'

'As soon as I've got something,' Ellroy answered, and exited the mayor's office.

Behind his desk, the mayor leaned back. His glance fell on the newspaper. Scowling angrily, he grabbed it and threw it into the wastebasket across the room.

'Mr Mayor?'

'Yes, Jean?' Presley glanced up at the door.

'You have the radio interview in fifteen minutes,' she reminded him.

'Thanks.' Charlie Presley nodded tiredly. He stood, then stepped into his small office bathroom and began to make himself presentable for his constituency.

The bar was called Dom's Ten Pin. It was the only one of

the beer and shot joints that had managed to survive the remodeling of the city. Set in the center of a block, on a cross street bisecting the town, it had opened fifty-six years ago, and had that weary countenance of a place that would last another fifty-six years.

Ellroy arrived fifteen minutes early. He took a seat at the far end of the bar and ordered a cup of coffee. The mud-colored brew was served in a chipped beer stein.

Ellroy was on his second refill when he saw Will Leland step through the front doors. Leland paused for a moment at the entrance, blinking as he tried to adjust to the dim lighting.

'Over here, Will,' Ellroy called out, and watched the other man smile and then walk over to him. Ellroy picked up his cup, wondering what Leland wanted.

'I think I'll have the same,' Leland said, nodding towards Ellroy's coffee. He turned to the detective, 'So, Tom, how you been?'

'Good. And you?'

'Fine. Everything's going great.'

'Yeah, I hear you've become a real hotshot in real estate.'

'I'm doing okay.' Leland nodded as the bartender placed his coffee in front of him.

'Still not drinking, huh?' Ellroy observed.

'Yep. Been five years now,' Leland said, adding generous portions of cream and sugar to his coffee. The mixture turned the liquid an unappetizing grayish-brown color.

'I have to admit I was a little surprised to hear from you.' Ellroy swiveled on his stool to face the other man. 'It's been what – two, three years now?'

'Yeah, just about that.'

'Made me wonder why, all of a sudden, I'd get a call from you.'

'And what'd you come up with?'

Ellroy grinned at the other man over the edge of his cup. 'Seems pretty obvious, Will.'

'How so?' Leland asked innocently.

'Listen, we've both been around the block a few times. Let's not play games with each other.' Ellroy paused, looking thoughtfully at the other man. 'Only thing I got on my plate is the Sawyer thing.'

'And the mayor.'

'That, too.' Ellroy nodded, still examining Leland closely.

'So what'd you decide, Tom?' Will turned to face the detective.

'Didn't decide anything.' Ellroy shrugged, reaching for his coffee. 'I figured I'd just listen to what you had to say, and then make up my mind.'

Leland abruptly swiveled around and looked over at the scarred pool table in the center of the room. 'Back when I was drinking, I used to hang out here pretty regularly,' Will said.

'Lot of us did.'

'Me more than most.'

Ellroy nodded, waiting for him to go on.

'Took me a long time to get myself back together after the strike.'

'Screwed up a lot of people.'

'But not you,' Leland said, catching Ellroy's gaze.

'I thought the whole thing was bullshit.'

'Yeah,' Will admitted. 'I remember your telling me that.'

'You should've listened.'

'Lot of things I should've done back then.'

'I don't know.' Ellroy shrugged. 'Seems as if you've done all right for yourself.'

'I'm okay,' Will said softly, then a moment later repeated it, as if trying to convince himself.

'What do you want, Will?'

'What's going on with the Sawyer thing?'

'Why?'

'Just something I promised someone I'd look into,' Will said casually.

'Anybody I know?'

'Maybe.'

'What makes you think I'd talk to you about this?' Ellroy asked, genuinely curious.

'Old times?' Will grinned.

'Try again.'

'Maybe because I can help you.'

'How?'

'I have connections you don't.'

'Bullshit.'

'Think about it, Tom. You're a policeman. People don't talk to the police, but they love talking to their realtor.'

'I don't think I've ever met anyone who confides in their real-estate agent before,' Ellroy said sarcastically. He reached for his cup. 'You're going to have to do better than that, Will.'

'Who do you think's behind this?' Will asked.

The abrupt change in conversation confused Ellroy for a moment.

'No comment,' Ellroy responded.

'Howard?' Will said softly.

Ellroy turned to look at him. 'That thought may have crossed my mind.'

'Well you can cross him out,' Will said casually, turning and waving to the bartender for a refill.

'Why?'

'He's the one who asked me to look into it.'

Ellroy waited until the bartender had moved away before he asked, 'Howard asked you?'

'Yes.'

'Maybe he's being cute.'

'No. It's not his style.'

'How would you know?'

'He's asked me for other things in the past.'

'What kind of things are we talking about, Will?'

'Things that don't have any bearing on the conversation we're having now,' Leland said, turning to Ellroy to make his point.

'Okay.' Ellroy nodded. 'I can live with that.'

'We could help each other, Tom.'

Ellroy turned to him. 'Yeah, we could, but I'll tell you something, Will, something that really bothers me about all of this' – he paused to examine the other man – 'is what do *you* get out of it?'

Leland glanced away without answering.

After a moment, Ellroy sighed and stood up. He threw a couple of dollars on the bar and started towards the door.

'Wait.'

Ellroy turned back.

'I want reinstatement,' Leland said quietly.

'I can't promise you something like that, Will,' Ellroy said softly.

'But you could talk to someone who could.'

'Will, for Christ's sake, you're better off where you are. Why would you even want—?'

'Yes or no?' Will interrupted.

Ellroy sighed. 'I can ask.'

'That's good enough for now.'

Ellroy stepped back to his stool. 'Tell me about Howard?'

'No.' Will shook his head. 'Not until you give me something.'

'I can make you, Will.'

'You can try.'

After a moment, Ellroy broke away from the other man's gaze. He nodded. 'All right, I'll get back to you sometime tomorrow.'

'Hey, Tom.'

Ellroy paused on his way towards the door.

'Thanks.'

'Sure,' Ellroy waved without turning, then stepped through the front doors.

Leland slowly finished his coffee, trying to decide if he'd played it the right way.

* * *

'Have you heard from Ricky?'

'No,' Jane said quickly, glancing up at her father.

Thomas stood in the doorway of her office at Howard Ltd.

'Why do you ask?'

'No reason.' He smiled dismissively, then turned and closed the door behind him.

Jane leaned back and closed her eyes, trying to still the sudden rush of adrenalin.

She rose and stepped over to the window. The offices of Howard Ltd occupied the whole twenty-eighth floor of the Pates building, which had been completed only last year on the ridge overlooking Lake Michigan. Jane's window commanded a view of both the lake and the yacht club.

She looked down at the majestic line of luxury boats in the harbor, trying to discern which was Crayton's. After a moment she returned to her chair.

The *Waukegan News* was spread out on one corner of her desk. The headline clearly explained her father's surprisingly good mood this morning. It had been a long time since Jane had seen him in such a mood. And it sadly reminded her of the way things had once been.

Pushing the newspaper away, Jane reached for the recent mall polls, collected and analyzed earlier that morning. The projection was almost dead even, but these polls had been taken before the release of this morning's news. Jane knew that once the public had time to digest the implications of last night's events, the polls would most assuredly swing in her father's favor. It didn't matter that these allegations were completely unproven; the average voter seemed more easily swayed by gossip than fact. And today's story would do more to bring in the vote for the mall, than any of the countless studies they had previously undertaken and published to enlighten the public.

Jane neatly gathered the recent polling sheets and carried them into her father's office.

'Don't even bother,' Thomas said, waving disdainfully at the files. 'I've got Hartford running another one this afternoon.' He smiled happily. 'That's going to be the one that counts.'

'When will he have the results?'

'Late this evening.'

'It looks good, doesn't it, Dad?'

'Yes,' Thomas agreed confidently. 'It looks very good.' He swiveled his chair and looked out at the cloudless sky.

The man from the park sat in a small café on Main Street. He had a cup of cappuccino before him, and the remains of a cream-cheese strawberry croissant. He pulled out a cigarette and carefully lit it as he looked out at the pedestrians on the sidewalk.

'Would you like anything else, sir?'

'No, thank you.' The man smiled, reaching out to accept the bill.

He left a four-dollar tip, then stepped out on to the sidewalk. Gathering his coat around him, he walked down Main Street, admiring the neatly maintained business area.

He smiled happily, thinking about what was going to happen to this area once the mall opened its doors.

A passing shopper caught and returned his smile.

He nodded to the woman, aware of her interested gaze.

It was a gaze to which he had long since become accustomed.

At twelve forty-three he stationed himself in the phone-booth in front of the First Federal Savings Building.

At exactly twelve forty-five the phone rang.

'Excellent job,' the voice complimented.

'Thank you.'

'Are we ready for the next step?'

'Not quite. It's going to take another day or two to set it up.'

'We don't have much time.'

'Don't worry,' the man from the park responded. 'It's just a matter of fine tuning.'

'All right, I'll leave it up to you.'

'You won't be disappointed.'

'I'd better not be,' the voice warned, then the caller abruptly hung up.

Eleven

The weather turned cold almost as soon as they crossed the Indiana State border. Autumn had come to the Midwest. Seemingly endless acres of cornfields bracketed each side of the interstate, but the browned, grotesquely twisted stalks were all that remained of the once gravid plant.

Ryan pulled over and tied down the collar of his leather jacket with a black shoelace.

'You okay, kid?'

'Fine,' Ricky muttered through chattering teeth.

Ryan grinned, then kicked up through the gears.

Twenty miles later, he turned off the interstate and followed the arterial into the business section of Scottsburgh, Indiana.

Ten minutes after that, he pulled over and parked.

'Jesus, it's cold,' Ricky said, hopping off the cycle and rubbing his arms.

'Why don't we get some coffee?' Ryan nodded to a diner on the other side of the street.

Without waiting for Ryan, Ricky hurried across the sidewalk and stepped into the restaurant. He took a table by the window, and sat there blowing on his hands. When his coffee arrived, he wrapped both hands around the hot cup and inhaled the steam.

'Still cold?' Ryan asked, sitting across from him, trying to hide his grin.

Ricky caught the smile and glared at him. 'It's okay for you. You got that on.' Ricky nodded at Ryan's leather jacket. 'But all I got's this.' He glanced down disgustedly at his lightweight cloth jacket.

Ryan shrugged and lit his cigarette.

'The cold doesn't bother you at all?' Ricky asked a few moments later.

'Not too much.'

'Christ,' Ricky gasped. 'I can't even feel my feet.'

'It's a good day to ride,' Ryan commented, peering out the window at the blue sky.

Ricky held on to his coffee cup.

'It'll get worse once we lose the sun.'

Ricky shuddered.

Outside the restaurant, Ryan nodded to a store across the street. 'Let's see if we can get you some warmer clothes.'

'Great.' Ricky followed him. He started to step into a men's clothing store, then abruptly stopped when he saw Ryan pass it by.

'Where you going?'

Ryan glanced back at him, and gestured down the street.

Hesitantly, Ricky turned and followed him down the block to a Salvation Army Store.

As they stepped inside, Ryan turned to him. 'Don't say it,' he warned.

'What?' Ricky asked innocently.

'"I've never been in one of these before",' Ryan mimicked, then he started towards the men's section.

'Well, I never have,' Ricky muttered.

Ryan browsed through the second hand books as Ricky carried an armful of clothes into the changing booth.

He was idly paging through an atlas when Ricky stepped out again.

'Looking good, kid.' Ryan grinned.

Ricky ignored the comment and stepped over to a full-length mirror.

Wearing a ratty black wool, full-length overcoat and a pair of brown cowboy boots, he stared in disbelief at his reflection.

'I can't wear this.' He turned to Ryan.

'Why not?' Ryan shrugged.

'I look ridiculous.'

Ryan sighed. 'Put your hands in your pockets.'

'Why?'

'Just do it.'

Reluctantly, Ricky shoved both of his hands into the pockets of the coat.

'How does it feel?'

'It feels stupid.'

'How does it feel?' Ryan asked again, glaring.

'It feels warm,' Ricky grudgingly admitted.

Ryan nodded wryly, and turned away.

At the check-out counter, he handed Ricky a pair of leather gloves.

Ricky smiled happily at them.

'Will we make it today?'

'Should.' Ryan stepped over to the bike. 'You ready?'

Ricky nodded and slipped on his gloves. He buttoned up his overcoat, then pulled a shoelace out of his pocket and tied down his collar.

Stepping up to the bike, he ignored Ryan's amused glance.

A few miles into the interstate, Ryan asked, 'You all right back there?'

Ricky, sheltered somewhat behind Ryan, and cocooned in his overcoat, grinned. 'This is great,' he yelled.

Ryan let the road take him.

By seven thirty they were on the north side of Chicago, and fifty-six miles from Waukegan.

Ryan felt the cold beginning to worm its way beneath his collar. He hunched forward, trying to avoid the wind.

Headlights splashed the dark road ahead and behind them. He suddenly stiffened as he heard the engine drag for an instant.

He leaned to the side, listening carefully.

The engine throbbed evenly, then fell off for a split second.

He spotted an exit sign two miles ahead, and dropped down to fifty. He heard the kid ask something, but ignored him as he took the exit and wheeled over to the side. He slowed and parked beneath a streetlight.

'What's wrong?'

'I don't know.' Ryan climbed off the bike and centered it on its main stand. He stepped away from it and stretched.

'What are you doing?'

'Letting it cool down,' Ryan answered, feeling the muscles pop in his neck and shoulders.

Ricky climbed off the bike and stepped over to the edge of the lighted rest area. He looked out toward the north.

Ryan glanced over at him.

Standing in the large overcoat, at the edge of the darkness, the boy looked hopelessly lost. For a moment Ryan felt the threat of another memory starting to intrude. He shook away from it.

'Almost home,' he called out.

'Yeah,' Ricky responded softly, without turning.

Ryan stared at him curiously.

Ricky turned and caught Ryan's gaze. He shrugged uneasily. 'I don't know what he's going to say.'

Ryan didn't have to ask who the boy meant.

'About what?' he asked instead.

'About jail and everything.' Ricky glanced away.

'Hey, kid, you've already done the hard part. The rest is just gravy.' Ryan reached for his cigarettes.

'He's still going to be pissed.' Ricky stepped over and took one.

'So?'

113

'He's my father,' Ricky explained.

'So?' Ryan said again.

Ricky examined him carefully.

'He's your father. What's he going to do to you? Ground you for a week?' Ryan added sarcastically.

'No.' Ricky shook his head. 'But he's going to be mad.'

'Hey, there's going to be a lot of people in your life who are going to be mad at you. If that's all you ever have to worry about, you'll be doing fine.'

'You don't understand.'

Ryan eyed him thoughtfully. 'Maybe I don't,' he said softly, then crouched beside his bike.

'What about *your* father? Where's he?'

'Dead.'

'I'm sorry.'

'Don't be. I wasn't,' Ryan replied curtly.

Ricky knelt down beside him. 'What about your mother?' he asked.

'Damn.' Ryan jerked his hand back and sucked on his finger.

'What about her?' Ricky asked again, a moment later.

'Dead.' Ryan carefully reached into the engine housing.

'Both of them are dead?'

'Yeah.'

'Didn't you have any brothers or sisters?'

Ryan suddenly paused. He stared blankly at the cycle in front of him.

He suddenly flashed on the small gathering of people standing around the grave site.

Palm trees dott̩d the cemetery, gently swaying in the Gulf breeze. The monotonic sound of the minister's voice. The casket slowly descending into the grave. The gravestone with the name NEAL RYAN *etched into its surface. The woman weeping; the two children huddled around her legs, turning.*

Turning until their eyes rose to meet his . . .

'Ryan!' Ricky yelled, reaching out and jerking Ryan's hand from the engine.

Ryan suddenly became aware of the scent of burning flesh. For an instant he saw the flames devouring the stilt-house, heard the screams coming from inside.

'Jesus, Ryan, what the hell did you do?'

Ryan shook his head, trying to clear it of the image. He saw Ricky crouched over him, examining his hand.

'What . . . ?'

'Your hand – look at it.'

Ryan glanced down at his hand. A blister had already begun to form on the back of it. He stared at it blankly, still beyond pain. The acrid stink of singed flesh overwhelmed all of his other senses.

'You all right?'

'Fine.' Ryan stood up and stepped away from the bike.

He found himself standing at the edge of the darkness, staring down at the highway below. He felt – more than saw – Ricky behind him, looking at him worriedly. He turned and stepped back to the bike.

'You okay?'

'Fine.' Ryan grunted, then crouched down again. He reached into the housing and began to trace the fuel line.

* * *

'Hit it,' Ryan called. He was hunched before the cycle.

Ricky sat on the bike and hit the throttle.

Ryan felt moisture beginning to bead along the fuel line.

'Back off.'

Ricky let go of the throttle and peered down at him. 'What is it?'

'Pet cock.'

'Oh.'

Ryan glanced up at him.

Ricky shrugged. 'Can you fix it?'

'Not here.'

'Can we keep going?'

Ryan rose. He sighed, looking at the bike appraisingly.

'Can we?'

'Yeah, but we're going to have to gas up again. We're losing a lot of fuel.' He glanced at Ricky. 'How many more miles?'

'Twenty-five maybe. No more than thirty.'

'You know how far we are from a gas station?'

'There's a station at the Lake Forest exit.'

'How far's that?'

'No more than five miles.'

'All right, why don't we try for there?'

Ricky scooted to the back as Ryan climbed on to the cycle. He checked the gas gauge. They still had a good half a tank.

Ryan kicked into gear and wheeled down to the interstate. He kept it a steady forty-five, reaching down often to check the fuel line. He could feel the spray of gas escaping from the carburetor head, but couldn't calculate how much they were actually losing.

The engine coughed, then steadied out, with the lights of the station in sight.

Ryan dropped down to thirty and hugged the shoulder.

The engine coughed again.

'It's dying,' Ricky said.

Ryan shook his head. 'It's just sick,' he yelled over his shoulder, then slowly turned the bike on to the exit ramp and up into the station.

'You gas it up,' Ryan directed, then stepped inside.

He paid for the gas and bought a roll of black electrical tape. He carried his purchase out to the bike.

'Is that going to work?' Ricky asked, crouching over to watch as Ryan taped the fuel line.

'For a while it should. All it's got to do is get us another twenty miles, right?'

This time when he pulled on to the highway, he kicked up to sixty-five, then leveled off at sixty.

Ten minutes later, they pulled into the outskirts of Waukegan.

'Where to?'

'Keep going. We'll take Grand Avenue into town.' Ricky pointed at the road ahead. 'It's only a mile or so up.'

Ryan heard the excitement in the kid's voice.

Ryan followed Ricky's directions through a maze of residential streets.

'Take a left,' Ricky suddenly shouted.

Ryan leaned into the bike and took the turn.

'Right there. That one with the lights on,' Ricky yelled.

Ryan examined the house ahead of them. He slowed as he approached the driveway. It was bracketed by a black wrought-iron fence. The house sat to the left of the drive. It was a three-story stucco home, with two dormers on the third floor, facing the highway. The first floor had a large sunporch that stretched across the front of the building. The inside of the house was brightly lit.

'Head down to the end.' Ricky pointed to the garage at the end of the drive.

Ryan pulled up in front of the building, and cut the engine.

Ricky quickly climbed off and started towards the house. Then he paused and glanced back at Ryan.

'You coming?'

'Kid, maybe I should just take off.'

'C'mon, Ryan,' Ricky implored. He stepped back beside the bike. 'You can't leave now.'

'Why not?'

'That's crazy. Your bike isn't even running.' Ricky paused to examine him. 'At least come on in for a while. Please?' He grinned nervously.

Ryan sighed, then climbed off the bike.

He followed Ricky up the drive. He could smell the stink of gasoline on his clothes.

As they approached the side door, the outside light suddenly flashed on. A moment later the door opened and a young woman stepped out.

'Ricky,' she cried, and rushed forward. She threw her arms around her brother and hugged him. 'I was so worried,' she gasped.

Ryan lit up a cigarette. The flare of the match startled the young woman. Without releasing her hold on her brother, her eyes quickly rose and settled on Ryan.

Ryan saw her stiffen.

'It's okay,' Ricky said, moving out of her embrace. He kept his arm locked around her waist and turned to Ryan.

'This is Ryan. He gave me a ride. And this is my sister, Jane,' Ricky said proudly, glancing at each of them.

'How do you do. I'm Jane Howard,' the young woman said coolly, pulling away from Ricky and offering her hand.

'Edward Ryan.' Ryan took her hand in his, feeling the delicate bones disappear within his grip.

'Richard, is that you?'

At the sound of the voice, both Jane and Ricky turned towards the house.

Jane suddenly became aware that she was still holding Ryan's hand.

She jerked her hand from his grip, threw him a quick apologetic glance, then turned to Ricky. She reached out to touch his arm. 'Don't say anything about the money. Just say that they released you on your own recognizance,' she whispered quickly, then glanced up at the door.

The man standing in the doorway was silhouetted by the hall light, making it almost impossible to discern his features.

119

'Richard, I've been wondering what happened to you.'

'I'm fine, Dad,' Ricky said, then turned and gestured to Ryan. 'This is Edward Ryan, Dad. He gave me a ride home.'

Ryan could feel the other man's eyes bore into him.

'Mr Ryan,' the man in the doorway acknowledged. 'I'm Thomas Howard. Why don't you step inside where it's a little warmer.'

Ryan followed Ricky and Jane into the house.

'It's nice to meet you,' Thomas said, offering Ryan his hand.

Ryan examined the man as they clasped hands.

Ricky's father was neatly dressed in dark slacks, a white shirt with only the top button undone, and a light brown cardigan sweater.

Ryan, wearing his road-worn jeans and boots, and black leather jacket, felt out of place standing beside him.

'Ryan dri ...' Ricky started, then stopped. He grinned at Ryan. 'Rides a motorcycle,' he corrected. 'We rode up from Middlesboro,' the boy added proudly.

Thomas glanced at Ryan appraisingly.

'Would you like a cup of coffee or something to eat?' Jane offered.

'Coffee would be fine, thanks.'

'Richard, why don't you help your sister with the coffee, and Mr Ryan and I will adjourn to the living-room.' Thomas smiled politely, then gestured to the hallway.

Ryan caught Ricky's worried glance, and nodded to him

almost imperceptibly. When he returned his gaze to Thomas, he saw his gesture had not gone unobserved.

'After you, Mr Ryan.'

Ryan started down the hallway.

'And, Richard,' Ryan heard behind him, 'take off that ridiculous outfit before you join us.'

'Yes, Dad.'

The hallway opened to a large room overlooking the back yard. A crystal chandelier hung from the center of the ceiling. Splinters of fractured light reflected colorfully from the crystal.

Ryan stepped over to the window and looked out. The dark glass mirrored his reflection back at him.

He turned and reached for his cigarettes as Howard stepped into the room behind him. He caught Thomas's annoyed glance as he waved distastefully to an ashtray on the sideboard.

'Why don't you have a seat, Mr Ryan.'

Ryan carried the ashtray with him to the couch.

Thomas sat across from him in an Eames chair. He leaned back, steepling his hands before his face.

'I want to thank you for looking out for my son.'

'I just gave him a ride.'

'I'm sure there was more to it than that.' Thomas smiled indulgently. 'Richard is somewhat naïve about the world.' He paused, looking over expectantly at Ryan.

Ryan shrugged and glanced around the room. 'Nice place,' he commented.

'Thank you.'

'You're welcome.' Ryan met the other man's gaze.

For a moment neither man seemed willing to be the first to break eye contact.

Ryan hit his cigarette.

'Ricky tells me you used to be the State's Attorney around here.'

'Two terms: eight years total.'

'Interesting,' Ryan observed. His bored tone contradicted his comment.

'For a man like you, I suppose it might seem so.'

'A man like me?'

'Someone, whom it would seem, may have had occasion to become acquainted with other State's Attorneys.'

'And just why the...?' Ryan paused as Ricky and Jane stepped into the room.

Jane carried a silver serving tray. Ricky helped her arrange it on the table between the two men. Ricky was now wearing a pair of gray slacks and white shirt.

Jane poured the coffee while Ricky passed the cups to Ryan and his father.

Ricky sat beside Ryan on the couch, while Jane carried her coffee over to a chair on her father's right. She deftly balanced cup and saucer on her knee.

Ryan ashed his cigarette. He glanced over and caught Ricky's surprised look. Without saying anything, he pulled out the pack and put it on the table between them. Ricky looked at it longingly, but made no attempt to pick it up.

'Mr Ryan and I were just talking about previous occupations,' Thomas said, smiling pointedly at Ryan.

Before Ryan could comment, Thomas turned to Ricky. 'So, Richard, the last message I received from you was a pitiful plea for help. How did you ever manage to extricate yourself from that situation?'

Only because he was looking did Ryan manage to catch the worried glance Jane threw at Ricky.

'They let me out on my own recognizance,' Ricky said quickly, with a sidelong glance at Ryan.

'How odd,' Thomas said, examining his son intently.

'Why's that?'

'Well, Richard, why on earth would they ever let a non-resident, with no ties whatsoever to the community, out on his own recognizance? It would be absolutely ludicrous for them to expect you to ever return for trial.' Thomas paused, then glanced over at Ryan.

'Wouldn't you agree, Mr Ryan?'

Ryan felt the combined focus of three pairs of eyes.

'Small towns.' He shrugged. 'Who knows what they'll do.'

'I see.' Thomas nodded thoughtfully, never taking his eyes from the other man.

'Do you?' Ryan couldn't help asking.

'Maybe more than you know, Mr Ryan,' Thomas challenged.

Before Ryan could comment, Jane interrupted, 'The two of you are probably both exhausted.'

'Yes,' Ricky quickly agreed. 'We've been riding since early this morning, and the bike's all messed up.'

'What's wrong with it?' Jane asked.

'The pep cock is—'

'Pet cock,' Ryan gently corrected.

'Yeah, right.' Ricky grinned. 'The pet cock's broken. We

wrapped it up with some tape, but it's not going to hold for too much longer,' the boy said knowledgeably.

Ryan hid his grin in his coffee cup.

'Can it be repaired, Mr Ryan?'

'Just Ryan.'

'Ryan.' Jane nodded.

'It needs either to be replaced or circumvented.'

'Circumvented?' Thomas repeated in surprise.

'Yes, Mr Howard, circumvented. Are you familiar with the word?'

'Oh, Mr Ryan.' Thomas laughed. 'I think I'm going to like you.'

After a glance at Ricky, Ryan bit back his immediate comment.

'Dad?'

'Yes, Richard?'

'I told Ryan he could stay over,' Ricky said, without glancing at Ryan.

'Why, of course he can. After all he's done, I wouldn't hear of anything else,' Thomas quickly agreed. 'I'm sure you're both exhausted. Why don't we continue our conversation in the morning?' Thomas stood and offered Ryan his hand.

'I want to thank you again for bringing my son home safely.'

'He would have been fine without me, Mr Howard.'

'Call me Thomas, please. Jane, why don't you show Mr Ryan to his room.'

'It's right this way, Mr Ryan.'

Ryan turned to follow her.

124

'And, Richard, I would like to hear more about your adventures. Maybe we could get together for lunch tomorrow,' Thomas said. His tone made it quite clear that this was not a request.

Ryan left the room before he could hear Ricky's response.

Jane glanced over her shoulder. 'This way, Mr Ryan.'

'It's just Ryan – or Edward if you don't like using the last name.'

'I'm sorry.'

'Don't be, Jane,' Ryan said, using her name for the first time.

He followed her up the stairs, trying to keep his gaze from the slim line of her legs and hips.

At the top of the stairs was a wide hallway. The walls and ceiling were painted white. The thick berber rug covering the floor was also a pure white.

'That's my father's room.' Jane pointed to a room at the end of the hall. 'And that's Ricky's,' she said, gesturing to the opposite end.

'And that one?'

'That's mine,' Jane said curtly, meeting his gaze for a moment.

She turned away. 'You'll be upstairs. I hope that's all right.'

'That's fine.'

Ryan followed her along the hall to another stairway.

The third floor of the house was in complete contrast to the second floor. It was all oak floors, and walled in knotty pine. The ceiling peaked, cathedral-style, above them.

Jane led him to a door centered in the corridor. She opened it, and motioned him in ahead of her.

The back half of the room was all glass. Opposite the window, was a large queen-size bed.

'The bathroom's right here.' Jane stepped over to a door to the side, and opened it.

Ryan caught a glimpse of gleaming black and white tile.

'There are towels and extra bedding in the closet, if you need them.'

Ryan glanced around the room, then became aware of Jane's expectant gaze.

'Is there an ashtray?'

'Yes.' Jane suddenly smiled. The smile was the first real one Ryan had seen her give. He was amazed at the difference it made.

'Let me just go downstairs and get you one.'

'No, that's all right. Don't go to any trouble. I can probably last the night without a cigarette.'

'Don't be ridiculous, Mr...' She paused, then corrected herself. 'Ryan, it's no trouble at all.'

Ryan watched her step out of the room, then he turned to the windows and looked out.

'So, what'd you think?'

Ryan turned to see Ricky step into the room. The boy walked over and sat on the edge of the bed.

'About what?'

'About my father. What'd you think of him?'

'He's okay.' Ryan shrugged noncommittally.

'Really?'

'Hey, kid, he's *your* father, not mine.'

'Yeah.' Ricky nodded, examining Ryan closely, trying to discover more.

Ryan shook his head, then reached into his pocket and threw him the pack of cigarettes.

Ricky grabbed them enthusiastically.

'It's hard to stop, once you start, isn't it?' Ricky grinned, inhaling deeply.

'That's what they say.'

'Ricky!'

They both turned to see Jane standing in the doorway. 'When did you start smoking?'

'I don't know.' Ricky shrugged sheepishly.

'Dad will kill you if he ever finds out,' she cautioned.

'Well.' Ricky smiled slyly. 'I guess I'll just have to be careful then.'

Jane turned to glare at Ryan.

'It wasn't his fault, sis,' Ricky said defensively.

Jane glanced at her brother skeptically.

'It wasn't, really.'

Jane sighed, then curtly handed the ashtray to Ricky. At the door, she turned. 'Goodnight, *Mr* Ryan,' she said emphatically, then whirled down the hallway.

'She's like that.' Ricky shrugged apologetically.

'It's okay, kid. She's probably got a point.'

Ryan stepped over and pulled a cigarette. He sat down and leaned back against the headboard. 'This is quite a place you got here.'

'Yeah, it's all right.'

Ryan glanced over at him.

'It's just so...' Ricky paused, trying to find the right word.

'Sterile?' Ryan offered.

'Yeah.' Ricky nodded. 'Everything's so neat. It drives me crazy sometimes.' The boy shifted and turned to face him. 'What'd my father say to you when you lit up?' he asked gleefully.

Ryan shook his head wearily.

'Well, what? What'd he say?'

'He told me I couldn't go to the prom,' Ryan said dryly.

Ricky cackled hysterically.

Watching him fall back on the bed, laughing, Ryan felt a tentative drag of memory. He was surprised at how easily he was able to push it away. He looked down in amusement at the kid, who was hugging a pillow to his chest and still laughing uproariously.

Ryan slouched back against the headboard.

'So who is he, Ricky?' Jane asked. She was seated on the top end of her bed. She wore a white robe tucked modestly beneath her legs. Her hair was still damp from the shower, and brushed cleanly back from her forehead.

Ricky sat further along from her.

'I met him in jail.'

'Oh, Ricky, I'm so sorry about that.' Jane reached out to touch his shoulder.

'It's okay. It wasn't your fault.' Ricky shrugged. 'What did Dad say about it?'

'Not very much.' Jane paused, then quickly added, 'He was really worried, though.'

'Was he?'

'Yes, I don't think I've ever seen him that worried before.'

Jane closed her eyes for a moment. When she opened them, she saw her brother eyeing her curiously.

'What?' she asked.

'If he was so worried,' he said uncertainly, 'then why was it *you* who sent the money?'

'You know how Dad is about money?' Jane reached out to reassure him. 'I just thought it would be better if he thought you got out on your own recognizance.' Jane felt her brother's eyes examining her closely. She kept her face impassive.

After a moment, Ricky smiled thoughtfully. 'He was *really* worried?' he asked again.

'Yes, as worried as I've ever seen him,' she said, knowing that her lies were easily transparent, but also knowing that in order for Ricky to see through them, he would have to *want* to see through them. And the one lie that Jane had managed to maintain over the years was the lie about their father's affections for them.

'Tell me about this Ryan person,' Jane said, changing the subject. 'He's a pretty rough-looking character.'

'He is, isn't he,' Ricky said proudly.

'How did you ever hook up with him?'

Ricky glanced away.

'What is it, Ricky?'

'When I was in jail...' Ricky paused. He took a deep breath before he went on. 'There were some other guys in the same cell, and they ... well they wanted me to...'

'Oh, Ricky,' Jane gasped, pulling her brother into her arms. She held him tightly.

'Nothing happened,' Ricky added quickly, pulling away.

'They didn't hurt you?'

'No.' Ricky shook his head. 'Ryan just came out of nowhere and beat the shit out of both of them. It was amazing, Jane. One minute it was like there was nothing in the world that could save me. And then, the next, Ryan comes off the top bunk like something out of a Clint Eastwood movie.'

'Thank God.'

'He's a nice guy, Jane.'

She stared at him.

'He is,' Ricky said emphatically.

'I'm so glad he was there, if he . . .' She shook her head She suddenly reached out and hugged him.

Ricky squirmed out of her embrace. He leaned back on the bed and began to idly pick at a stray thread. 'You know what Ryan said about the whole thing? He said I was lucky.'

'Lucky?' Jane repeated incredulously.

'Yeah.' Ricky turned to her. 'He said there was a lot worse that could've happened.'

'Like what? Death?' Jane said sarcastically, then caught her brother's sober gaze.

'Yeah, that's exactly what he said.' Ricky nodded.

Jane returned her brother's glance, while her thoughts raced furiously to the man upstairs, wondering just who it was they had allowed inside of their home.

* * *

'Edward Ryan,' Howard said into the receiver. 'Richard met him in Middlesboro, Kentucky – in the city jail.'

Will bit back his astonishment that Thomas's son had been in jail, and forced himself to concentrate on what the other man was saying.

'See what you can find out about him. I want as much information as possible by tomorrow morning.'

'That is going to be difficult at this time of the night, sir.'

'I'm not interested in how difficult it's going to be, Will. I'm only interested in results.'

'Yes, sir.'

'Good. I expect to hear from you by no later than nine o'clock tomorrow morning, with a preliminary report.'

'I'll—'

Howard hung up before the other man could respond. He smiled thoughtfully as he walked out of his office and climbed the stairs to his room.

Lying on his bed, he stared up at the ceiling, thinking about the man upstairs and how he might be put to use.

Twelve

'There was twenty thousand in cash,' Detective Ellroy said, glancing up from his notebook.

'That's all?' The mayor shrugged, unimpressed.

'No.' Ellroy shook his head. 'You don't understand, Mr Mayor. Sawyer also had a checking and savings account with a combined total of twelve thousand dollars, plus he owned his home outright.' Ellroy noticed the mayor's still confused expression. He sighed wearily, then added, 'There's no way he should have had that kind of cash lying around, judging from his salary.'

'The man was a policeman for almost thirty years.'

'Doesn't matter.'

'Why couldn't he have simply saved that much money over the years?'

'He could have, but why would he leave it lying around in a safety-deposit box. Plus he paid off the mortgage on his house two years ago. That came to ...' Ellroy checked his notebook '...eighty-four thousand dollars.' He looked up at the mayor. 'His house was just assessed at a hundred and ninety. Sawyer had a real-estate agent out there just a month ago, to find out what it was worth.'

'So what does this mean?' Presley asked thoughtfully.

Ellroy sighed. 'Means Sawyer was taking from somebody.'

'But you don't have any idea who?'

'No, I don't. I haven't been able to find anything with a name on it.'

'So essentially, we're right back where we started?'

'Not completely,' Ellroy corrected. 'At least now we do know he was *taking*. What we don't know is from whom.'

'This doesn't help me, detective,' Presley said softly.

'It doesn't hurt you either, Mr Mayor. I talked to the district attorney about the case.'

'On whose authority?'

'Mine,' Ellroy said, holding the mayor's gaze.

Presley was the first to glance away. He ran a hand across his eyes, then leaned back in his chair. 'I'm sorry, Tom. This whole thing has been making me crazy. Go ahead. Tell me the rest.' The mayor nodded for the other man to go on.

'There's no case. There's no indication of any malfeasance on your part. The only evidence of any wrongdoing was the note found on Sawyer's body, and so far there's absolutely nothing to back it up. Cramer said he wouldn't even consider taking any action.'

Presley swiveled his chair around to look out the window. A steady stream of headlights drove down the north shore, headed towards downtown.

'I also went through title and deeds, and there isn't anything there either.'

'Doesn't matter.' The mayor shrugged without turning.

Ellroy looked over at him curiously. He could see the mayor's reflection in the window.

'I need irrefutable proof that none of what Sawyer claimed was true.' The mayor turned. 'The election is less than three weeks away. If I can't find something to completely exonerate me, I don't think I'm going to be able to swing it.'

'We're still looking.'

The mayor smiled painfully. 'What do you think your chances are of finding something in the next two weeks?'

'Not good,' Ellroy reluctantly admitted. 'But I'm not giving up on it, Mr Mayor. Whoever was paying Sawyer is probably the same guy who took him out.'

'Probably,' the mayor agreed. 'But you don't have much time to find him.'

'We'll get him,' Ellroy vowed.

'I'm sure you will – eventually.' Presley nodded. 'But I don't think it's going to matter to the town.'

'There is one other possibility.'

'Yes?'

'Will Leland. He used to be on the force, but he was one of the officers let go during the strike.'

'What about him?'

'He's offered to help.'

'How?'

'He says Howard hired him to look into Sawyer's death.'

'Howard was the first one I thought might be behind this. If he wasn't, then why would he care?' The mayor asked softly.

135

'That would be interesting to find out.'

'What does Leland say?'

'Nothing yet. He wants something in return.'

'What?'

'Reinstatement.'

Presley leaned back thoughtfully. After a moment, he leveled his gaze at the detective. 'What do *you* think?'

Ellroy shrugged. 'Leland was a good cop. He just got caught up with the wrong group.'

'What about now?'

'I don't know.' Ellroy shook his head.

'Do you think he can help?'

'He can't hurt.'

'What about reinstating him?'

'I'm not sure.'

'Why?' the mayor asked curiously.

'It's too pat. There's something not quite right about it.'

'What?'

'I don't know.' Ellroy shrugged. 'It's just a feeling I got talking to him. There's more to this than he's admitting.'

'Can he hurt us?'

'I don't know,' Ellroy admitted.

The mayor swiveled his chair from side to side. He paused, looking thoughtfully over at the other man. 'I'll tell you what we'll do, Tom. Offer him what he wants. Let's see what he's got. But make it clear to him that unless he comes up with something, there's no deal.'

'I think he already understands that.'

'We'll make damn sure he does,' the mayor said.

'I'll talk to him tomorrow, then get back to you.'

'Thanks, Tom. I appreciate it.'

Ellroy rose and started for the door. He paused indecisively, then turned back.

'What?'

'You ought to try to get some rest.'

The mayor smiled sadly, then shook his head. 'Thanks for the concern, Tom. But I'll get all the rest I need, in two weeks and four days.'

Mayor Charles Presley waited for the detective to leave his office.

When he was gone, he sighed wearily, then swiveled his chair around and looked down at the bustling activity of his town.

Roberta finished work at three fifty-two in the morning. She showered, then toweled off, standing in front of the hotel mirror. As she wiped the moisture from her body, she examined her reflection critically.

At twenty-eight, her body had already begun to show the debilitating effects of gravity and of her career. She figured she had another year or two before she would either be forced to get out of her profession or to become less discriminating.

She lit a cigarette, not particularly pleased by either option.

She dressed and left the hotel at four thirty. She made her usual stop at the Greek all-night diner on Madison Street. She took a corner booth in the back and ordered breakfast. Two men were seated at the counter, glumly sipping coffee. A young couple sat in one of the booths near the door. Their eyes seemed unnaturally bright, and their gestures were exaggerated and frenetic.

Roberta lit another cigarette after she'd finished her breakfast. She sipped her coffee, calculating her profits for the night. She'd run six tricks through the room that evening. At fifty bucks a shot, plus an extra two hundred for specialties, her gross had been five hundred. The room had cost her fifty-two fifty.

Call it a four fifty night, she figured happily. Not bad for a Wednesday. The oncoming weekend would only get better.

Roberta stretched, feeling the pull of muscles in her thighs and stomach. Her last trick had worked her hard. The son-of-a-bitch had kept holding back, until finally she'd been forced to go through her whole repertoire of techniques to get him off. The twenty-buck tip he'd finally left hadn't seemed near enough for all the trouble he'd put her through. But she'd smiled politely and taken it, carefully committing his face to memory. Next time, she figured, she'd price accordingly.

She finished her coffee leisurely, looking forward to the thought of home and bed.

She walked the ten blocks to her condo, set in a quiet residential area a little outside of town. As she fitted the key to the security door, she heard a sudden movement behind her. She whirled around.

'Jesus,' the man sighed in relief. 'I'm so glad some-one finally showed up. I've been stuck out here forever,' he said, smiling up at her from the bottom step.

Startled by his sudden appearance, Roberta cowered back against the door.

The man stepped out of the shadows and into the light. 'Don't be afraid,' he said reassuringly. 'I locked myself out. I came down with the dog, and someone had left the door open. Before I knew what was happening, he took off through that door like a shot.' The man shook his head in irritation.

Roberta examined him suspiciously. He was barefoot, wearing only a shirt and pants.

Seeing the direction of her gaze, the man shook his head in frustration. 'I didn't even put shoes on. I was just going to get the mail. It never occurred to me that I'd end up outside.'

Roberta brought her gaze back up to his face. Meeting his eye, she immediately relaxed.

The man smiled. His smile charmed her.

'My name's Raymond,' the man from the park said, stepping up closer to Roberta. 'I'm in 405.'

Roberta smiled back at him, then turned and opened the door.

'I can't tell you how much I appreciate this,' Raymond said, once he'd stepped inside the foyer.

'That's okay.' Roberta nodded, unable to help herself from glancing over at the mailboxes. She spotted the box for 405.

Raymond Burlinger was the name printed in the slot.

'Listen, I don't mean to be forward,' the man said shyly,

'but there's no way I'm going to be able to sleep for a while. Why don't you let me repay you with a nightcap? What do you say?' he asked, looking over at her sincerely.

Roberta looked into his startling blue eyes and found herself nodding and smiling back at him.

'Great,' he grinned, then gestured toward the elevator.

Roberta entered the elevator, then turned and watched him step in behind her. As he punched the button for the fourth floor, she couldn't help wondering how she'd never noticed him before. He looked like a cross between Robert Redford and Paul Newman.

Raymond smiled at her as the elevator doors opened.

And Roberta, feeling the intensity of his smile, did something she hadn't done in almost fifteen years.

She blushed.

The man gestured her ahead of him, and watched hungrily as the woman stepped into the hallway.

He followed behind, admiring the line of her neck and shoulders – smiling in anticipation at the thought of how neatly his hands would fit around the delicate stem of her neck.

He glanced at his watch, then shuddered excitedly. He figured he'd have hours to discover all the secret places where Roberta could be hurt.

Working for most of the night, Leland managed to come up with a fairly clear picture of Edward Ryan. As each new piece of information came in, he found himself becoming more and more curious about Howard's interest in the man.

By six thirty in the morning, he slumped back in his chair and lifted the file.

He read the completed file for the first time, bringing together all the bits and pieces of the puzzle he'd acquired throughout the night.

The composite picture of the man provided by the file before him amazed him.

Will had run background checks before for Thomas Howard. They were usually undertaken to discover the personal and financial assets of various businessmen. That was what Will had expected to find in Edward Ryan's background. But what he had uncovered, instead, was pure *outlaw*.

Leland leaned back, staring up thoughtfully at the ceiling, trying to figure out just what Howard had planned for someone with Edward Ryan's unique abilities.

Thirteen

In that nebulous stage between waking and sleeping, Ryan felt the tug of memory.

Neal, standing by the side of the old wooden pier, a fishing pole in his hand, looking over excitedly at Ryan.

Ryan, unable to stop a smile, noticing the two miss-matched socks on his brother's feet.

Neal's furious look of concentration as he now crouched over his fishing-pole and stared into the brackish water of the bay. The way the sunlight splashed around him. His excited squeal as his pole suddenly wobbled and dipped forward.

'I got one, Eddie. I got one,' Neal screamed, and Ryan watched as Neal suddenly threw his pole to one side and dipped both hands over the edge of the boat to grab the fish.

The two of them walking up to the stilt-house. Neal proudly climbing the stairs, dragging the fish up the steps.

The face of their father in the doorway. The drunken rage quickly turning into a sneering grin as he glanced at the fish, then back at Neal.

'Fucking amberjack, kid. What the hell you going to do

143

*with that, 'cause you sure the fuck aren't bringing it into this
house?'*

*The sound of the door slamming closed. Neal whirling
around and racing down the stairs.*

*Ryan, alone on the steps, looking down at the fish, but
seeing only the tears streaking across his little brother's face.*

Ryan opened his eyes and climbed out of bed. He
stepped into the bathroom and showered and shaved.

He quietly descended the stairs, feeling the silent house
close around him.

In a cupboard over the refrigerator he found the makings
for coffee. He started a pot, then stepped over in front of
the sink and looked out the window. The sun had just
started to top the eastern horizon. The front lawn was
delicately laced with frost.

Ryan went to pour a cup of coffee, then carried it back to
the window.

Sunlight now stretched across the front yard. It glinted
brightly off the melting traces of frost.

Ryan lit a cigarette and refilled his cup, then continued
staring out the window. Remembering.

Remembering that other house: that house that had once
been his home.

His and Zella's.

The last time he had seen it had been the morning he'd
returned from the hospital.

Moving through rooms that had suddenly seem to have
grown large and empty, searching for something, for
someone that would never be there again.

Zella.

Glancing over at him shyly, reaching out to take his hand and press it to her face.

'It's all right, Edward. It's all in the past. What happened then doesn't mean it will happen now.'

Looking into her face, seeing all the things he had never thought he would see. And, once recognizing them, feeling it all fall away, feeling himself finally able to let it go.

And then the nightmare of the hospital, the nightmare that seemed to never—

'I didn't realize you were down here.'

Startled, Ryan whirled around in a crouch. His coffee splashed over his hand and on to the floor.

Jane gasped and stepped back.

Ryan sighed, then ran a hand over his face.

'I'm sorry, I didn't mean to . . .' He shrugged. 'I was just daydreaming.'

'You okay?' Jane asked softly.

'Fine.' Ryan turned and grabbed a paper towel. He stooped to mop the floor. He glanced up to see Jane eyeing him curiously.

'It's okay.' He smiled reassuringly.

After a moment Jane returned his smile. She stepped around him to the coffee pot.

'How come you're up so early?'

'Couldn't sleep.' Ryan shrugged, noticing her properly for the first time. She wore a white robe bunched tightly at her waist. Her hair was casually pushed back from her forehead and tucked behind her ears. Without make-up, she seemed younger and more vulnerable.

'I have to admit you did scare me for a minute.'

145

'Sorry.' Ryan rose and dropped the paper towel in the wastebasket. He picked up his coffee and glanced out the window.

'It's nice, isn't it?'

Ryan looked at her.

'The frost,' she explained, nodding out the window. She turned back to him. 'Do you get any in California? Ricky told me that's where you're from.'

'Sometimes. One year it even snowed.'

Jane glanced over, incredulously.

'Honest.'

'I just can't imagine that. I always think of California as being perpetually hot and sunny,' Jane said, clasping her cup to her chest with both hands.

'You've never been there?'

'No, I've never been any further west than St Louis,' she said longingly.

'Why?'

'I don't know.' Jane shook her head. 'There just never seemed to be time.'

'You should try making time. There's a lot of country out that way.'

'Have *you* done much traveling?'

Ryan turned back to the window.

'Maybe more than I should,' he said softly, then, catching her inquisitive glance, he suddenly smiled. 'You interested in learning about motorcycle maintenance?'

'Excuse me?'

'I need some help with the bike. You feel like getting your hands a little dirty?'

'I don't know anything about engines.' Jane smiled tentatively.

'Well, here's your chance to learn,' Ryan said, putting his cup down and starting toward the door. He paused in the hallway and glanced back at her.

After a moment, Jane suddenly grinned. 'Let me change first,' she said, then darted out of the kitchen and up the stairs.

'That thing's the carburetor?' Jane pointed, glancing over at Ryan for approval.

'Yep.'

She grinned. 'And that's the pet cock?'

'Right.'

'That's what you're trying to fix?'

'No.' Ryan shook his head, then rose to his feet. 'That's what I just fixed.'

'It's done?' she asked incredulously.

'Should be.' Ryan nodded, glancing over at her. She now wore a pair of faded blue jeans and a man's long-sleeve white shirt.

'You want to try it?'

'Me?' Jane took a step back.

'Sure.' Ryan smiled, and motioned her towards the bike. He flipped the fuel cock, pulled the choke, then turned the key.

'Just hit that button there,' he said, pointing to the starter.

'And then it's going to blow up, right?' Jane grinned at him.

'If it does, I'll be really disappointed.'

'That's nice to know,' she commented dryly.

Ryan motioned her to the bike.

Jane hesitantly reached out and pushed the button. The bike turned over but didn't catch.

'You have to hold it for a little longer,' he explained patiently.

'How much longer?'

'Until it starts.'

Jane gave him an exasperated look, then reached for the button. This time Ryan took her hand and held it against the starter until the engine caught.

'It works,' Jane cried out happily, grinning up at him.

Ryan nodded, then crouched beside the engine housing. He reached inside and traced the fuel lines, checking for any leaks.

'Is it okay?'

'Seems to be, but I need to take it out on the road to be sure. You want to come along?'

'Oh, I don't know about that.' Jane took a step back, her glance traveling from Ryan to the motorcycle.

'I'll go slow.'

'Promise?'

'Absolutely,' Ryan vowed.

Jane gritted her teeth, indecisive.

'If you'd feel more comfortable driving, I'll ride in back,' Ryan offered.

Jane glared at him. Then, straightening her shoulders, she stepped over to the side of the bike.

'What do I do?' she asked firmly, and Ryan smiled and told her.

'This is great. Can't you go any faster?' Jane screamed into his ear.

Ryan crouched over and hit the throttle. The bike leaped forward.

Jane squealed delightedly as they raced down the highway.

They sat in a window booth, in a small diner on the outskirts of town, and ordered breakfast. Jane kept glancing through the window at the motorcycle parked in front.

'I want one.' She grinned across the table at Ryan.

Ryan shook his head in amusement.

'I think I want to get something a little bigger, though,' Jane said thoughtfully. 'Yours is a little too slow.' Then, catching his glance, she quickly added. 'No offense.'

'None taken.' Ryan sighed, and reached for his coffee.

Their breakfast arrived a moment later. While Ryan was still cutting his bacon, Jane had already finished her plate of scrambled eggs and was stealing pieces of his toast.

Ryan glanced over at her as she stared out the window at the motorcycle. It was difficult to match the woman sitting across from him from the prim and proper woman he had met the evening before. Her flushed features and wind-blown hair seemed in direct contrast to the carefully maintained personality he had seen last night.

'How long have you been riding?'

'Off an on for almost fifteen years. I got my first bike when I was seventeen.'

'Weren't your parents upset?'

'No.' Ryan leaned back and pushed away his plate. 'By then I was on my own.'

'At seventeen?'

Ryan nodded.

'That's the same age as Ricky is now,' Jane said thoughtfully. 'I can't imagine *him* on his own.'

'I think you'd be surprised at what your brother is capable of handling.'

'He told me what happened,' Jane said, nervously toying with her fork. 'In jail.'

Ryan shrugged and reached for a cigarette.

'I wanted to thank you for helping him.' Jane glanced up. Her gaze caught and held his.

'It's no big thing.' Ryan pulled his gaze away to look out the window. He felt her eyes examining him.

'Where do you come from, Ryan?'

'Florida.'

'Whereabouts?'

'Small town west of Miami.'

'What's it like there?'

Ryan turned to meet her gaze.

'Pretty empty,' he said softly, then quickly turned and waved the waitress over for their check.

Jane climbed on the back of the cycle and wrapped her arms around his waist.

Ryan pulled out on to the highway and raced up through the gears.

'You know...' Jane said, leaning forward.

Ryan could feel her lips against his ear.

'...I wish I could just ride forever.'

Thomas Howard pulled out the last page of Will Leland's report from his fax machine. He carried the four-page report over to his desk and began to read.

When he finished, he became aware of the sound of voices coming from the drive. He swiveled his chair and looked out.

Ryan and Jane were seated on the motorcycle. Ricky stood beside them, grinning excitedly.

Noticing a similar smile on his daughter's face, Thomas frowned as he watched her climb off the back of the bike.

Thomas glanced down at the file before him, then back out the window at Ryan.

He watched as Ryan pulled out a cigarette. As he cupped the match and raised it to the cigarette, he seemed to pause and stare directly into Thomas's eyes.

'So what'd you think, sis?'

'I think we're going to have to get one,' Jane announced.

Ricky nodded enthusiastically and glanced over at Ryan.

Ryan looked up towards the house, then casually took out his cigarettes again and offered them to the kid.

Ricky quickly took one and lit up.

Howard leaned forward as he saw his son light up the cigarette.

His gaze traveled to the man who had given it to him, then back to his son.

Richard's affectionate smile was easily discernible even from the window of Thomas's office.

He fingered the file thoughtfully, still thinking of various ways he could use Mr Ryan.

Smiling, Thomas put the file in his bottom desk drawer. He heard the sound of the front door opening and closing, then the excited murmur of voices entering the house. He rose, straightened his suit coat, and went out to join them.

Jane quickly excused herself and rushed up the stairs to change.

In the shower, she let the steaming water cascade down over her head and shoulders. She could still feel the rush of adrenalin that hit as the cycle had first taken off. The sudden burst of speed had thrilled her. It was beyond anything she had ever felt before. And, having felt it once, she couldn't imagine never experiencing it again.

She quickly toweled off and began to dress. As she straightened the hem of her skirt, she caught sight of herself in the mirror. Suddenly, the plain blue skirt and white blouse seemed boring and unappealing.

Unbuttoning the blouse, she stepped over to her closet and peered inside. She settled on a short black skirt and a yellow silk top.

Examining herself in the mirror, she was pleased with the

effect. While it wasn't too daring, there was no way anyone could possible think of it as conservative.

'Wow,' Ricky offered, as he passed her on the stairs. 'You're going to wear that to the office?'

'And why not?' Jane asked imperiously.

'I don't know.' Ricky shrugged sheepishly. 'It just seems a little different from what you usually wear.'

'Too much, you think?' Jane asked, suddenly feeling uncomfortable with the short skirt.

'No, it looks great, sis. Wear it,' Ricky encouraged.

Stepping into the kitchen, her gaze immediately shifted to Ryan. She caught his appreciative glance before he quickly looked away.

'You *are* going to the office, aren't you, Jane?'

Jane turned to her father. 'Of course.' She felt his eyes examining her critically. She kept her face impassive, determined not to give in to his silent disapproval.

'Well you should be on your way, then,' he finally said, turning away from her.

'Are you coming?'

'In a while.' Howard waved absently. 'I would like to talk with Richard first.'

After a last reproachful look, he turned and disappeared into his office.

'Will you be leaving today?'

Ryan turn to face her.

Jane felt the intensity of his gaze. It seemed to last only a moment before it inexplicably dimmed.

'Yeah,' Ryan said softly, then glanced away.

'Then I guess this is goodbye.'

Ryan nodded, turning back to her. Again, there was a moment when Jane felt his interest, but, as before, it seemed to abruptly disappear.

'Thanks for the help with the bike.'

'Thank you for the ride, and for what you did for my brother,' Jane said, offering her hand.

Ryan took it, feeling her hand move in his. He released it reluctantly.

'Take care, Jane.'

'You, too, Ryan,' Jane said softly, then turned and walked out of the house.

Pulling out of the drive, she paused to glanced one last time at the motorcycle. She could still feel the vibration of it running through her body, and she could also still feel the almost dizzying warmth of the man sitting in front of her.

The man from the park – who was now calling himself Raymond – glanced over at Roberta. She bore little resemblance to the woman who had, only a few hours before, met him at the front door of the condo building.

She was sprawled naked across the bed. Her hands and feet had been tied to the bedposts. A pool of blood had formed in the pit of her stomach. Whitish pieces of fat and bone glistened in this sanguinary puddle.

Raymond listened carefully at the door before he opened it and stepped into the hallway. He took the stairs to the lobby, and exited the building without being seen.

He stopped at a phone-booth two blocks from the condo and dialed the number he had memorized.

He didn't allow the voice on the other end to speak, but

quickly passed on his message, then hung up the receiver and stepped out of the booth.

He walked down to his car and climbed inside. He slouched back in his seat and stared out through the windshield at the condominium.

Thirty minutes later, he saw the car he'd been waiting for turn on to the block. Without waiting to see it pull up and park, Raymond hurried out of his car and back to the phone-booth.

As the other car stopped in front of the condo, Raymond smiled and made his second call.

Fourteen

'You're something of an anomaly, Mr Ryan.' Thomas paused and peered expectantly over his desk.

They were seated in Howard's office. Ryan sat across from him, and returned his gaze impassively.

'Anomaly,' the older man repeated thoughtfully.

'It's a good word,' Ryan finally offered in response.

Thomas beamed at him. 'It is, isn't it? I try to learn at least one new word a day. Do you like words, Mr Ryan?'

'No, not too much.' Then, seeing the other man's expression, he explained, 'I find them pretty useless.'

'And why is that?'

Ryan shrugged. 'Most people use them just to remind themselves that they're there.'

'That's quite true.' Thomas nodded approvingly. 'But in your case, I don't think that would be necessary.'

Before Ryan could respond, Thomas went on. 'Looking the way you do, I'm sure you command attention wherever you go.' He paused, meeting the other man's eye.

Ryan held his gaze.

'A man who looks like you is either possessed of great

vanity, or simply doesn't care. Which case are you, Mr Ryan?'

'Maybe neither.' Ryan shrugged.

'I don't think so.' Thomas leaned forward. He picked up a brown manila folder. 'I think it might be the latter,' he said, leveling his gaze at Ryan.

'And why's that?'

Thomas smiled, then suddenly threw the file towards the other side of the desk-top. 'I took the liberty of making a few calls last night.'

Ryan picked up the folder and quickly paged through it. When he was finished, he casually replaced it on the desk.

'You've had quite a checkered past, Mr Ryan.'

'Life was hard in Florida,' Ryan said tonelessly, reaching for a cigarette. He lit up.

'It seems to have been hard wherever you've been.'

Ryan felt the other man's eyes boring into him. He forced himself to remain calm.

'I was especially interested in the murder indictment. You were, what, thirteen years old?'

'About that.' Ryan nodded.

Thomas looked over at him speculatively.

'What do you want, Thomas?' Ryan asked, softly emphasizing the other man's first name.

'What makes you think I want something?'

Ryan nodded at the folder on the desk. 'You wouldn't put out this kind of effort unless there was something you figured you could get in return.'

'That's very astute of you.'

'Thanks,' Ryan said dryly.

'What I want is simply this. I would like you to stay for another couple of weeks.'

Ryan's surprised glance amused the other man.

'Not what you expected, is it?'

'No,' Ryan said truthfully. 'Not after that.' He nodded to the file. 'I would have thought you'd want the exact opposite of me.'

'This.' Thomas glanced disdainfully at the file. 'This is nothing more than a paper biography. I think it has very little to do with the person it's attempting to describe. It's only the bones, Mr Ryan. It's not the body.'

Ryan looked over at him closely. 'And if I don't stay?'

Thomas shrugged. 'That's your choice, Mr Ryan,' he said matter-of-factly.

'No threats?'

'No.'

Ryan stubbed out his cigarette. 'I assume this is more than a simple invitation.'

'Possibly. That remains to be seen.'

'This has to do with the mall vote, doesn't it?' Ryan said, and caught Thomas's look of surprise.

'Ricky told me about it on the way up here.'

'Then you know how important it is to me.'

'Yes, and I also know how important it is to the other side to see it doesn't happen.'

'That's certainly true,' Thomas agreed.

'If I stayed, what would you expect me to do?' Ryan asked curiously.

'That I can't say. It would depend on what happens.'

159

'You're looking for some *heavy* work, aren't you, Thomas?'

'I don't have any idea to what you're referring,' Thomas said innocently.

Ryan glanced over at him skeptically. He sighed, then shook his head. 'As you mentioned, Mr Howard' – he nodded to the file – 'that's just the bones. It's not the body.' Ryan rose to his feet. 'I'm sorry, but I think I'll take a pass on the offer.'

Ryan glanced out the window. Sunlight shafted through the browning leaves of an oak tree. 'Weather's turning on me, and I'd like to be far enough south before the snow hits.'

'That's your choice, Mr Ryan.'

'It is, isn't it,' Ryan said, turning to meet the other man's eye. After a moment, he broke away and stepped towards the door.

'Oh, Mr Ryan, there is one more thing you might find of interest,' Thomas said casually.

'Yeah, what's that?' Ryan turned.

'You might like to know that you've finally been cleared of your mother's death,' Thomas said, eyeing him intently.

Ryan whirled around.

Thomas smiled triumphantly at the shocked expression on the biker's face.

'What are you talking about?' Ryan demanded hoarsely.

'I neglected to include this last page.' Thomas reached into his desk drawer and pulled out a single typewritten sheet.

Ryan reached over and wrenched it out of his hand.

'As you can see, they closed the case only a couple weeks ago.' Thomas paused to take the full measure of enjoyment from the other man's discomfort. 'It would seem your brother Neal shared some of your more violent proclivities.'

Ryan raised his glance from the paper and leveled it at Thomas.

Startled by what he saw in the other's eyes, Thomas quickly drew back.

Ryan shredded the paper, then turned to the door.

Stepping into the hallway, he heard the ring of Howard's phone behind him.

Ricky passed him as he started up the stairs.

'Hey, Ryan—' Ricky's grin quickly disappeared as he caught sight of Ryan's face. He watched as he silently climbed the stairs.

Mystified by his friend's expression, Ricky hurried along the hall.

His father was just stepping out of his office.

'Dad, what happened with—?'

'Not now, Richard. We'll talk later,' Thomas said brusquely, shrugging into his coat and starting for the door.

Ricky watched as his father hurried out the door and down the drive to his car. He turned and looked up at the empty stairs. Hesitantly, he started back towards them, then, remembering the bleak set of Ryan's features, slowly turned and went into the kitchen.

Ryan staggered into his room and sprawled across his bed. He stared up at the ceiling. For a moment he caught the greasy scent of smoke. He tried to pull away from it, but it held him and dragged him down into the darkness...

His ribs were tightly taped when he returned from the hospital, which made it difficult to breathe. Every breath sent a lance of pain through his chest, and reminded him again of his father's fists smashing into his side. Of the drunken smile that cruelly twisted his father's lips. Of the whimpering of Neal, lying curled up on the porch, hugging his knees as he watched his father batter his older brother to the ground.

Ryan stumbled up the drive. He saw his father's truck parked in front of the house, and crept down towards the dock. Only when he was out of sight of the house did he call out softly for Neal.

He couldn't find his brother. He looked everywhere, until finally there was only one place left to look.

The house.

Where his father was.

Steeling himself, Ryan started up the path from the dock. He suddenly caught the scent of smoke. It was a greasy odor that had a meaty pungency to it. It was like nothing he had ever smelled before.

The wind carried it down to him. He glanced up to see a thunderous black cloud, spiralling into the air. For a moment he thought it was an oncoming storm – before he suddenly realized what it actually was. He wrapped a protective arm around his ribs and raced up the path to the house.

By the time he got there, the fire had completely engulfed the main floor of the house. Smoke poured from the windows and blossomed from the roof. The stilted structure beneath the house only added oxygen to the rapacious flames.

Ryan glanced at the drive and saw his father's truck still parked in place. He heard a window shatter and turned back to the blaze.

Suddenly he saw Neal stumble out from the mangroves to one side of the house. He raced over to his brother's side.

'He's dead.' Neal smiled. Tears, blackened with soot and smoke, streamed from his eyes.

Ryan stared at him, then glanced at the house, then back to his brother.

'He's dead,' Neal said again.

Ryan opened his mouth to say something. What it was he was about to say he never found out, because at that moment both brothers turned to see their mother's car weaving up the driveway.

Neal started forward eagerly, then abruptly froze as he watched his father stagger drunkenly out of the halted vehicle.

Ryan heard Neal's broken sob. He stepped up to him and gently reached out.

At his touch, Neal whirled around and glared at him. His gaze held a combination of horror and hate. For a moment Ryan wasn't sure where either emotion was directed.

'What have you done?' his father screamed.

Ryan turned. Before he could defend himself, the man grabbed him and threw him to the ground. He lashed out with his boot.

'What the fuck have you done, you little prick?'

Ryan curled up, trying to protect his already battered ribs. He peeked out from between his arms to see Neal gazing down at him with that same intense expression on his face. Ryan started to call out to him, but his father's boot crashed into the side of his head and sent him spinning into darkness.

When he awoke again, he was in the city jail, awaiting trial for murder.

Three weeks later the indictment was dropped, due to lack of evidence.

Ryan never told anyone what actually happened.

'Neal,' Ryan whispered hoarsely, and he twisted on the bed. His forehead was beaded with cold sweat.

He lunged to his feet and staggered into the bathroom.

Crouched over the sink, splashing water on his face, he lifted his gaze to meet the bleak expression waiting for him in the mirror.

'Jesus Christ,' Mayor Presley growled, disgustedly throwing the morning's paper on his desk. He glanced up to see Jean standing in the doorway.

'Is everything all right?' she asked hesitantly.

'Did you see this?' the mayor demanded, picking up the paper and thrusting it in her direction.

'Yes, sir.' Jean glanced away.

'That goddamn Alder. I can't believe he had the audacity to pull something like this.'

'It's not that bad. It's only...' Jean started, but quickly stopped when she caught her boss's expression.

She backed out of the office, gently closing the door behind her.

Presley slumped back in his chair. He ran a hand across his face, then picked up the newspaper.

The headline read LEWIS AND CONSTANTINE DUMP PRESLEY.

The article below detailed how councilmen Lewis and Constantine had thrown their complete support behind the mall project.

On page four, in a small paragraph at the bottom of the page, was a six-line article reporting the exoneration of Mayor Presley on all charges of malfeasance in the Sawyer case.

Disgustedly, the mayor threw the newspaper into his wastebasket. He started to reach for the phone, then stopped himself.

He knew that if he talked to Alder now he'd just make matters worse. The smart thing to do was to calm down, he told himself, then tried to believe it.

He was leaning back in his chair, taking deep breaths, when Jean suddenly burst through his door, without knocking.

Startled, the mayor peered at her incredulously.

'The radio,' Jean cried, without apologizing for her unprecedented entry.

Further surprising him, she dashed across his office to the small Sony radio on his filing cabinet. She flicked it on, then quickly dragged it through the stations.

'Jean, what the—?'

'Shut up,' Jean ordered, without even glancing in his direction.

'Now, just one—'

Jean turned and held up a cautioning finger. 'Listen,' she told him.

Presley was about to inquire just what the hell she thought she was doing, when the announcer broke through the silence.

'Thomas Howard, of Howard Ltd, was picked up for questioning in the murder of an alleged prostitute this morning. Our station received an anonymous call earlier this morning, about Howard's involvement with this woman. Our reporters discovered Thomas Howard in the room with the mutilated body of the prostitute. Only moments ago, Howard was escorted out of her apartment building by the police. At this time it is not believed that any charges have been filed against Howard. Thomas Howard is the driving force behind the mall issue presently facing the city. He started his real-estate empire ...'

Jean switched the volume down and turned to the mayor.

'When?' Presley gasped, still stunned by the announcement.

'Nine o'clock this morning.'

Presley nodded thoughtfully, still trying to digest this news. He glanced up to catch Jean's eye.

'Thank you.' He nodded appreciatively.

Jean smiled warmly. She stopped at the door and turned to him.

'Would you like me to get Detective Ellroy on the line?' she asked assuredly.

'Yes, Jean.' The mayor offered her a grateful smile. 'I think that would be an excellent idea.'

'I do, too,' Jean replied, then quickly ducked out of his office.

Presley grinned in consternation.

A moment later, when he picked up the phone, all traces of his amusement had vanished.

'What the hell's going on, Tom?' he asked – then heard the detective's weary sigh before he began to explain exactly what had taken place that morning.

Fifteen

Jane was seated at her desk. The morning paper was spread out before her.

'Ms Howard, both Mr Crayton and Mr Lewis called,' Margaret informed her.

Margaret Ansel stood in the office doorway. She was the secretary used by both Jane and her father.

'Mr Crayton called at eight o'clock, and Mr Lewis called at eight thirty.'

'Any messages?' Jane asked, glancing at her watch. It was eight forty-five.

'Both of them would like you to return their calls as soon as possible.'

Sighing, Jane nodded, then said, 'Would you get Mr Lewis for me first, please?'

Jane turned and looked out at Lake Michigan. An east wind whitened the tips of the waves. She picked up the phone as soon as it buzzed.

'Did you see it?' Councilman Lewis asked without preamble.

'Yes,' Jane responded, glancing again at the headline.

'What'd you think?'

'It looks good.'

'How good?'

'Very good.'

'Has he seen it yet?'

'No, not yet. My father usually doesn't see the paper until he arrives at the office.'

'He'll be pleased.'

'I'm sure he will,' Jane agreed.

'Is he going to be home tonight?' Councilman Lewis asked softly.

Jane closed her eyes. 'Yes,' she lied.

'Maybe tomorrow night, then,' Lewis said, disappointed.

'Yes, tomorrow.' Jane nodded. 'Call me.'

'I will,' Jeffrey Lewis promised, then hung up.

Within moments, Jane's phone buzzed again.

'Yes?'

'Would you like me to put that call through to Mr Crayton now, Ms Howard?'

'No, not just yet.'

Jane swiveled her chair to face the window. She looked out again at the dark water. Her thoughts kept straying to the powerful surge of the motorcycle beneath her, and the promise it seemed to offer as it whipped along the road.

'What the hell do you mean, you didn't know?' Donald Alder glared across his desk at Mike Petersen.

Petersen, a twelve-year veteran with the paper, with two years' experience on the night desk, shrugged uncomfortably.

'Goddamnit, where the hell were you?'

'It didn't come over the scanner, Don, until they were already out there.'

Alder snorted disgustedly.

'There was nothing I could do about it,' Petersen tried to explain.

'That's no excuse.' Alder thrust a finger at the other man's chest. 'You were in charge of the desk, so you should have been on top of this.'

'How?'

'How the hell do I know?' Alder said furiously. 'That's your job, not mine.'

Shaking his head in disgust, Alder took a deep breath, then leveled his gaze at the other man. 'What have you got so far?'

'They've got Howard downtown. He's still being questioned. He hasn't been charged with anything, and there's been no formal statement by—'

'By anyone but that goddamn radio station,' Alder angrily interrupted.

'Don, there was nothing I could do about that,' Petersen insisted, leaning across his editor's desk. 'WEVU got an anonymous call, and they sent someone out. Even *they* didn't know what they were going to run into.'

'What do you mean?' Alder asked curiously.

'I talked to Jon Harris over at the station, and he said all the caller told them was that they might be interested in how one of the principals of the mall issue spent his leisure time.'

'That's all?' Alder asked incredulously.

171

'According to Harris, that's all the man said. That's why they didn't go there with any of their main guns. They sent that Maynard woman over, the one who does the gossip show.'

'Well she's doing a hell of job on it,' Alder said, slumping back in his chair.

'I got two guys covering the station, and I've got another one out at the scene,' Petersen offered. 'Nothing's going to get by us.'

'That does us a hell of a lot good now.' Alder sighed in frustration. 'Okay, take off. I've got it covered.'

Petersen quickly slipped out the door.

Alder leaned back thoughtfully, trying to figure out how to handle this story.

If not for the radio, he could have buried it in the back pages. But now it would be almost impossible to play it down. Howard was suddenly vulnerable, and if Howard was vulnerable, what would happen with the mall issue?

'So, you got a phone-call at...' The detective paused to refer to his notebook. 'About eight thirty. Is that right?'

'Yes.' Thomas quickly nodded.

He was seated in the interrogation room. Before him was a stainless-steel table bolted to the cement floor. Sitting across from him was a detective who made little effort to hide his disbelief. Another detective paced to one side of Thomas, forcing him to twist uncomfortably in his chair to answer his questions.

'And the caller informed you that he had important

information about the death of Detective Sawyer – is that correct?' The detective paused to look down at Howard.

Thomas nodded.

'Please answer verbally,' the detective, seated in front of him, requested, nodding to the tape-recorder on the table between them.

'Yes.'

The seated detective smirked.

Before Thomas could react to this smirk, the other man asked, 'Why, Mr Howard, would this person call *you*?'

'What do you—?'

'Why would anyone with information about an ongoing investigation call you rather than the police?'

'I don't know.'

'Bullshit,' the detective in front of him said softly.

'It's true,' Thomas contended.

'So, after receiving this call, you immediately drove to...' Again the detective paused to look at his notes. 'To 781 Genesse Street, and went up to apartment 401.'

Thomas nodded, then, glancing at the recorder, quickly spoke: 'Yes, that's exactly what I did.'

'How did you get inside?'

'What?'

'How did you get into the building?'

'I don't understand.'

'It has a security door. It takes a key to get inside,' the detective seated across from him challenged.

Thomas turned and met the man's belligerent stare. 'It was open. I just—'

'And then, once you were inside, you went up to apartment 401 – is that correct?' the other detective asked.

Thomas swiveled around as the man stepped behind him.

'Yes, that's all I did. I just stepped into—'

'That door was open, too?' the other detective asked sarcastically.

Howard twisted around again.

'And then, once you were inside, you immediately called the police?'

'I was about—'

'But, lo and behold, before you even had time to dial our number, we were already there,' the detective taunted.

'It's what happened. I don't care what it sounds like. It's—'

'Lets try this again, Mr Howard.' The standing detective sighed wearily, and stepped around in front of him. 'Why don't you tell us one more time about your morning.'

Thomas leaned back and closed his eyes, struggling to maintain control.

'Mr Howard?' one of them prompted.

'I got a call at about eight thirty this morning, and the man said—'

'You're sure it was a man and not a woman?'

'Yes.'

'Because that sure the hell wasn't a man up there spread across the bed.'

'I know that.'

'Though,' the detective shrugged reasonably, 'it was

pretty difficult to tell after what had been done to her.' He leveled his gaze at Howard.

'I didn't do that. I had nothing whatsoever to do with what—'

'Tell us about your morning, Mr Howard.'

'I already told you. I got the call at around eight.'

'I thought you said it was eight thirty.'

'It was eight thirty.'

'You just said it was eight.'

'I said it was *around* eight.' Thomas gripped the edge of the table.

'So around eight, or eight thirty' – the seated detective rolled his eyes in disbelief – 'you got a call.'

'I want my lawyer,' Thomas said tightly.

Both detectives examined him intently.

'You haven't been charged with anything, Mr Howard,' the standing detective then said softly. 'A lawyer, at this point in the investigation, might not be your best move.'

Thomas met the other man's gaze. 'I want my lawyer,' he repeated more firmly.

'It's *your* choice, Mr Howard.' The detective shrugged, leaving little doubt about his feelings regarding this request.

A moment later, both detectives rose and left the room.

Thomas waited until the door closed before he shut his eyes and tried to focus his thoughts. He'd always prided himself on his ability to concentrate on *solutions* rather than problems.

Thomas leaned back in his chair and tried to see beyond his present situation to a probable solution. But he found it impossible to pull his thoughts away from the bare room around him. The green concrete walls, etched with obscene graffiti, kept pulling him back to his predicament.

He closed his eyes, trying to force the room away.

He suddenly saw the woman again. The bright splash of blood across her stomach. The whitish pulp of her entrails glistening loosely in the sanguinary pool formed between her hips.

Thomas groaned and buried his face in his hands.

'What do you think?' Detective Ellroy asked.

The detective, who had earlier been seated across from Howard, leaned forward to look through the one-way mirror into the interrogation room. He examined the man inside for a moment, then turned to Ellroy.

'The guy's bullshitting.'

'You think he did it?'

The detective turned back to look in at Howard. After a moment he shook his head. 'Nah. Guy's too much of a fucking pussy. Who ever chopped that broad, enjoyed it. This guy' – the detective nodded disgustedly at Howard – 'probably washes his hands every time he gets a hard-on.'

'Then what's he hiding?' Ellroy wondered.

'I don't know. Something.' The detective shrugged, then turned back to look in at Howard.

Ryan grabbed his duffel bag. He paused at the door to look around the room, then turned and started along the hallway. On the second floor, he stopped in front of Jane's room. After a moment, he shook his head and headed towards the stairs.

At the top of them he paused to light a cigarette. He inhaled deeply, letting the smoke bite into his lungs.

'Ryan!' Ricky suddenly screamed, and a moment later darted out of the kitchen.

The kid swung around the bannister and paused at the bottom step, staring up helplessly at Ryan.

Ryan looked back at him, struggling against a surge of memory.

'It's Dad!' Ricky cried. 'He's been arrested.'

After a moment, Ryan forced himself to walk down the remaining stairs to the boy's side.

'Tell me?' he said softly, reaching out to tentatively touch the boy's shoulder.

Sixteen

Jane heard the squeal of her tires as she turned the corner and pulled into the public parking lot. Her front wheels rammed against the concrete divider. She twisted and pulled the key out of the ignition. She wrenched up the emergency brake, then scrambled out of her car.

Across from her stood the downtown police station. She raced to the front door and into the building.

'I'm looking for Thomas Howard,' she said breathlessly to the policeman at the front desk.

'Down the hall and to your right. It's the third...'

Jane turned and raced down the hallway. She took the first right, then abruptly stopped as she saw Ricky and Ryan standing in front of one of the offices that lined the short walkway.

Ryan was casually leaning against the doorframe, talking to someone inside. Ricky stood nervously beside him.

'Sis,' Ricky called, turning to face her.

'What's going on? I just heard about Dad over the radio.'

'I don't know. I can't get anyone to tell me anything,' Ricky said helplessly.

Jane glanced over his shoulder at Ryan, who was talking to someone seated at a desk.

'Thanks.' Ryan nodded to the other man, then turned and spotted Jane. 'It's okay,' he told her reassuringly.

'What do you mean it's okay? Where's Dad? And what's he doing in here?' Jane demanded.

'C'mon.' Ryan gestured to the entrance. He reached out to take her arm. 'We'll talk about it outside.'

'Ryan.' Jane shrugged impatiently away from his grip. 'I want to know what's happening. Right now.'

'Jane, please.' Ryan met her eye. 'You too, Ricky. C'mon, we'll go outside to talk about this.' He took them by the arm and led them through the front doors.

'What's happening?' Jane halted a few steps outside the door.

'Everything's all right.' Ryan pulled out his cigarettes. He offered one to Ricky.

'Is Dad okay?' Ricky asked worriedly, pulling out a cigarette. He then fumbled with a match.

Ryan gently took the matches from him and lit them both up.

'He's all right,' Ryan said calmly, glancing at each of them. 'He hasn't been charged with anything. They're just questioning him.'

'About what?'

'About a murder,' Ryan said, turning to Jane.

'What on earth would he know about a murder?'

'I don't know, Jane. I don't think at this point that anybody is very clear about what's going on. Your father just happened to be on the scene.'

'What do you mean he was on the scene? I just left him at home forty-five minutes ago.'

'He went out,' Ricky said abruptly.

Jane turned to him.

'Right after you left, he took off somewhere.'

'Where?'

'I don't know.' Ricky shrugged. 'He was in hurry, though.'

'What's that supposed to mean?' Jane glared at Ricky.

'I didn't mean anything by it,' Ricky quickly amended. 'I was just saying he was in a hurry.'

'I know that. I'm sorry.' She reached out to touch his shoulder. 'I just don't understand what's going on.' She turned to Ryan. 'Do you?'

'All I could find out was that a woman was murdered sometime this morning.'

'He was with us all morning.'

'Not *all* morning,' Ryan said softly.

'What are you suggesting?' Jane asked sharply.

'Nothing.' Ryan shook his head. 'I'm just telling you what I found out so far. Your father was on the scene when the police arrived. At the moment all they're doing is trying to find out why he was there.'

'What do mean, at the moment?'

'Exactly what I said, Jane. That's all that's going on right now.'

Jane met his gaze, then abruptly turned away. She turned back an instant later, to see Ryan place a reassuring hand on Ricky's shoulder.

'Have you talked to him?'

'No.' Ricky shook his head. 'They wouldn't let me.'

'What about a lawyer? Does he need—'

'He's already requested one,' Ryan interrupted. He dropped his cigarette and carefully stubbed it out with his boot. 'I think they're going to release him any time now.'

'Did they tell you that?'

'No, but it's the impression I got from the detective I talked to.'

'I don't understand any of this,' Jane said tremulously.

Ryan looked over at her.

'Why would they...? I mean, Dad, why...?' She glanced at Ryan, then at her brother.

'Sis.'

'It's okay, Jane.'

Jane shook her head and turned away again. She stared out blankly at the parking lot.

A moment later she felt Ryan reach out to touch her shoulder. At his touch, she quickly turned and wrapped her arms around him, burying her face in his chest.

'Anything?' Ellroy asked, listening to the static across the radio band.

'Nothing,' the detective on the scene reported back. 'She was hooking, though. We found her book, plus some pretty interesting toys.'

'What about Howard? You got anything that places him?'

'We got a woman on the first floor who says she saw him pull up in front of the building at about eight thirty or so.'

'What'd Maloney say? He give you any kind of time frame?'

'Between one and nine a.m.'

'That's a hell of a lot of help.'

'He can give us more after the autopsy.'

'How good's this woman?'

'Good. I ran her around a little, but she knows what she saw.'

'All right, keep on it – and let me know what you come up with.'

'What're you going to do about Howard?'

Ellroy snorted, 'What do you think,' and he disconnected.

Thomas jerked forward at the sound of the door opening.

Ellroy stepped inside.

Thomas looked up at him anxiously.

Ellroy in turn examined him closely, surprised at the abrupt change in his demeanor. Gone was that superior look of invulnerability. All that remained was a frightened old man.

'My lawyer...' Thomas said hesitantly.

'You won't be needing him,' Ellroy responded.

'Why?' Thomas asked fearfully.

'We're letting you go.'

'Thank you.' Thomas sighed. He started to rise, then paused, glancing meekly up at the detective.

'Can I go now?' he asked apologetically.

'Yes, Mr Howard. You can go now – though we would like to get a statement from your son and daughter about your whereabouts this morning.'

'Of course. That's no problem at all,' Thomas quickly offered.

'Good.' Ellroy nodded, then gestured to the door.

Howard glanced at him gratefully.

Ellroy followed him down the hallway towards the front entrance. As they approached the front doors, Thomas suddenly froze as he glanced through the window.

Standing outside were Ricky, Jane, and Ryan. Ryan had his arms around Jane. Ricky stood close beside them.

'Dad,' Ricky shouted, suddenly spotting his father.

Jane turned, then quickly pulled away from Ryan.

Howard stepped through the front doors as both Ricky and Jane rushed over to him.

'Are you all right?'

Thomas nodded.

'You sure?' Jane asked, eyeing him worriedly.

'I'm fine.' Thomas cleared his throat. 'Fine,' he said again. His gaze locked on Ryan.

Ryan looked at the detective now stepping through the front doors.

'Ms Howard, Richard, I'd like to ask you a few questions if I could?' Ellroy requested, then turned his gaze to the stranger. He examined him closely. 'And you, too, Mr...' He paused, waiting for the other man to offer his name.

'Sure.' Ryan nodded.

Ellroy studied him for a moment longer, then he held open the door and gestured them inside.

'Edward Ryan?' Ellroy asked.

'Yes.'

'Where you from, Edward?'

'California. And I prefer Ryan.'

'Whereabouts?'

'Los Angeles.'

'What do you do out there?'

'Bike shop.'

Ellroy looked carefully over his desk at the other man.

'Motorcycles?'

'Yeah.' Ryan smiled.

'So what brings you up here?'

'Visiting.' Ryan shrugged. He reached into his pocket for his cigarettes, then paused to glance up at the detective.

Ellroy pushed an ashtray across the desk towards him.

Ryan lit up, then slouched back in his chair.

'When was the last time you saw Mr Howard this morning?'

'Eight twenty.' Then, at Ellroy's surprised glance, he added. 'I've had some time to think about it.'

'Did you see Mr Howard leave the house?'

'No.'

'So you can't say exactly what time he left home?'

'No, but as I said, the last time *I* saw him was at eight twenty.'

'Where?'

'In his office at home.'

'You were in there with him?'

'Yes.'

'Doing what?'

Ryan paused to look at the other man. 'Talking,' he finally replied.

'About what?'

'That part of the investigation?'

'Anything I say is part of the investigation.' Ellroy glared. 'What were you talking about?'

'I forget.' Ryan shrugged. 'My memory isn't what it used to be.'

'You didn't seem to have any problem remembering the time.'

'No, I didn't.'

Ellroy leaned back to examine him. 'You always like this with the police?'

'What makes you think I've had that many opportunities to find out?'

Ellroy grinned. 'Call it a shot in the dark.'

Ryan returned his smile. 'Okay.' He nodded. 'I met Ricky down in Kentucky and gave him a ride home.' He shrugged. 'That's all there is to it.'

'You're sure about the time?'

'Positive.'

'All right, that'll do it.'

Ryan started to rise.

'But, you know, Mr Ryan, I will be running you through the computer.' He held Ryan's gaze. 'That going to be a problem for you?'

'Not that I know of.' Ryan turned to the door. He hesitated, then turned back to the detective. 'I don't know if this means anything, but as I was leaving his office I heard the phone ring.'

'What time was that?'

Ryan smiled. 'Eight twenty.'

'You hear any of the conversation?'

'No, nothing.'

'Okay, Mr Ryan, thanks – and we'll be in touch.'

Ryan left the room, feeling the detective's gaze follow him.

In the front hall he found Jane waiting for him.

'Ricky took Dad home,' she explained. 'What did they ask you?'

'The time I saw him last.' Ryan shrugged, then became aware of her gaze. 'What?'

'What did you tell them?'

'The truth.' Ryan returned her gaze.

Jane glanced away and stepped through the front doors.

A moment later, Ryan followed.

Ellroy spotted Leland seated at a table in the back of the bar. He ordered a coffee and carried it over.

'Sorry it took me so long to get back to you, Will.' Ellroy pulled out a chair and sat down.

'No problem, Tom,' Will replied. 'You've had a pretty busy morning, from what I hear.'

'Yeah.' Ellroy sighed. 'It's been something, all right.'

'You find anything?'

'Just a body, and I could have easily done without that.'

'Pretty bad?'

'Real bad,' Ellroy said, raising his cup of coffee.

'You got anything on Howard?'

'Nothing.' Ellroy carefully replaced the cup on the table.

He looked over at Will. 'But what about you – what do you have?'

Leland grinned and shook his head. 'Not until—'

'You got it. I talk to a few people, and if you can produce anything to clear up this Sawyer thing, you'll be reinstated.'

'How come so easy?' Leland asked suspiciously.

Ellroy shrugged. 'There's a lot riding on this, Will. You know that. So what do you have for me?'

'I have this.' Leland smiled as he pulled a folder from beneath the table. 'I thought it might save you some trouble.' He handed it to Ellroy.

Inside, printed at the top of the first page, was the name RYAN, EDWARD.

'What is this?'

'Some guy Howard's got out at his house now. He says Ryan helped his son out of a jam down in Kentucky.'

Ellroy nodded absently as he skimmed through the file.

'Guy's got quite a past, wouldn't you say, Tom?'

'Yeah,' Ellroy grunted.

'Interesting thing that he shows up just about the same time everybody starts dying.'

'When'd he get into town?'

'Few days ago.'

'How many days?'

'I don't know exactly. I do know Howard called me *two* days ago to run a check on him.'

'So that would make it after Sawyer was killed.'

'Yeah, but not before the woman.'

Ellroy stared across the table at the ex-policeman.

'What do you know about the woman, Will?' he asked softly.

Leland shrugged innocently. 'Just what I heard on the radio.'

'And what was that?'

'She was hooking.'

'And?'

'And nothing else,' Leland said sharply. 'What are you trying to say?'

'Nothing. Just asking some questions.'

Leland looked over at him speculatively.

'What else can you tell me 'bout Howard?'

'Not much more.'

Ellroy sighed, then leaned back in his chair. 'Then what are you offering me, Will? What are we doing sitting here, if you don't have anything?'

'I didn't say I *couldn't* get anything.' Leland grinned. 'I just said I don't have anything right now.'

Ellroy pushed his coffee away. He stood up and glared down at the other man. 'Don't fuck around with me on this, Will.'

Leland watched the detective stalk out of the bar. He smiled when he noticed that Ellroy hadn't forgotten to take the file with him.

Seventeen

'I don't understand any of this,' Jane said softly.

Ryan turned to look at her.

They were parked in the lot at the public beach. In front of them, a line of sand dunes drifted down to the water.

Jane abruptly opened her door and stepped outside. Ryan watched the wind whip her hair around her face.

As she started across the sand, he opened his door and climbed out.

He caught up to her as she paused at the edge of the lake. The north wind rolled coldly across the water.

'What was he doing there?' she asked, turning to face Ryan.

'I don't know, Jane.' He shrugged and tightened the collar of his jacket.

'He said he received a phone-call.'

'Yeah.'

'Why would someone want to do that to him?'

Her eyes searched his face.

'From what Ricky tells me' – Ryan paused. He stooped to pick up a stone. He skimmed it across the surface of the waves – 'there's a lot at stake here right now.'

'You mean the mall?'

'Yeah.' Ryan picked up another rock and sent it out over the water.

'Is money that important?' she asked softly, still looking out at the lake.

'Money.' Ryan shrugged. 'And power.'

Jane turned and started to walk along the shore.

Ryan walked beside her.

'It's all he's interested in anymore,' Jane said, keeping her eyes on the sand before her.

Ryan glanced at her silently.

'Ever since my mother died, it's the only thing that seems to matter to him.' Jane sighed, then shook her head. 'He wasn't always like that. I can remember when everything was different.' She suddenly stopped and turned to Ryan. Her eyes rose to his, searching.

'But it's getting harder, you know. It's getting almost impossible to remember who he was, when all I can see is who he's become.' She abruptly glanced away and continued to walk.

Ryan followed.

They moved along the shore until it stopped at the concrete breakwater. Jane paused at the foot of the embankment and looked out at the lighthouse at its end.

'That used to be *my* place,' she said softly. 'That's where I would always go when something was bothering me. I remember when my mother was sick, I used to walk out there and just sit, trying to figure out what was going on. And when she died...' Jane paused. She took a deep breath. It caught in her throat.

'When she died,' she continued more firmly, 'I came down here.' She turned to Ryan. 'I stayed there the whole night, just sitting, thinking. And when I finally went home, I remember stepping into the house, thinking how angry my father was going to be with me.' Jane snorted bitterly. 'But, you know,' she said quietly, turning away from Ryan to look out again at the lighthouse, 'he never even noticed I was gone.'

They walked wordlessly back along the shore. As they approached the car, Jane handed Ryan the keys.

He opened her door, then stepped around the front of the car and climbed behind the wheel.

He pulled out and drove them back to the house.

After carefully locking the door of his office, Howard quickly stepped behind his desk. He stared intently down at its heavy oak structure, lightly running his hands across its surface as if trying to assure himself of its solidity.

He then leaned back in his chair and surveyed his private domain. The rich polished wood and carpeted floor were worlds beyond the interrogation room he had been forced to inhabit for most of the morning.

'This is real,' he said softly, touching his desk, trying to push away the ever-threatening image of the woman tied across the bed.

Thomas noticed a folder placed crookedly across the surface of his desk. He smiled, then reached out to straighten it. He carefully began to align it with the desk's edge.

He paused when he noticed a slight tremor in his fingers. He slowly raised his hand before him and stared at it.

He heard the sound of a car door opening, and whirled around to see Jane's car in the drive. He watched as Ryan climbed out of the driver's side and moved to open the other door.

He watched the two of them walk up the drive. He noticed that they were deep in conversation.

He peered intently through the window, wondering what they were saying to each other, wondering if they were talking about him.

'Ryan,' Thomas suddenly whispered, then stepped around his desk. He opened the bottom desk drawer and pulled out the biker's file. He turned to the first page and began to study it.

He traced each sentence with his finger. He paused once to smile when he noticed that his fingers were no longer trembling.

'He's in his office.' Ricky shrugged helplessly.

'Is he okay?'

'I don't know, sis. He won't talk to me.'

'What do you mean he won't talk to you?'

'Just what I said. As soon as we got home, he went in there.' Ricky gestured to the office door.

'Dad, are you all right?' Jane called.

'He's being really weird, Ryan.'

Ryan turned to the boy.

'It's like...' Ricky faltered. He glanced away. 'It's like he's afraid or something.'

'Dad?'

'Yes, Jane?' Thomas responded through the closed door.

Jane sighed in relief. 'Are you okay?'

'Fine, Jane. Just doing some work.'

'Why don't you open the door?'

'I'd rather be alone right now, Jane. I'm sure you understand.'

'You sure you're okay?'

'Just fine, Jane. I'll be out in a little while.'

Jane leaned against the door.

'What're we going to do?' Ricky asked, glancing from his sister to Ryan.

'I don't know, Ricky.' Jane shook her head, then looked over at Ryan.

'Give him some time alone,' Ryan suggested, feeling their eyes searching his.

'Is he going to be all right?' Ricky asked uneasily.

'He'll be fine,' Jane said determinedly, then turned and started towards the kitchen. 'I don't know about you guys, but I need some coffee.'

Ryan stood beside his motorcycle. He held a cup of coffee and a cigarette. Steam rose from the cup into the cold autumnal air.

'You're not leaving, are you?'

Ryan turned to see Ricky walking towards him.

'You're going to hang around for a while, aren't you, Ryan?' Ricky asked uneasily.

'I don't know, kid.' Ryan shook his head. He glanced

around the yard, noticing the fallen leaves decorating the frost-burned grass. 'Weather's turning on me. I don't leave soon...' Ryan finished his sentence with a shrug.

'Just stay for another day or so.'

Ryan glanced at the boy.

'Please?' he asked.

'All right.' Ryan nodded.

'Great.' Ricky grinned, then reached over and plucked a cigarette from Ryan's breast pocket.

Ryan watched him light it, noticing the concentrated effort the kid put into it.

'What?' Ricky asked, after glancing up to catch his smile.

'Nothing.' Ryan grinned back at him.

'So what do you think happened to him?' Ricky asked.

They were walking through a residential section of town, on their way to a corner convenience store.

Ryan stopped to light a cigarette before he replied, 'Maybe he suddenly realized he was vulnerable.'

'What'd you mean?'

'He was in jail, kid. That's a hard thing for some people.'

'But he wasn't arrested or anything?' Ricky pointed out.

'No, but he could have been. Maybe that's what scared him.'

'Why? He didn't do anything.'

'Doesn't matter.' Ryan shook his head. 'Sometimes all it takes is the threat.'

'But he's Thomas Howard. He used to be the State's Attorney. He isn't just some guy.'

'That's right.' Ryan nodded.

A block later. 'You know, when I was in jail...' Ricky paused.

Ryan turned to examine the boy.

'I was pretty scared.' Ricky turned to look at Ryan.

'Hell, kid, everybody's scared sometime. It's just what you do with it.' Ryan crushed his cigarette out beneath his boot.

'You ever been afraid, Ryan?' Ricky asked. He waited for Ryan to turn before he added, 'I mean really afraid?'

'Yeah.'

'When?'

Ryan met his glance for a moment, then turned away.

'When I had something to lose,' he muttered softly, feeling the boy's eyes still on him.

Jane waited until she saw Ricky and Ryan disappear through the back gate before she turned and walked over to the office door.

She knocked.

'Yes?'

'Are you okay, Dad?'

'Jane?' Thomas called out hesitantly.

'Yes,' she responded, then heard the sound of footsteps. A moment later the office door swung open.

Thomas quickly waved her inside.

Jane stepped into the room, hearing the door being closed and locked behind her.

'I need to talk to you,' Thomas said curtly. He stepped behind his desk and pointed her to a chair.

For a moment all Jane could do was stare at him.

Thomas wore the same clothes he had worn that morning. Both were wrinkled and soiled with perspiration stains. His hair was disheveled and awry.

'Dad, are you all right?' Jane moved around the desk toward him.

'Please,' Thomas ordered, gesturing again to the chair in front of his desk.

Jane slowly backed away from him.

'Be seated.' Thomas smiled brightly. He waited for Jane to sit before he calmly clasped his hands on the desk in front of him.

'I know you may think I'm acting a little strange.' Thomas gave a short bark of laughter. 'But I can assure you that everything is just fine. It's going exactly the way I planned.' Thomas leaned back and peered at her thoughtfully. 'I will admit, reluctantly so' – he winked at her – 'that there have been a few incidents that I hadn't quite taken into consideration. One of these being that wom—' Thomas stopped abruptly. His smile slowly faded. It was replaced with a blank stare.

'Dad?' Jane asked worriedly, rising from her chair.

Howard quickly recovered, and motioned her to be seated again. His smile returned. 'There is something of which I think you need to be cognizant,' he said, savoring the word. 'Cognizant,' he repeated, smiling happily.

'Dad, why don't you rest for a while? You've had a—'

'Jane.' Thomas interrupted. 'There is work to be done.

We can't rest now. Later, when we've accomplished everything we've set out to do, then we can rest. Do you understand?' he asked sternly.

'Yes.'

'Good. Then I think there is something which you need to consider.' Thomas reached into his bottom desk drawer and pulled out a folder. He glanced at it briefly, then offered it to her.

'What is this?'

'Information that I think you'll find very interesting.' Thomas glanced around the room, then brought his gaze back to his daughter. 'We have to be careful, you know. There are a great many people who would like to see us fail.' Howard suddenly pushed himself to his feet.

His sudden movement startled Jane. She looked up at him anxiously.

'Now, I want you to consider that file, and later this afternoon I would like to discuss it with you.' Thomas stepped around his desk.

'Where are you going?'

'I've had a busy morning,' he said, straightening his shirt. 'I think I might rest for a little while. If anything of any importance arises . . .'

'I'll call you, Dad,' Jane promised.

'Good.' Thomas nodded, then strode across the floor of his office. At the door, he turned back to her. 'Be sure and lock this door, Jane. You never know,' he added enigmatically, then turned and disappeared around the corner.

Jane listened to his footsteps starting up the stairs. After she heard the sound of his bedroom door opening and closing, she sighed and leaned back in the chair. For a moment she stared around the office blankly, trying to understand what had happened to him. Wondering desperately what she could do about it.

She glanced at the folder in her lap. She opened it and saw the name at the top of the first page.

She crouched over and began to read.

When she had finished, she slowly put the folder back in her father's desk and stepped over to the window. She looked out at the surrounding trees, suddenly noticing the bare branches and the profusion of leaves littering the yard.

Mayor Presley examined the latest poll taken on the mall referendum.

'It's only five percent,' Jean offered helpfully, noticing his expression. 'And there's still almost two weeks left before the vote.'

'I know,' Presley said wearily.

'And you also have to consider what took place this morning. That hasn't yet had time to sink in with most of the people.'

'You really think it's going to make a difference, Jean?' Presley looked over at his secretary.

'Yes.' She nodded. 'I think it's definitely going to hurt Howard's argument.'

'Why?' Presley asked curiously.

'The crime aspect. You've been talking about that right from the very beginning. I think people will see the correlation between the loss of business and what will happen to the downtown area.'

'I hope you're right.' The mayor sighed, pushing the new statistics away.

Jean turned and started for the door.

'Could you get me Mr Huntington, please?' Presley called after her.

'Charlie, how are you?' Christian said cheerfully, as Presley picked up the phone.

'Not so good, Christian. Have you seen the latest poll?'

'Five percent.'

'That's right.'

'You know, Charlie, once I come on board, I can easily swing another fifteen percent into your camp.'

'I know that, Christian. I was just wondering when you plan on making your announcement.'

'I think right now might be a little premature. I think we would be much more effective if we waited a few days before the election. The way things are going at the moment, I don't know if my endorsement will get the proper coverage.'

'Just as long we don't wait too long, Christian.'

'No chance of that, Charlie. You know where I stand on this issue. I don't want that damn mall built any more than you do.'

'I know that. I'm just worried – with everything else that's happening – that interest in this issue is slowly being re-directed,' the mayor said, then paused to listen to Christian's hearty laugh.

'Charlie, you worry too much. You know how fickle the people are. Today's news is tomorrow's garbage. There's always another story to captivate the voting public.'

'Well, I don't want them to be *too* captivated. I want them out at the polls and voting *against* the mall.'

'They will, Charlie. Don't worry.'

'I've always been a worrier, Christian. You know that.'

'It's what makes you such a good mayor,' Christian replied easily. He hung up the phone and stared across his desk at his brother-in-law.

'How's it look?'

'Very good.' Christian nodded, eyeing the other man thoughtfully.

'What is it?'

Christian raised his gaze to his brother-in-law's eyes. As always, he was somewhat discomfited by the other man's intense gaze.

'Nothing.' Councilman Huntington shook his head, glancing away. 'I think it's time we set up a meeting with Will.'

John Caldwell, owner of Caldwell Construction, smiled in anticipation. 'When?' he asked excitedly.

'Tonight.'

'Both of us.'

'Oh yes.' Christian grinned. 'It wouldn't be the same without you there.'

The man from the park smiled back happily at his brother-in-law, and at the thought of the night's work ahead of him.

Eighteen

They met at the Yacht Club for lunch. Detective Ellroy arrived first. He was shown to the mayor's table, overlooking the lake front. He was halfway through a bottle of Heineken before the mayor appeared. Ellroy watched him weave his way through the tables, pausing to shake a hand or offer a smile to other diners.

As Presley pulled out his chair, he caught sight of the detective's bemused smile.

'What's so funny?'

'Nothing.' Ellroy shook his head.

'No, what?' Presley asked again, picking up his napkin and placing it neatly in his lap.

'Just watching you.' Ellroy gestured vaguely. 'Work the room.'

The mayor sighed wearily. 'It's all a part of the job, Tom.'

'You do it well.'

'I don't have any choice.' Presley stared across the table, trapping the detective's gaze.

Ellroy, understanding this tacit warning, picked up his menu.

They busied themselves with the process of ordering, neither man anxious to broach the reason for their meeting.

'I think this is only the second time I've ever been here,' Ellroy said, glancing around the restaurant.

'When was the first?'

'My daughter's wedding.' Ellroy nodded to the far side of the room. 'She was married right there, almost eight years ago.'

'She still live in town?'

'No, she moved away a couple of years ago. Her husband got a job offer out on the west coast.' Ellroy shrugged and picked up his beer. 'It was too good to pass up.'

'You ever hear from your wife, Tom?' Presley asked softly.

'No,' Ellroy replied curtly.

Presley nodded and looked out at the lake. When he turned back to the table, he caught the detective's inquisitive glance. He sighed, then leaned back in his chair. 'I was hoping we could avoid it for a while.' He smiled ruefully. 'It's kind of nice to pretend that we're just having lunch, and that all the rest of this mess was long past us.'

Before Ellroy could reply, the waiter appeared with their lunches.

Presley looked distastefully at the club sandwich before him. 'I don't even know why I ordered this. I'm not very hungry,' he said, pushing his plate away.

Ellroy paused with his own sandwich.

'No, go ahead. Eat, Tom. I didn't mean to put you off.'

Ellroy carefully replaced his sandwich on the plate and smiled across the table. 'I was just being polite. I'm not very hungry either.'

The mayor returned his smile and picked up his martini glass.

Examining it thoughtfully, he said, 'You know I only allow myself one of these a day.' He looked across at Ellroy. 'But I'll tell you something, Tom. Today I think I could do with a few more of these babies.'

'Another beer wouldn't hurt me either.'

'All right.' Presley grinned. He waved the waiter over and ordered another round.

When their drinks arrived, Presley settled back in his chair and gazed at the detective. 'As much as I hate to ask, you might as well tell me what's going on so far.'

'I wish I had better news for you, Mr Mayor.'

'Charlie,' the mayor corrected.

Ellroy nodded, without pausing. 'But there haven't been any developments in the Sawyer case. I've been back and forth over his financial records, and I've done a search of every case he's handled over the last two years.' Ellroy leaned back, toying with his beer bottle. 'And there just isn't anything there – or, if there is, it's something I can't see. The only thing I can definitely say is that he was taking, though who from and how often I don't have any idea.'

'What kind of money are we talking about?'

'It's hard to tell. He's got the whole thing so tied up in his house and car, and everything else he owns, that it's hard to get any kind of feel for it. But I would think we're talking at least low six figures.'

'You can't get anything from his friends or family?'

'No family, no children. His wife died about four years ago. Cancer.'

'Maloney come up with anything?'

'No.' Ellroy shook his head. 'He found powder burns on the side of his head and residue on his palms. We matched the type on the note with one of the machines down at the station. Whole thing looks like a suicide.'

'Then what's bothering you about it?'

'The circumstances are just a little too convenient for me.'

'How so?'

'The note was clearly directed against you. In my twenty years on the force, I've never known anyone who's pulling the plug to write anything like that. It's always that "poor me" shit.'

Mayor Presley plucked the olive from his martini glass. He looked at it thoughtfully, then raised his glance to the detective.

'Let's call it a suicide,' he said softly, then popped the olive into his mouth.

Ellroy shrugged. 'It's up to you.'

'There going to be any repercussions with that, you think?'

'No, not the way it stands now. Maloney's findings will back you up.'

'I can't afford any problems with this, Tom. I don't want anyone coming back at me and accusing me of sweeping this one under the carpet.'

'The way it reads now, suicide is the only possibility.'

'Good, now what's going on with Howard?'

'Not much more than what I told you this morning. We've had a little more time to look into the woman's background. She's got a paper tail on her for the last eight years, all soliciting charges. There's no doubt she was in the life.'

'You find anything out about the phone-call?'

'Nothing. It was logged into the radio station at eight forty-five. They had someone out there within five minutes.'

'So where does that leave us?' Presley asked.

Ellroy shrugged. 'Almost where we started.'

'Almost?' the mayor asked curiously.

'Well, the one thing we can be sure about is that there's someone out there who doesn't much like you *or* Howard. And the only thing the two of you have in common...'

'Is the mall referendum,' the mayor completed for him.

'Right.' Ellroy nodded, then finished off his beer.

'Flitz?' Ricky said, reading the name off the side of the tube.

Ryan reached over to take it from the boy's hand. He opened it and squeezed out a line of grey putty on his rag, then began to apply it to his exhaust pipes.

Ricky crouched down to watch.

'What's it do?'

'It protects the chrome. Keeps it from rusting.'

Ricky nodded thoughtfully. He reached out to touch the grayish smear, already beginning to coagulate on the chrome.

Ryan slapped his hand away.

'It's got to dry,' he told him.

'I just wanted to see what it's like,' Ricky pouted.

'You want to do it?'

'Can I?' Ricky bounced to his feet.

'Just put it on smoothly, and don't use too much of it, all right?'

'Sure.' Ricky grinned, reaching for the tube and rag.

Ryan leaned against the side of the garage and watched Ricky apply the protectant.

He suddenly flashed on an image of Neal, crouching over the hull of their boat, trying to apply a sheet of fiberglass. For a moment the image was so vividly before him, that he could almost feel the hot sun and smell the musty odor of the bay.

Neal, bending over, his tongue caught between his teeth in concentration. The way he suddenly whirled around and grinned at Ryan.

'Look it, Eddie. I did it,' he cried excitedly.

Ryan, moving over to examine the boat, feeling his younger brother's eyes on him.

Turning to him, smiling, reaching out to touch his shoulder.

Neal, showered with sunlight, smiling happily back at him. Then the sound of the truck pulling into the drive.

Neal's smile disintegrating.

Their father's voice: the drunken shout.

The sound of their mother's cry.

Neal turning to him – and all that was left on his face was the fear.

'Like that?'

Ryan shook away from the image. He came back to the sight of Ricky crouched before the bike, looking up at him anxiously.

'What?'

'Is this okay?' Ricky asked impatiently, pointing to the exhaust pipe.

Ryan stepped over to the bike. 'It looks good,' he said, then, unable to help himself, reached out to touch the kid's shoulder.

Ricky glanced up at him, smiled, then turned back to the bike.

Ryan stepped away and pulled a cigarette. He lit it, squinting against the smoke.

As Ricky worked the handlebars, Ryan heard the sound of the front door. He glanced up the drive to see Jane walking towards them.

She wore jeans and a black windbreaker over a white shirt. It was the same outfit she had worn that morning when they had taken their ride.

With her gaze fixed on Ricky, Ryan examined her as she walked up to her brother. Her hair was pulled back over her shoulders. A single dark strand fell forward across her forehead. She reached up casually and pushed it back.

'How's Dad?'

'He's resting now.'

'Is he okay?' Ricky paused to look at her.

'He's going to be fine, Ricky. He was just a little shook up.' Jane smiled reassuringly. She glanced over at Ryan, then quickly turned away when he met her gaze.

'What're you doing?'

'Have to put this on the chrome, or else it'll start to rust,' Ricky said knowledgeably.

'Oh.' Jane smiled, watching her brother's hand move across the handlebars. 'Run into a lot of rust, do you?' she teased.

Ricky glanced up at her, then blushed. 'Well, that's what Ryan said.' He shrugged.

Ryan waited for her glance.

She continued to watch her brother, until he pulled back to examine the bike. He reached over to dab at a spot, then looked inquisitively at Ryan.

'It looks good, kid. You did a great job.' Ryan nodded, stepping over to the bike beside Jane.

He ran his fingers along the handlebars, then stooped down to examine the exhaust pipe. He suddenly became aware of Jane standing next to him. His shoulder brushed against her leg.

She quickly stepped away.

'You going to take it out?'

'Yeah, I was thinking I might look around.'

'Can I come?'

'Sure, it's all right...'

'Ricky, why don't you stay with Dad?' Jane interrupted.

'Why can't you?'

'I want to talk to Ryan for a little while,' Jane replied, without glancing in Ryan's direction.

'C'mon, sis.'

'Ricky,' Jane cautioned.

'Jesus, I never get to do anything,' Ricky pouted, then turned and stomped up to the house.

Catching Ryan's amused glance, Jane shrugged, then stepped over to the bike. Her fingers nervously traced the line of the handlebars.

'What's going on?' Ryan asked softly.

'Nothing.'

'C'mon, Jane, what is it?'

'Let's go for a ride,' she said abruptly.

Before Ryan could respond, she'd climbed on to the back of the bike.

Ryan pulled out of the drive and on to North Sheridan Road.

'Take a left at the light,' Jane directed.

Ryan turned, then followed her directions out of town. As they rode west, they passed through small residential developments that gradually gave way to open fields.

Jane directed him off the main highway and on to a black-topped road.

Ryan silently followed her lead.

Two miles into the road, Jane asked him to pull over and stop.

Ryan wheeled the bike over to the shoulder and killed the engine. They were surrounded by untended farmland. The earth, once rich with corn and soy beans, now splayed out around them in all directions, twisted with weeds and rocks.

Jane swung off the bike and stepped to the side of the road.

Ryan kicked down the stand and moved over beside her.

'All of this' – Jane pointed out at the fields; her gesture encompassed the whole western horizon – 'is where the mall's going to be.' She turned to look at Ryan. 'It's going to be the largest in the country. Over four million square feet. It's going to have twelve theaters, twenty-eight restaurants, and over three hundred stores. It's going to be the biggest thing that's ever hit this area.'

Ryan nodded, reaching for his cigarettes.

'My father's been working on this for almost three years now.'

Jane paused to look out at the empty fields.

Ryan examined her, noticing the determined line of her jaw, the dark strand of hair falling across her forehead.

He started to raise his hand, then abruptly turned and stepped away.

'There's nothing out here,' he said harshly.

Startled, Jane turned to him.

Catching her glance, Ryan shrugged, then said more softly, 'There's nothing here, Jane. The town's all behind us.'

'But we can bring it out this way. It's the only way the town can grow.'

'Why does it have to grow?' Ryan asked curiously.

'Because it's the way things are. Everything changes,' she said, looking at him intently.

'Does it?' Ryan asked quietly.

'Yes.' Jane nodded.

'Maybe.' Ryan stepped back to the bike. He swung his leg over it and waited.

A moment later she climbed on behind him.

This time Ryan picked their route. He drove back to town.

He pulled up on a side street and parked.

Without saying anything, they started to walk towards the downtown section.

They stopped at a sidewalk café, and took a table looking out at the street. Jane ordered a cappuccino and a croissant.

Ryan wrapped his hands around his coffee cup, letting the warmth take away the chill from handling the bike.

He lit a cigarette and watched the throng of shoppers moving along the sidewalk. He felt Jane's eyes on him and turned to her.

'You can't tell me anything about growth and progress,' Ryan said quietly. 'I'm from Florida, Jane. I know what it means.'

'And what's that?'

'Money – that's all it comes down to. No one's trying to improve anything; they're just looking to make a buck.'

'That's not true. What my father wants to do will benefit the whole town.'

'Will it?' Ryan challenged. 'What about this part of town? What's going to happen to it? You think it's going to survive that kind of shift to the west?'

'There's no reason it shouldn't.'

'Right.' Ryan snorted sarcastically. 'You're going to put in over four million square feet of shopping space twelve miles west of the downtown area, and you think it isn't going to be affected.'

'It doesn't have to be. All it has to do is change and compete.'

'How the hell can it compete against something like that?' Ryan demanded bitterly.

'Why are you so angry?' Jane asked softly, meeting his eye.

'I'm not.' Ryan shrugged, breaking away from her glance. He reached for another cigarette.

Ryan paused after they rose from their table. He watched her weave her way through the other tables to the sidewalk.

Sighing heavily, he stepped out to join her.

They walked slowly down Main Street, stopping to look in the windows.

'Thanksgiving's only three weeks away,' Jane mentioned.

Ryan grunted in response.

'Where do you spend Thanksgiving, Ryan?'

'Home,' Ryan said curtly.

Jane's eyes lingered on his face.

She turned and began to walk.

'California?'

'Yeah.'

'You have family out there?' she asked carefully.

'No.'

'Your family still in Florida, Ryan?'

Ryan turned to her. 'What about you?' he asked, avoiding her question. 'What do you do for Thanksgiving?'

For a moment she held his gaze, then quickly walked away.

Ryan caught up to her at the corner.

'What was that all abo—' He stopped when she turned to face him.

Wiping angrily at her eyes, Jane merely shook her head and moved back towards the bike. Ryan followed.

'I want to go home,' she said abruptly, without meeting his glance. She climbed on the back and waited.

Ryan nodded and started up the bike.

He pulled away from town and stopped at a traffic light. Before him was Lake Michigan. To his right was the Howard house.

The light changed, and Ryan gunned the engine and ran straight ahead.

He parked at the foot of the breakwater.

'I want to go home, Ryan,' Jane repeated, carefully enunciating each word.

Ignoring her request, he climbed off the bike, then turned and offered her his hand.

Examining him closely, Jane hesitated, then reached out to take his hand.

It wasn't until they had started to walk out to the lighthouse that Ryan suddenly became aware that he was still holding her hand.

He gently released his grip and felt a sudden rush of cold air shift across his palm. Jane walked on ahead of him.

When Ryan reached her, she was seated at the base of the lighthouse. Her legs dangled over the water's edge. Ryan sat down beside her.

'I don't want to hurt my father,' she said softly, looking out at the water.

'Why would you hurt him?'

'I don't know.' Jane shrugged, still avoiding his eye. 'But I just don't want that to happen.'

'I don't understand.'

Jane turned to him. Ryan started to turn away, but she quickly reached up to touch his cheek. She gently forced his gaze back to hers.

'Jane . . .'

'Don't,' she said softly, touching his lips, then hesitantly leaned forward.

Ryan felt her lips press softly against his. He closed his eyes, trying to push back the sudden flush of memory.

Zella.

Reaching out to him, offering him something that he had never thought possible.

The harsh glare of the hospital lights, the agonized twist of her face.

Ryan jerked back.

'Please,' Jane whispered softly. Her hand again rested against his cheek.

Ryan shrugged away from her touch. He pulled a cigarette and took his time lighting it.

He stood up and leaned against the lighthouse, aware of her gaze following him.

'I know you, Ryan.'

He looked down at her.

'I know all about you. I know what you feel, and what you're afraid of.'

Ryan was unable to turn away from her eyes.

'You know why?' She smiled painfully. 'Because I'm

almost as afraid as you are.' She turned to look out at the lake again.

'You . . .' Ryan paused.

'What?' She turned to him.

'Nothing.' Ryan shrugged wearily, also staring out at the cold waters of the lake.

'There's more to living than just surviving, Ryan,' Jane said quietly.

Ryan felt her eyes still searching his face. He kept his gaze locked on the lake.

Jane pushed herself to her feet. She brushed off her jeans, then reached out to touch his shoulder. 'C'mon, we need to get back.'

Ryan turned. Her eyes were waiting for him. He felt a brief flash of memory, but it quickly disappeared and left him staring only at the woman before him.

Almost violently, Ryan suddenly reached out and pulled her against him. He held her fiercely, using her body to push away all the memories that seemed to suddenly threaten him.

Nineteen

Will Leland glanced at his watch. It was seven twenty-two. He had another eight minutes before his guest was supposed to arrive.

When the call came in, earlier that day, he hadn't been particularly surprised. He'd been expecting to hear from him, had even begun to wonder what was taking him so long. At the sound of that voice at the other end of the phone, Will had felt a measure of relief, realizing that everything was going according to plan.

His plan, right from the beginning, had always been fairly straightforward – or at least as straightforward as Leland could make it. What Will expected to accomplish – dealing between the two political factions – was more than just reinstatement, though that was certainly a part of it. He wanted to be the sole controlling head of the Waukegan Police Force.

When he first realized that this might be a possibility, he had shied away from the idea, unable to see how he could possibly make it work. But the harder he had tried to push the thought from his mind, the more it had seemed to take root. Until finally, eight months ago, he'd decided to test the waters. He wouldn't commit to anything, he reassured himself. He would simply put out a few feelers to see if the opportunity was there.

His first tentative approach to Sawyer had been a positive one. Sawyer's impending retirement had made him stupidly greedy. He was willing to listen to any offer, no matter how dubious, that might promise him a measure of financial relief.

Realizing how Sawyer could be put to use, Leland had cautiously begun to look around for a benefactor. To make the venture a successful one, he would need someone with both money and political power. He had been surprised at how easy this had proved.

By the time he had finished his research on the predominant political powers in Waukegan, it had not been a question of *who*, but *which one*. All of the men Leland had investigated had proven to be mutable. It was simply a matter of discovering which of them would be open to the size of the scheme Leland had in mind.

This had taken a little longer to uncover. Leland needed a precarious balance of caution and determination to make his plan a viable one.

After reducing his list to five names, Leland decided to approach his selection from a different direction. He began to research each man's family. Within a matter of hours, he'd found the perfect partner to his plan.

Surprisingly, the biggest drawback to his approach had been the modest reward that Leland expected to reap. His man had found it difficult to believe that all Will wanted out of this deal was control of the police force. This disbelief had forced Leland to reveal the true depths of his feelings about his summary firing from the force.

Recounting the two years of hell he had spent trying to put his life together, chronicling the loss of his wife, his home, and just about everything else he had ever valued, had brought back all the bitterness he had tried to bury over the intervening years. His ready anger had surprised him as much as it did the man he was trying to convince.

Within twenty-four hours of his explanation, he'd found the partner he'd been looking for.

Funneling the money to Sawyer had been easy. The man's greed had far outshadowed any sense of caution he might have once had.

Setting him up hadn't bothered Will in the least. Sawyer was a bad cop. He wouldn't be someone Will would want to employ, once he took over the force. Easier to get rid of him now than to draw it out over a long legal battle, Will had rationalized.

Setting up Thomas Howard had been ridiculously easy. The man, for some reason Leland couldn't fathom, seemed to be under the illusion that Will was easily manipulated. Will found the whole charade immensely amusing. Howard's sense of invulnerability and power had made him weak and anemic. He was there to be had, and Will and his partner were more than willing to do the taking.

The sound of the bell pulled Will away from his thoughts. He rose and stepped over to the door.

'Will.' Christian nodded, stepping into the house. Behind him trailed his brother-in-law, John Caldwell, head of Caldwell Construction. It had been that link between the two men that had first attracted Will to Christian.

Going through the city bids, he'd found an inordinate amount of projects allocated to Caldwell Construction. Many of them were granted on bids that weren't at all competitive. One of the few bids that Caldwell had failed to get was the one for the planned mall project. It had been that, more than anything else, that had first made Will contact Christian.

'How are you, John?'

'Very good.' Caldwell smiled, then stepped around Will and followed his brother-in-law into the living-room.

Will closed the door, as always surprised by the man's easy charm. It was an illusion that Leland had quickly discovered could be a deadly one.

Stepping into the living-room, he found Christian already at the side bar, helping himself to a glass of brandy. Caldwell was leaning against the mantelpiece.

'I hope you don't mind,' Christian said, waving the glass before him.

'No, not at all. Can I get you something, John?'

'No, I'm fine, Will. I think I'll just coast.' Caldwell grinned.

Will nodded, then sat down across from Christian. 'So what's up?' he asked, clasping his hands before him.

'Well,' Christian said thoughtfully, swirling the brandy around in his snifter. 'I think we're ready for our next step.'

'Have you heard anything more about Howard?'

'Yeah.' Will nodded at Caldwell. 'I talked to Ellroy earlier today and, from what he tells me, Howard was pretty shook up.'

'What else did Ellroy have to say?'

'He's getting a little impatient over the Sawyer thing.'

'Tough shit.'

Leland glanced sharply at Caldwell. The man's easy smile contradicted his words.

Will shrugged and turned back to Christian. 'When are you going to make your endorsement?'

'Odd you should ask that. The mayor asked me that very same question earlier today.' Christian smiled in amusement.

'And what'd you tell him?'

'I told him I thought it would be a little premature right now. I want to wait until a few days before the election to secure the optimum impact.'

'You still think you can carry it?'

'If I don't, Will, we're all fucked.'

Caldwell snorted disgustedly.

'What about Lewis and Constantine?'

'They're ready.'

'You're sure you can swing this?' Will asked, leveling his gaze at Christian.

'You do worry, don't you?'

'There's a lot to worry about.' Will nodded, not taking his eyes off the other man. 'The mall's only part of it. *Your* part. It's the next step that concerns me.'

'Will.' Christian smiled reassuringly. He crouched forward, cradling his snifter in his hands. 'I've got it covered.

Both Constantine and Lewis are more than ready to vote for impeachment if the mall fails. With those two, plus the backing of Alder, the town's ours.' Christian paused, then added. 'And the police force is *yours*. Is that what you want to hear?'

'Yes.' Will sighed.

'I have to admit, I am still somewhat surprised at how little you want out of all of this.'

'We've already been through this, Christian.'

'But there's such a lot of money to be made here. It worries John a little.' Christian nodded to his brother-in-law.

Will turned to see Caldwell's smile waiting for him.

'He doesn't quite trust people who are able to control their greed. They make him...' – Christian paused, searching Will's eyes – 'uncomfortable.'

'I told you, right from the start, that's all I want. You guys can keep whatever you make off the mall deal. I'm not interested in the money. I just want—'

'Revenge.' Christian smiled.

'If that's what you want to call it.' Will shrugged. 'That's as good a name as any.'

'Revenge I understand,' Caldwell said, stepping away from the mantelpiece and moving behind Will.

Will felt uncomfortable having him behind him, but Christian's taunting gaze held him in place. He felt a trickle of perspiration begin to bead along his ribs.

'Who built this place?' Caldwell asked curiously.

Relieved at the opportunity to turn, Will swiveled in his chair to face the other man.

Caldwell was standing in the doorway, running his hands along the trim.

'I don't have any idea.'

'Shitty work,' Caldwell pronounced, moving along the wall, examining the ceiling.

'Why?'

Caldwell snorted disdainfully, then went back to his examination.

'There was something I wanted to ask you, Will.'

Leland turned to face Christian.

'I hope you don't mind,' Christian smiled, 'but it's something I've been worrying about.'

'Yeah, what's that?'

'You mentioned once that you had tapes of all of your conversations with Howard.'

'Yes.' Will nodded, watching the other man carefully. He heard Caldwell's disgusted snort as he discovered yet another flaw in his house.

'I know this is probably ridiculous of me, but I was wondering if you might also have tapes of *our* conversations as well.'

'That's a possibility you might want to keep in mind, Christian,' Will said carefully, locking eyes with him.

'Oh, it most definitely is, isn't it, John?'

'Most definitely,' Caldwell said into Will's ear.

Startled, Will jerked forward in his chair.

Caldwell's hands suddenly closed around his shoulders and forced him back.

'I want those tapes.' Christian said, without a trace of his previous sociability. 'And I want them now.'

'C'mon, Christian, what's this all about? If we don't trust each other, we're not going to get anything out of this.'

'Where are the tapes?'

'They're safe.'

'From whom?'

'From everyone.' Will glared at him.

Christian nodded to Caldwell.

Before Will could turn, Caldwell slammed a fist into the side of his face.

It was only Caldwell's grip with his other hand that kept Will in place. Feeling a trickle of blood worm it's way across his lip, Leland raised his eyes to Christian.

'This isn't going to do you a damn bit of good, Christian. Something happens to me, those tapes'll burn you,' Will threatened.

'Only if you don't tell me where they are.'

'That would be pretty fucking stupid of me, wouldn't it? I tell you anything and I'm dead.'

'See, Will.' Christian crouched before the other man. 'That's where your thinking is all confused.'

Will lashed out at him with his foot.

Christian easily batted it away and continued. 'You're dead, anyway. The only question is how you're going to die.'

'You mother fu—'

Caldwell suddenly released him.

But before Leland could move, Caldwell clapped both hands across each of Will's ears.

Leland screamed as the pressure burst his left eardrum. He sagged forward, trying to escape from the pain.

Caldwell jerked him back against the chair.

Will raised his head to see Christian standing before him. He could see his lips moving, but couldn't hear what the other man was saying.

He watched as Christian shrugged disgustedly, then nodded to his bother-in-law.

'No,' Will screamed, sensing the movement behind him.

Caldwell's knuckles slipped into the joint on each side of Leland's jaw and began to grind into the muscle.

Unable to hear his screams, Leland could only look down helplessly to see his legs spasming before him.

'Where?' He barely managed to hear Christian shout.

Caldwell suddenly released him.

Will sagged forward, feeling blood trickling from his nose and ears. Will tried to raise his head, but the slight movement sent a sharp stab of pain shooting through his jaw and head.

'Where are they?'

Will felt Caldwell's hands grip each side of his head. He tried to pull away, but the knuckles began to grind into his jaw. The pressure made it impossible for him to scream. All he could do was moan and writhe helplessly in his chair.

'Stupid place to put them,' Caldwell said disdainfully, standing in Leland's closet. 'We would have found them anyway.'

'I think that was the point,' Christian said thoughtfully.

At his brother-in-law's glance, Christian explained, 'I think he figured they were well enough hidden for a cursory examination, but if something happened to him they would eventually be found by *someone*.'

Caldwell shrugged, then knelt down and began to sort through the tapes.

'They're all labeled,' he said over his shoulder.

'That makes it so much easier.' Christian turned and looked over at the bed.

Leland was sprawled across it. His face was splattered with coagulated blood. His jaw was swollen and discolored. His left hand spasmed uncontrollably.

Christian glanced at his watch.

'Hurry up, would you. It's getting late. I've got an early morning tomorrow,' Christian said impatiently.

Caldwell replaced the top of the shoebox and stood up. He turned and handed the box to Christian.

Christian glanced into the box, then tucked it under his arm. He turned and looked over at Leland.

The ex-policeman moaned feebly.

'You'll take care of him?'

'Yes.'

Christian turned to see his bother-in-law's smile.

'Don't get too playful with him.'

Leland moaned phlegmily. A bubble of blood-tinged saliva appeared on his lips.

'I don't think he's going to be too much more fun,' Caldwell said sadly.

'Just dump him somewhere where we don't have to worry about him for a couple of weeks.'

'I know just the place.' Caldwell grinned.

After Christian left, Caldwell stepped over to Leland

and examined him. He reached out with a finger and gently prodded the man's swollen jaw. At his touch, Leland groaned and struggled weakly to shift away.

Caldwell grinned down at him.

He went into the living-room and picked up the empty brandy glass. He took it into the kitchen, then carefully washed and replaced it in the cabinet. He stepped back into the living-room and carefully examined the room. He stepped over to the chair Will had sat in and wrinkled his nose distastefully at the damp urine stain.

He reluctantly reached out and turned the cushion. The other side was still dry. Satisfied, Caldwell stepped back into the bedroom.

Leland had managed to roll over on to his stomach. He was lying half off the bed. A few feet from him was a nightstand with a telephone on it.

Caldwell smiled approvingly at him, then stepped over and reached down for him.

Ignoring Leland's constant moans, he hefted him to his feet and dragged him to the front door. At the doorway, Caldwell propped Will up against the wall, then he turned and walked back into the bedroom. He came out a moment later, smoothing out the marks Leland's feet had made across the carpet.

He carried Leland outside to his car and opened the back door.

Steadying him against the car, Caldwell smiled in anticipation. He waited until he saw Leland's eyes begin to open before he raised his fist and smashed it into the other man's jaw. Will sagged against the car door.

Caldwell threw him across the floor in the back, then returned to the house and locked the door. He came back to the car whistling happily.

CALDWELL CONSTRUCTION announced the sign planted in front of the work site.

Caldwell backed his car up to the footings, then climbed out. He pulled Leland from the back seat and dragged him across the rubble to the edge of the footings. There he balanced him on top of a ridge of dirt, then settled back on his heels and waited.

Five minutes later, Leland moaned and opened his eyes. The pain immediately forced him to close them again. It was the slap across the face that made him reopen them.

He saw Caldwell crouching before him, grinning excitedly.

He moaned. He tried to speak. His words came out thickly through the broken joints of his jaw.

Caldwell reached over and gently turned his head.

For a moment all Leland saw was the darkness. It shifted and began to take shape. When he realized what he was seeing, he screamed. The high-pitched keening sound, more animal than human, echoed around him.

At the sound of his scream, Caldwell pushed him over the edge.

Leland toppled into the hole dug at the base of the footings.

Caldwell started up the backhoe and steered it over. Whistling tunelessly, he slowly began to move the mound of dirt over the edge and into the hole below.

He paused once when he thought he heard another scream, but, after listening carefully for a moment, reluctantly decided it must have only been his imagination.

Caldwell turned off the backhoe and stepped over to the edge of the footings to look down.

Satisfied, he turned away and walked to his car. He backed away from the site, glancing over at the concrete mixer parked at the side of the road, all ready for use early tomorrow morning.

Twenty

'*There's always something else,*' *she'd said sadly, then, seeing his confusion, explained. 'Nothing ever lasts. And if there isn't anything to replace it, then there isn't any reason to go on.*'

Ryan stepped over to the side of the bed and knelt beside her.

'*What is it, Eddie?*'

He shook his head, committing every feature of her face to his memory, until it was burned so indelibly within him that it would never disappear.

'*Eddie?*' *Zella said softly, reaching over to cup his face.*

'*We don't need anything else. We'll never need anything else,*' *Ryan said fiercely, clasping his hand over hers, pressing it against his cheek.*

'*No,*' *she sighed, coming into his arms. 'We'll always have each other.*'

'Ryan?'

Ryan turned from the dark plane of the window.

Jane was lying on her side, looking at him. She wrapped the sheet around her chest, then pushed back a strand of hair. 'What are you doing?'

'Couldn't sleep.'

'Come back to bed. It's cold.'

Ryan closed his eyes, trying to push away the flush of memories.

'C'mon,' Jane called softly.

Ryan stepped over to the bed.

Jane raised the sheet and looked up at him expectantly.

Ryan climbed in beside her. Her arms came around him.

'You're freezing,' she said, rubbing his back and arms.

Ryan felt her hand move across his chest to his chin.

Her fingers traced his lips, then rose and lightly moved across his jaw and forehead. She leaned forward and pressed her lips against his. He felt the heat of her body rekindling. Her legs shifted, enclosing his own.

'Ryan,' she whispered, pressing against him.

And Ryan, without effort, found his hands beginning to move across her body, touching and probing, until she gasped and drew him inside.

'Tell me?'

'What?'

'Tell me about her. Please?'

Ryan turned. The darkness made a pale blur of her features. Her hair shrouded her face.

'Who?'

'Zella.'

Ryan grunted and shifted away.

'No.' Jane grabbed his arm and held him. 'Tell me what happened.'

'What are you talking about?'

'My father told me,' Jane said, feeling his eyes fixed on her.

'She died,' Ryan said hoarsely, then glanced away.

'When?'

Ryan sighed. 'A long time ago.'

He shifted and sat on the edge of the bed.

Jane followed. She wrapped her arms around him and leaned against the warmth of his back.

'Were you together a long time?'

'Yes.'

'It must have been hard for you.' Jane said quietly, feeling the beat of his heart beneath her cheek.

Ryan looked at the window. He saw a single skeletal branch outlined against the night sky.

'She's still there,' Jane said, then a moment later whispered, 'Isn't she?'

Abruptly, Ryan turned and took her in his arms. He held her tightly, closing his eyes, trying to force the memories away.

'It's okay,' Jane whispered sadly, touching his hair, letting her hand rest on the back of his neck as she held him.

They stood before the window, looking out at the frost covering the back yard.

Sharing the sheet, arms wrapped around each other, they watched the sunlight begin to trickle across the grass.

'I have to go.' Jane turned to look at him.

Ryan nodded. His eyes searched her face.

'It's okay.' Jane smiled, then, touching his lips, turned and quickly shrugged into her robe.

As she turned at the stairs, she glanced back up to see him standing in the doorway watching her. She smiled, then quietly moved on down.

Stepping on to the second-floor hallway, she gasped as she sensed movement behind her. She whirled around to see her brother standing outside his door, staring at her.

'Ricky?' she whispered, clutching her robe tightly to her chin.

Without answering, he slipped back into his room and closed the door.

'I'm fine,' Howard insisted. He stood just in the kitchen doorway looking over at his son.

Ricky leaned against the sink with a cup of coffee in his hand.

'You want some coffee, Dad?'

'Please.' Thomas stepped further into the kitchen. 'You're up early this morning,' he remarked, as Ricky handed him a cup.

'Couldn't sleep.' Ricky shrugged.

Thomas raised his cup.

'Are you going into the office today?'

'Why wouldn't I?' Thomas responded quickly, fixing his gaze on the boy.

'I don't know. I just thought ...'

'Thought what, Richard?'

'Well, after yesterday ... I thought you might want to just take it easy for a while.'

'There's work to be done, Richard. There's no time to waste.' Thomas sipped his coffee. 'That's something you're going to have to learn.'

'Yes, Dad.'

'Is your sister up yet?'

'No,' Ricky answered, quickly turning away.

Howard glanced impatiently at his watch.

They both turned as they heard footsteps coming down the stairs.

Ryan stepped into the kitchen.

'Good morning, Mr Ryan.'

'How you feeling?'

'Is there any reason I shouldn't be feeling fine?' Thomas asked imperiously.

Ryan shrugged and stepped over to the coffee pot.

Ricky quickly shifted out of his way.

Ryan tried to catch his eye, but the boy avoided his glance.

'I'm late,' Thomas said, putting his cup on the counter. He straightened his tie, then turned to Ricky.

'When your sister finally wakes, would you please inform her that she's needed at the office.'

Ricky nodded.

After a last nod towards Ryan, Thomas turned to the door.

'Hey, kid—'

'Dad,' Ricky called, pointedly ignoring Ryan. 'Maybe I could help out today.'

Thomas turned to look at the boy speculatively.

'I mean, I'm not doing anything today.' Ricky shrugged vaguely. 'And I might as well start learning the business.'

'I think that's an excellent idea, Richard. Why don't you get changed and we'll drive down to the office together.'

The boy smiled enthusiastically and darted through the kitchen door.

Howard glanced over at Ryan, then abruptly turned away – but not fast enough to hide the small triumphant smile that creased his lips.

Ryan stood at the kitchen window and watched as Ricky, dressed in a suit and tie, trailed alongside his father down the drive.

As they pulled out, Ryan caught sight of the boy's face peering at him through the windshield.

'Where *is* everyone?'

Ryan turned to see Jane standing in the doorway.

'Work.'

'What?'

'They just left.'

'Ricky, too?' Jane exclaimed.

'Yeah.' Ryan nodded.

'Jesus.' Jane shook her head, then smiled. 'I guess that means we have the whole house to ourselves.'

'Listen, I wanted to talk to you about—' Ryan started.

Before he could finish, Jane had moved across the floor and wrapped her arms around him.

'What were you saying?' she said, pressing her body against his.

'Nothing.' Ryan shook his head, then reached up and gently pushed back a strand of dark hair. His fingers lingered on her forehead.

As soon as Howard stepped through the front door of his office, all vestiges of the previous day vanished. Here he was in total control. There was no sense of the vulnerability he had so suddenly experienced yesterday. Surrounded by all the accoutrements of his success, Thomas felt an overwhelming sense of his own importance. He was a man who was going to change the shape of the city, and there wasn't anyone or anything that would stop him.

'Margaret, I believe you know my son, Richard. He's going to be working with us today,' Howard explained, glancing over proudly at his son.

Ricky nodded shyly to the woman.

'Welcome aboard.' Margaret smiled.

'Can you pull up all the data on the mall project. I'd like Richard to familiarize himself with it as soon as possible.'

'Certainly, Mr Howard.'

After his secretary had left, Thomas turned to his son. 'Now that you've become part of Howard Ltd, we'll have to see about setting you up with your own office.'

'You mean I get my own office?' Ricky said eagerly.

Thomas smiled at the boy's enthusiasm and nodded.

'That's great, Dad.'

'Why don't you take Jane's office for the time being, and I'll have Margaret bring you in that information. Just take your time with it, Richard. There's no hurry.' Thomas paused to glance at his watch. 'Why don't we plan on lunch about twelve, and then we can review what you've read so far. How does that sound?'

'That sounds great.'

'Good.' Thomas nodded. 'If you have any questions before then, you just give me a call, all right?'

'That sounds real good, Dad.' Ricky grinned happily. He turned, then stopped at the door.

'Dad?'

'Yes?'

'Thanks.' Ricky ducked through the doorway.

'Mr Howard?'

'Yes, Margaret?'

'I've got Councilman Lewis on line two.'

'Thank you.' Howard picked up the phone. 'Jeffrey, how are you?'

'Fine, Thomas. How are you doing? I heard about that mess yesterday. Everything all right now?'

'Everything's fine, Jeffrey. It was no problem. I was just helping out the police with their investigation.'

'That's all?'

'Yes, that's all there was to it.'

'Jesus, that radio station made it sound like you were headed for the chair.'

'That's been taken care of, Jeffrey. I don't think we need to worry about any more problems from that front.'

'We've got to watch ourselves. We don't want to get too confident,' Councilman Lewis said carefully.

'No, we certainly don't want that, do we, Jeffrey?' Howard agreed.

'Reason I'm calling is that I tried to get a hold of Jane yesterday, and couldn't seem to get through to her.'

'She's been very busy lately,' Howard offered thoughtfully.

'I realize that,' the councilman quickly responded. 'But I would like to get together with her and go over a few things before the election takes place. We don't want any mistakes here, do we, Thomas?' the councilman added pointedly.

'No, we don't. Why don't I talk to her and have her give you a call later this afternoon?'

'That would be fine, Thomas. I'd really appreciate that. Why don't we get together for lunch sometime next week. How's that sound?'

'Sounds good. I'll give you a call later in the week.'

Howard replaced the phone and buzzed Margaret.

'Would you get my daughter on the phone, please?' he requested, then leaned back and waited.

'There's no answer, sir.'

'Keep trying,' Thomas said impatiently, wondering just what Jane thought she was doing. Losing Lewis's support could cost them the whole election.

Thomas suddenly froze when he remembered the sight of her and Ryan walking up the drive together.

'Mr Howard?'

Thomas pulled away from his thoughts and glared across the room at Margaret.

'What is it?'

'This just came in over the fax machine,' she said bewilderedly.

'Well, what is it?'

'I think maybe you should take a look at it, sir.'
She stepped over to his desk and handed him the sheet of
paper.

Howard grabbed the paper and examined it. He glanced
up at Margaret in confusion.

'I don't know,' she answered his tacit question. 'There
wasn't any return address or phone number.'

'This is utterly ridiculous. Someone's playing games.'
Thomas angrily shredded the paper and threw it in his
wastebasket.

He rose and stalked over to the window.

SELL OR BE SORRY was what the fax read.

Thomas didn't have the faintest idea what it meant.

He picked up the receiver and dialed Will Leland's
number.

After the seventh ring, he hung up, glaring in irritation at
the phone.

'Dad?'

'Yes,' he said irritably.

Surprised by this abrupt response, Ricky took a step
back.

'Well, what?' Thomas demanded.

'I was just wondering . . .' Ricky paused.

'Wondering what, Richard?'

'Well, what this means?' Ricky stepped over and handed
Thomas a file.

Thomas glanced at it impatiently, then shrugged dismissively. 'They're the property deeds for the mall project,
Richard,' Thomas said condescendingly.

'Well, yeah, I know that. But what about this one?'

Ricky leaned over the desk and pulled out the bottom sheet in the file.

'Who's C & H?'

'What are you talking about?'

'This, Dad. Look.' Ricky stepped around the desk and handed his father the document. 'It looks like an offer to buy the land.'

'Where did you find this?'

'It was in that file.'

Thomas turned back to examine the offer. Outlined on the sheet before him was all the land presently surveyed and planned for the mall project.

At the bottom of the sheet, in the line designated for the offering price, was the figure of $52.00.

'What the hell is this?' Thomas exclaimed, glaring up at Richard.

'I don't know, Dad, honest. I just found it in that stuff Margaret brought in.'

'Margaret!' Thomas shouted.

'What is *this*?' he demanded once she stepped into his office.

'I don't have any idea, Mr Howard. All of these files were in Jane's computer. I didn't have anything to do with—'

'Get me Jane, right now,' Thomas ordered.

'What does it mean, Dad. What's going on?'

'Don't worry about it, Richard. Just go back and continue with what you're doing.'

'But what about—'

'Richard,' Thomas interrupted. 'Go back to work.'

'I can't reach her, Mr Howard.'

'Well, keep trying, goddamnit,' Thomas yelled, then picked up the offer and began to examine it once again.

Twenty-One

'That's it.' Jane pointed to the two-story white house across the street.

They were parked on the side of a gravel road in Venetian Village. 'The Village', as Jane referred to it, was about twenty miles north-west of Waukegan. Though unincorporated, the Village was firmly bounded by three lakes: Sand Lake to the north, Lake Miltmore to the west, and Fourth Lake to the south.

She climbed off the bike and turned to point to the north. 'That's Sand Lake. When I was kid, we used to walk down to the old pier and swim. I remember my mother would always wear this yellow summer dress, and she'd sit on the end of the pier and dangle her legs in the water as she watched me.' Jane turned to smile at him. 'It was great, even my father was happy then.'

'What happened?' Ryan swung his leg over the bike and lit a cigarette.

'She died.' Jane shrugged and turned away. A moment later she stepped back to the bike.

'How old were you?'

'Thirteen. Ricky was only three.' Jane rested her hand

on Ryan's leg. She looked up at him, then glanced over at the house.

'We were all so happy here,' she said softly, then, shaking her head, climbed on to the back of the cycle.

They followed the gravel road out to the main highway bisecting the Village. They turned west, and rode out through the small farm communities dotting the county.

By midday they were both chilled from the ride. They pulled over to a small home-style café in Wadsworth.

Stepping into the diner, they encountered a momentary silence as the farmers and their wives turned to examine them.

Jane, feeling self-conscious beneath this close scrutiny, kept her eyes locked on the floor and quickly slid into a window booth. Ryan sat down across from her. They ordered coffee and the daily special: meatloaf and mashed potatoes.

'Doesn't it ever bother you?' Jane asked, clasping her hands around the warmth of her coffee cup.

'What?'

'They way people look at you.'

Ryan shrugged.

'I don't think I like it very much.'

'What?' Ryan grinned. 'Being a biker chick?'

Jane laughed, then suddenly stopped when she became aware of the stares. She blushed and glowered across the table. 'Don't do that.'

'What's *that*?'

'Make me laugh.'

'Why?'

'I don't want people to look at me.'

Ryan leaned back to examine her. 'I don't know how they could stop themselves,' he said softly, holding her gaze.

Jane smiled, then blushed and glanced away.

They rode back towards Waukegan on one of the three main highways leading into town. Fifteen miles from town, Jane suddenly leaned forward.

'Pull over.' she shouted, pointing to a side road leading up to a hill.

Ryan took the turn and followed the road upwards. As he crested the ridge, he saw a small Catholic church perched on the top, hidden from the highway below.

'Park on that side. I want to show you something,' Jane said into his ear.

Ryan pulled over to the far side of the lot and parked.

Jane quickly swung off the bike and stepped over the concrete dividers. She walked out to the east edge of the ridge, then turned and waved Ryan over.

'See that,' she said, pointing towards the farmland before them. 'That hill over there?'

Ryan looked out at the distant hill which rose at the far edge of the field. Behind it was a thick grove of trees.

'That used to be *my* place.' Jane turned to look at him. 'That's where I used to come when I wanted to be alone.'

On the peak of the hill stood a solitary pine tree.

'I've never showed that to anyone before,' Jane said softly.

Ryan turned to find her gaze waiting for him. He put his arm around her shoulder. Jane leaned against him.

In Waukegan they bought two cappuccinos to go, and carried them down to the waterfront. They walked out to the lighthouse and sat looking out at Lake Michigan.

'Last night,' Ryan started, 'you said your father told you something about me.'

Jane nodded.

'What did he tell you?'

'He asked someone to look into your background.' Jane shrugged, eyeing him closely. 'He's got a whole file on you. He showed it to me.'

Ryan turned to look out at the lake.

'What did it say?'

'What do you think it said?' she asked, and for a moment thought he wasn't going to answer.

'Usual horror stories.' Ryan shrugged.

'Not so usual, Ryan.'

'No, I guess not.'

'Was it that bad?'

'Bad enough.'

'You did all right, though.' Jane swiveled around to face him. 'You went to school. You started your own business. You came through it okay.'

This time he didn't answer. He dug into his pocket and pulled out a cigarette.

'It's all in the past, Ryan.' Jane reached out to touch him. 'None of it matters now.'

'Right.' Ryan snorted, then shook his head. 'It's always the past, Jane, that hurts the most.'

'Only if you let it.'

'I don't think it's that easy.'

'It is,' Jane insisted. Her eyes searched his face. 'The past only has the power we allow it to have.'

Ryan shrugged and hit his cigarette. He let the smoke burn into his lungs before he released it.

After a moment Jane turned away. She picked up her empty styrofoam cup and began to absently pick at it.

'Tell me about Neal?'

'What's to tell.' Ryan shrugged. 'He's dead.'

Ryan started to rise, but Jane quickly caught his arm and pulled him back.

'Tell me. Please?'

'He was my little brother.' Ryan flicked his butt out into the water. He watched the waves take it and wash it against the breakwater.

'He was four years younger than I was, and there wasn't a damn thing I could do to help him,' he said bitterly.

'But you tried.'

'Trying doesn't mean shit.' Ryan met her gaze, then abruptly stood up. A moment later he reached down to help her to her feet.

Jane took his hand and stepped into his arms. 'It's okay,' she whispered.

Ryan held her, staring blankly out at the water.

'Mr Howard,' Margaret said hesitantly. She stood in the doorway of his office. Thomas and Ricky had just returned from lunch. The two martinis Thomas had consumed had managed to retrieve his earlier confidence. He'd decided that the fax transmission, and the offer to buy, were nothing more than mischievous pranks that would easily be explained once he located Jane.

'Yes?'

'There's another one,' Margaret said helplessly, stepping over and handing him the new message.

THE OFFER HAS BEEN RECONSIDERED. THE NEW PRICE IS NOW $45.00. TAKE IT, OR ELSE SUFFER . . .

'Did you call the phone company?'

'Yes, Mr Howard.'

Ricky appeared in the doorway.

Thomas turned to him. 'What is it?'

'Nothing.' Ricky shrugged. 'I just had a question about one of the files.'

'Give me a minute, would you, Richard. I'll be right with you,' Thomas said expansively, still feeling the effects of the martinis.

He turned back to Margaret.

'There's no way of tracing these two calls, but they can put in a trap-and-trace on anything else that comes in,' Margaret informed him.

'How long will it take them?'

'I already called and set up an appointment for this afternoon.'

'Good, let's get that done as quickly as possible. I've had enough of this.' He glared at the fax transmission.

'You got another one?'

'Yes, we did, Richard.' Thomas sighed disgustedly.

'Who would do something like that?'

'I don't have any idea, but we're going to find out very soon,' Howard said, then glanced up at his son. 'Now what was your question?'

Ricky spread the file out on the desk before his father. 'I was wondering why you never bought *this* section of land? This lot 487?' Ricky pointed to a small corner of the surveyed property.

'No reason to.' Thomas smiled, then, seeing his son's confused expression, explained. 'Once the referendum passes, we can, by virtue of eminent domain, have legal access to that piece of property.'

'Couldn't you have done that with the rest of the land?'

'No, in order to use that legal process, we have to have clear-cut deed to three-quarters of the property. Unfortunately, Richard, that particular section of land is the only lot that works out logistically.' He paused to glance over at his son.

'I still don't get it.' Ricky shook his head in confusion.

'You see, Richard, everything else we bought was sold in whole sections. This was the only piece of property that fit the designated legal interpretation for eminent domain.'

'Who owned it?'

'A very helpful friend.' Howard grinned.

'You going to run this?' Petersen asked.

'No, I think we're going to hold off for a while,' Don Alder replied.

The article in question was a one-page editorial on the need for the mall.

'I want to back off for a day or two. This whole issue is becoming a little too complicated.' Catching the night editor's inquiring glance, Alder explained. 'We've got two bodies on the fringes of this upcoming referendum: Sawyer and that woman they found yesterday.'

'Barbara Arnold,' Petersen supplied.

'Right.' Alder nodded. 'I want to go a little more slowly with this for the time being. We still have almost two weeks to run the editorial. Let's wait for the dust to clear a little before we commit ourselves any more completely.'

'That's going to be tough, Don. We've been behind this thing from day one. I don't know if our suddenly taking a step back is going to carry a lot of weight.'

'Nothing wrong with rethinking an issue,' Alder said lightly, glancing pointedly at the door.

Taking the hint, Petersen nodded and stepped out of the acting editor's office.

Alder keyed his computer and saved the editorial for possible future use.

Thomas and Ricky were seated in Thomas's office at home. They both turned at the sound of Ryan's motorcycle coming up the drive.

Howard watched as his daughter swung off the bike, then waited for Ryan to dismount. The two of them walked up to the house together.

Thomas turned to see Ricky staring out the window at the two of them.

'Get your sister for me, would you, please?' Howard requested.

Ricky hurried through the office door. Avoiding Ryan's eye, he told Jane that she was wanted in their father's office.

'Richard, wait outside, please.'

Ricky turned and closed the door.

'What is it, Dad?' she asked.

'Where were you today?'

'I took the day off.' Jane shrugged

'I needed you at the office,' Thomas said quietly. 'We only have twelve days before the vote.'

'You had Ricky there. I thought it would—'

'Did you, Jane? Did you think at all, or are you letting your hormones do your thinking for you?'

'What's that supposed to mean?'

'I think you know perfectly well what it means.'

'No, I don't. Tell me.'

'It's rather obvious that you and Mr Ryan have formed some kind of attachment. Even your brother is aware of it.'

'So what?'

'So I'd rather you didn't continue with this ridiculous charade.'

'I don't think it's that ridiculous.'

'It's absurd, Jane,' Howard said angrily. 'The man is a murderer, for God's sakes.'

'He is not a murderer, Dad. You're the one who showed me his file. You know perfectly well he didn't have anything to do with what happened then.'

'Jane,' Thomas said placatingly. 'I don't want to get into an argument with you over this. That man is trouble. Regardless of what he's done or hasn't done, his life is a total shambles. He stumbles from one disaster to another, and I will not have a daughter of mine associating with someone like that.'

'And what do you plan on doing about it?' She glared across the desk at her father.

'Oh, that's rather simple.' Howard smiled without a trace of amusement. 'I'll see to it that Mr Ryan is quickly and most efficiently shown the fastest way out of town.'

Jane held his gaze, then whirled around and started for the door.

'Jeffrey called me today,' Thomas said quietly.

She froze.

'He said he'd been trying to get a hold of you recently.'

Jane slowly turned to meet her father's glance.

'And what did you say?'

'I said you were probably very busy and would return his call as soon as you could.'

She took a step towards him, then halted.

'I really think you should do that, Jane.' He held her eye until she looked away. 'It would make me feel much more confident about your Mr Ryan.'

Jane's glance dropped to the floor.

'Is that the deal, Dad?' she said softly.

Thomas waited for her to look at him. 'Call him, Jane,' he prompted. 'Let's not turn this whole thing into something ugly.'

Without responding, she turned and stepped out of his office.

Ryan leaned against the window-frame of his room. He watched Jane walk down the drive to her car. A moment later the lights flashed on and she pulled out of the entrance.

Ryan lit a cigarette, staring down thoughtfully at the empty drive. He heard footsteps outside his door and turned.

'I want to talk to you,' Ricky said, stepping into the room.

Ryan nodded. He stepped over and sat on the edge of the bed. He pulled out his pack of cigarettes again and threw them to the boy.

Ricky caught the pack and moved over to the window. He pulled out a cigarette, then threw the pack back to Ryan.

'What is it?'

Ricky turned to the window. He twirled the cigarette nervously between his fingers. 'I saw Jane last night,' he said without turning.

'So?'

Ricky whirled around to glare at Ryan. 'What do you mean, *so*? I saw her sneaking downstairs.'

'She's a big girl, kid. She wants to sneak around,' Ryan shrugged, 'that's her prerogative.'

'What do you mean by that?' Ricky challenged.

Ryan met his eye. 'There was no reason for her to sneak around,' he said quietly.

'She was with you.'

'Yeah.'

'I don't—'

Ryan shook his head wearily, interrupting the boy. 'Don't say it, Ricky.'

'Say what?'

'Say what you're going to say. Your sister knows what she's doing.'

'I don't want her to get hurt.'

'No one wants anyone to get hurt.' Ryan paused, then added, 'But someone always does.' He glanced over at the kid.

'I want you to leave her alone.'

'Do you?'

'Yeah, I do.'

Ryan broke away from the boy's gaze.

'Okay.' He nodded thoughtfully.

'That's it?' Ricky asked in confusion.

'What'd you expect?' Ryan rose and stepped over to the boy. 'I'm not going to fight you over this. You feel that strongly, then maybe I should back off.'

'Don't you care about her at all?'

'Kid, we're not talking about me *or* your sister here. We're talking about you. Only thing you've told me is what *you* want.' Ryan stepped over to the window and stood beside him.

'But...' Ricky started, then stopped. He turned to Ryan helplessly.

'You ask for something, kid, you better be prepared to get it.'

256

Ricky stepped over to the bedside table and stubbed out his cigarette. 'Do you want to keep seeing her?' he asked quietly.

Ryan turned to face him.

'*Do* you?' Ricky repeated.

'Yeah.'

'Okay.' Ricky nodded. 'It's all right with me.'

'Thanks,' Ryan reached out to grip the boy's shoulder.

They walked down the stairs together. Thomas was already seated at the dinner table, waiting for them.

'Where's Jane?' Ricky asked.

'She had a prior engagement,' Howard said, a slight smile on his lips.

Ryan examined the smile, then turned away.

'And how was your day, Mr Ryan?'

'Fine.' Ryan sighed, pulling out his chair and sitting down.

'How nice,' Thomas replied, with the smile still in place.

At exactly 7:01, as Thomas was reaching for his coffee cup, the phone rang in his office. After a quick glance at his watch, he excused himself from the table.

He closed the door to his office and stepped over to his desk. Only after he was comfortably seated did he reach for the phone.

'Howard Limit—' was as far as he got before the voice interrupted.

'Don't speak. Just listen.'

'What the—?'

'I said *listen*. This is the last time I'll tell you.'

Thomas forced back the angry words. He heard a click at the other end of the line, then a moment later he heard his own voice coming back at him. '*Will, I want you to go out and have a talk with Steven Garcia. He seems to be having trouble making up his mind whether to accept my most generous offer. Please get back to me as soon as Mr Garcia is ready to accept it.*' Stunned, Thomas listened to a distant whir of sound.

The noise abruptly halted. A moment later he heard his voice again. '*Will, please inform Mr Garcia that all hospital bills for both himself and his family will be covered in our original offer.*'

'Do you need to hear more, Mr Howard?' the voice said sarcastically.

'Who are you, and what do you want?'

'You should have taken our first offer, Mr Howard. While fifty-two dollars might not have seemed like much, it's more than we're willing to offer now.'

'What are you talking about?'

'Twelve-fifty, Mr Howard, and I'll get back to you tomorrow about the details of our transaction.'

'Are you out of your mind. Do you think I'm going to give you everything I've worked for—?'

'It's your choice, Howard. Take the deal, and the tapes, or I'll see that someone else gets them. Someone who may not have your best interests at heart.'

'You have *nothing*!' Thomas shouted into the receiver. 'You don't have one bit of legal evidence.'

'That's true,' the voice replied reasonably, 'but do you

really think that matters? These tapes will ruin you. They may not put you in jail, but you'd be finished in the business.'

'No one will believe it,' Thomas challenged.

'*Everyone* will believe it. And when they do, you're finished. Take the deal. We're not greedy. All we want is the land. You can still make something out of the lease agreements. I'll be talking to you, Tommy. You take care, now.'

'I will not even consider...' Thomas began, then suddenly stopped when he realized he was talking to an empty line. He slumped back in his chair, feverishly trying to comprehend what he'd just heard.

He grabbed the phone and quickly dialed Will Leland's number.

The phone was picked up on the second ring.

Without waiting for the other man to respond, Thomas began to speak. 'Will, I just received a call from some idiot who demanded that I relinquish all deed to the mall property.' He paused breathlessly, waiting for Will's customary polite response.

'Tommy,' the voice that he'd just heard gently chided, 'you have to think these things through a little more carefully. I'm the idiot you were just talking about. And that cost you another ten dollars on the deal. You're now down to two-fifty.'

'Who the hell are you?'

'A man who's going to make you very unhappy unless you do what you're told. Be talking to you,' the voice said agreeably, and hung up.

259

Thomas slammed the phone back into its cradle.

'Dad?'

Ricky stood in the doorway. Behind him, Thomas saw Ryan still seated at the dining-room table, fumbling with his cigarettes.

'Are you all right?'

'Yes.' Thomas nodded. He ran a hand across his face, trying to pull his thoughts together.

'You sure?' Ricky took a step into the office.

'Yes, I'm fine,' Thomas responded emphatically. He glared at Ricky, then suddenly transferred his gaze to Ryan.

'Are you—?'

'Mr Ryan,' Thomas called out, ignoring his son.

Ryan rose and stepped over to the office door. He leaned against it and looked inside.

'Get out.' Thomas waved his son out of the office, and impatiently gestured Ryan into the room.

Ryan sat in front of his desk.

Howard leaned forward and fixed his gaze on the other man.

Ryan examined him closely.

'I want to talk to you, Mr Ryan. I think I have a little job that you might be interested in doing for me.'

Ryan started to reply, but Thomas quickly cut him off.

'Nothing illegal. Just a small service you can render to repay our hospitality.' He leveled his gaze at the other man. 'You would be helping both Jane and Richard,' he added softly.

Ryan met his eye.

A moment later he nodded almost imperceptibly, and said, 'Why don't you tell me about it?'

Twenty-Two

'I've thought about leaving her,' Councilman Jeffrey Lewis said thoughtfully. He was lying on his back on the motel bed. His arms were crossed behind his head.

'But I realize that if I do, everything I've worked so hard for would be gone. I'd never be re-elected,' the councilman concluded sadly. He glanced across the room.

Jane was unbuttoning her blouse. Her shoes and pantyhose were already on the floor.

The councilman watched as she pulled off her blouse. Then she reached for the zipper on the side of her skirt.

'Do your bra first.'

Jane caught his smile, then reached for the clasp and unclipped her brassiere. She hung it over the back of a chair, feeling the man's eyes following her every move.

She unzipped her skirt and stepped out of it. She hung it neatly on the chair, then turned towards him.

'That's very nice, Jane. You look wonderful,' he said softly, eyeing her hungrily. He patted the bed beside him. 'Come, lie down.'

Jane took a deep breath, then walked over to the bed.

Councilman Lewis pulled her down beside him. He

263

propped himself on his side and reached for her. His hand moved across her stomach to her breasts.

'Your father's worried about the vote,' he said absently, rolling her nipples between his fingers.

Jane nodded. She stared up at him impassively.

'I don't know why he's so worried. He has a lock on it.'

'Not yet, he doesn't,' she said.

'Oh, I think he does.' The councilman nodded. He leaned forward and nuzzled the side of her neck.

Jane pulled away.

'What?' the councilman asked.

'The latest polls indicate only a five percent margin.'

'Yes, but that's without Christian.' Councilman Lewis smiled and reached for her again.

'What are you talking about?'

'Well, with me, Constantine, and Christian, he has more than enough support to swing the referendum,' Lewis murmured, as he returned to the side of her neck. He ran his hands along her hips.

'Christian is supporting my father?' Jane asked incredulously.

'Of course he is. Didn't . . . ?' Lewis suddenly paused. He pulled back to examine her. 'You didn't know?'

Wordlessly, Jane shook her head.

'I thought you . . .' Lewis abruptly sat up and leaned back against the headboard.

'Why would Christian back my father on this? He's a good friend of the mayor's?'

'I don't know.' The councilman shrugged. He reached to

the bedside table for his glasses. He put them on and turned to Jane. 'I thought you were aware of Christian's support. I probably shouldn't have mentioned it.' Lewis smiled uneasily.

'I don't understand why Christian would support my father, or why my father wouldn't tell me.'

'Maybe it was something he simply forgot to mention.'

Jane turned to the councilman. She suddenly smiled.

Lewis, mistaking her smile for one of acceptance, took off his glasses and reached for her.

Jane slipped away from him and stood beside the bed.

'What're you doing?' he asked as she stepped across the room and picked up her skirt.

'Getting dressed.'

'Why?'

Jane paused to meet his gaze. 'Because I'm going home,' she said matter-of-factly.

'Jane.' The councilman shook his head. 'I don't think that's such a good idea.'

'And why not?' Jane asked calmly. She zipped up her skirt, then picked up her bra and blouse. She stepped into the bathroom to put them on.

'Because there's a lot at stake here.' The councilman's voice followed her. 'We don't want anything to happen now to rock the boat.'

Jane smiled at her reflection in the mirror. She brushed back her hair and stepped back out of the bathroom. The councilman was still seated on the bed, and Jane examined him closely. She no longer found his nakedness repulsive. It seemed only pathetic to her now.

'You're dressed,' Lewis exclaimed in disappointment.

'Yes.'

'Well get undressed and come back to bed.'

'No.' She smiled.

'Jane,' Lewis cautioned. 'I think your father needs my support, as well as yours,' he said pointedly.

'Yes, he does,' Jane quickly agreed. 'But I think he also needs your discretion.'

'What is that supposed to mean?' Lewis asked angrily.

'I don't think he wanted that bit of information about Christian to become public knowledge, or else I would have already known about it.'

'So what? You're his daughter. Who are you going to tell?' Lewis challenged.

'Oh, I wouldn't have to tell anyone.' Jane shrugged innocently. 'But information like that has a tendency to leak out from the most surprising sources.'

'What are you saying?' Lewis asked, for the first time sounding unsure of himself.

'If this were to go public, you seem to be the only one with any knowledge of it.' She paused to look over at him speculatively. 'Who do you think my father would blame?'

'What is this – blackmail?' Lewis snorted in disbelief.

'Yes, that's exactly what it is.' she stared at him defiantly, then turned and started for the door.

'I'm going to tell him, you know,' Lewis called to her back.

'No, you won't.' Jane turned. 'You won't say one damn thing to him. Because, if you do, Jeffrey, I swear, I'll bury you.'

'You wouldn't!' Lewis retorted.

'Wouldn't I?' Jane replied, meeting his eye. A moment later she shook her head disgustedly. 'You know what really surprises me the most, Jeffrey,' she said softly, 'is that I've been a part of this whole sordid little affair right from the beginning. Why on earth I would ever condescend to sleep with someone as sleazy as you, for my father or anyone else, is absolutely beyond me.'

'You can't talk to me that way. Just who the hell . . . ?'

Jane laughed at him. 'Jeffrey, cover yourself. You look disgusting,' she said, then quickly turned back towards the door. She stalked out, leaving it open behind her.

Councilman Lewis glanced fearfully out at the parking lot, then quickly scrambled to the side of the bed and cowered behind it.

It was the first time Detective Ellroy had ever been invited into the mayor's home. The expensive furnishings and lush grandeur of the lakefront house made him vaguely uncomfortable – which, in turn, irritated him. He had always thought that he was long past being impressed by material wealth.

Mayor Charles Presley sat across from him, on the couch. Each of them had a frosted stein of imported beer, set on cork coasters on the glass table between them. The mayor leaned back casually against the arm of the couch, and crossed his legs.

'Relax, Tom, and tell me what's going on,' the mayor said reassuringly, well aware of the other man's discomfort.

Detective Ellroy nodded and reached for his beer.

It was one of the many attributes Mayor Presley had acquired over his long career in politics: the ability to put people at ease. It was something he had long ago recognized as being absolutely essential in currying favor with the voting public.

Detective Ellroy carefully replaced his beer stein on the coaster and pulled out his notebook. He glanced over.

'Go ahead,' the mayor prompted.

'On the face of it, we have two incidents that appear completely unrelated. If I were investigating both the Sawyer and Arnold cases, I wouldn't even consider a link between the two.'

'But what about the calls to the radio station and the newspaper? That was obviously set up from whoever got to these people,' Presley interrupted.

'Yeah.' Ellroy nodded. 'But it's not enough to shape a whole investigation. Anyone could have done it. You have a fairly controversial issue before the city. I doubt there's anyone around who doesn't recognize this. It would be the perfect way to muddy up what actually took place.'

'What's your point, Tom?'

'My point is that for either of these people to get whacked is not unreasonable. Sawyer was taking, and the woman was hooking. Neither represents the best long-term plan for eventual retirement.'

'You don't think there's any connection? Is that what you're saying?'

'I think that it's something we have to consider.'

'I have.' The mayor nodded. 'And I've rejected that conclusion. I think the anonymous calls irrefutably tie them together.'

'Not necessarily. The woman could have been done by someone who was aware of what had happened to Sawyer, and figured he'd do the same thing with her.'

'I don't buy that.'

'Neither do I.' Ellroy smiled.

'Then what the hell are you saying, Tom?'

Ellroy shrugged. 'I'm not really saying anything, Mr Mayor. I'm just throwing out possibilities.'

'Try Charlie for me, would you, just once.'

'Charlie,' Ellroy said.

'Thanks. Now tell me the rest of it.'

'Okay, I just wanted to point out that option before I continue. The other angle is that there's someone out there who has a personal interest in the mall issue, and has targeted both you and Howard.'

'That makes more sense to me.'

'I agree, but the only problem with that is why is he after both of you? Why hasn't he just gone after one side or the other, rather than trying to take you *both* down?' Ellroy leaned back thoughtfully. 'That's what I don't understand.'

'Maybe it's simply because we don't have enough information yet.'

'You could say that about any investigation.'

'I agree, but this one is a little more relevant to me right now,' the mayor commented dryly. He reached for his beer. 'You haven't come up with anything?'

'No, not a thing. I can place the woman at a downtown

restaurant at five thirty but from then, until we found her at the condo at eight forty, is a mystery. No one saw anything.'

'Didn't you tell me Howard said the door was open?'

'Yes.'

'So whoever did it had to have done it at her place.'

'Yeah, but that doesn't help.'

'Maybe he was waiting for her there?'

'If he was, that doesn't help your case any. That would point to his being one of her regulars.'

'No boyfriends, I take it?'

'No. She was running around with some guy a while back, but we checked him out and he's clean.'

'Anything more about the anonymous call?'

'Nothing.'

'What about Sawyer? You find anything more on him?'

'Just the money – that's it. We can't trace any of it to anyone. There's just nothing to find or, if there is, we haven't been able to come up with it yet.'

The mayor sighed. He slumped back in the couch, wearily.

'There's something else that you might want to consider.' Ellroy paused.

'Somehow that doesn't sound too encouraging, Tom.'

'No, it isn't.'

'What?'

'If you're right about this, that there's someone out there after you, then whoever it is is probably not done yet. You still got another week or so before the election. There's plenty of time to pull something else.'

'You're right: that isn't good news.' The mayor glanced

out at the lake. He turned back to the detective. 'You get anything from Leland?'

'No.' Ellroy shook his head. 'I haven't been able to get a hold of him. I was thinking of stopping by his place after I leave here.'

'What exactly has he offered so far?'

'Only that he could help.'

'With just the Sawyer thing?'

'That's what he said, but I got the impression he was holding out a lot more.'

'What about this Ryan character? You come up with anything on him?'

'Nothing that ties him in to either Sawyer or the woman, but his background is sketchy enough to make me certainly keep him in mind for anything else that happens around here.'

'Why's he with Howard?'

'He hooked up with Howard's kid.'

'Richard?'

'Yeah. Kid got himself into some kind of jam down south. Wasn't anything major, but I guess Ryan helped him out.'

'And Howard's just repaying the debt?' the mayor said sarcastically.

'Yeah, I agree, it doesn't sound too much like him, does it?'

'No, not at all. Maybe you should keep a closer eye on this Ryan fellow.'

'Already done. I've had someone on him for the last couple of days.'

271

'Anything?'

'No, just he and the daughter riding around together.'

'This guy's really worked his way into that family, hasn't he?' the mayor said thoughtfully.

'That's the way it looks.'

'I wonder why. Maybe he thinks there's something there for him.'

'That's a possibility,' Ellroy admitted

'Well, keep watching him then.' The mayor replaced his beer glass on the table. 'What are you planning on now?'

'I thought I'd go over to see Leland – see what he has to say.'

'Okay, Tom.' The mayor rose to his feet.

'Again, I want to let you know how much I appreciate this. I won't forget it.'

The mayor stepped around the table and ushered the detective to the front door.

'Call me after you've talked with Leland.'

'I'll get back to you later tonight,' Ellroy promised, then turned and walked down the drive to his car. He climbed in and pulled out of the entrance, aware of the mayor standing in the doorway watching him.

The road ended abruptly at a ravine. Ryan pulled over to the side and parked between a van and a pick-up truck. He climbed off his bike and stepped over to the ravine and peered down. It bottomed out twenty feet below him. Both the bottom and sides of the ravine were overgrown with trees and shrubs.

Ryan pulled a cigarette and turned away. The house he wanted stood at the center of the street. One side of it bordered the edge of the ravine.

He lit his cigarette and walked along the block to the front door. He knocked, then leaned back, thinking over his earlier conversation with Thomas.

Howard's fear had surprised him. The dramatic changes Ryan had observed in the man over the last few days were startling. Gone was the seemingly imperturbable sense of superiority. And what had replaced it was a growing sense of vulnerability and fear.

Ryan knocked again. He listened, then a moment later stepped back to re-check the address.

Satisfied that he had the right place, Ryan examined the dark house.

He stepped off the porch and walked around to the side. With the edge of the ravine only feet away, he followed a well-used path to the back of the house.

He knocked at the back door, then pressed his face to a side window and peered inside at a small breezeway.

Then he stepped back and thoughtfully examined the whole structure.

After a moment he carefully shredded his cigarette and returned to the door. He had just reached up to the edge of the doorframe when he heard the sound of a vehicle on the road in front.

Ducking down, Ryan quickly slipped over to the side of the house and peered out towards the front.

A car pulled up and parked at the curb. A moment later a man stepped out and started up the walk.

Ryan examined the car closely, then turned his gaze to the man. It was too dark to make out his features, so Ryan concentrated on the way the man moved. Looking for it, he easily spotted the slight bulge over the man's right hip.

Ryan carefully backed away from the house towards the ravine. Spotting a tree a few yards down the incline, he steadied himself along the edge, then slowly let himself fall forward.

His hands came into contact with the tree before he hit the ground, he used the trunk to stop his fall. Bracing himself between the lip of the ravine and the tree itself, he quietly eased himself down the ravine until he was hidden from view.

Crouched behind the trunk, he heard the sound of footsteps coming along the path. A few moments later he saw the policeman step over to the back door. The man knocked, then leaned forward impatiently against the window.

'Will?' the policeman shouted. He stepped back to examine the house, in much the same way Ryan had done only minutes before.

He knocked again, then, sighing wearily, turned and started back along the path to the front of the house.

Ryan waited until he heard the sound of the car heading up the road before he climbed back up the slope.

Wiping his hands on his jeans, he stepped back over to the door. He ran his fingers along the trim, searching for wires. Not finding any, he began to circle the house.

At the front of the house, he peered in through a side

window, searching for the tell-tale alarm light. Seeing only the darkness, Ryan started around to the rear of the house again.

He stepped up to the back door. Bracing his shoulder against it, he took a deep breath, then suddenly threw his full weight against the wood. There was sharp cracking sound as the door buckled. Without pausing, Ryan lashed out with his foot and kicked it open.

Regaining his balance, he quickly moved round to the front of the house and crouched down, peering out at the road.

He waited there fifteen minutes before returning to the rear of the house.

Pushing the back door aside, Ryan stepped quietly into Will Leland's house.

Detective Ellroy pulled into his drive, parked his car, and started to climb out. It was as he opened his car door that he suddenly remembered the reflected flash of his own headlights in front of Leland's house.

With the door half open, he paused, trying to decide what bothered him about that brief flash of light.

He leaned back in his seat and closed his eyes. Mentally, he conjured up an image of the road and tried to recreate the scene. Skimming the surface of his memory, trying not to force it, he saw the line of cars parked along the side of the road: the van and, in front of that, the pick-up truck.

The flash of his headlights had angled well off to the side of the truck-bed, where there shouldn't have been any reflective surface.

What was it? And why the hell was it bothering him so much?

Ellroy stepped out of his car. He suddenly froze when he caught sight of his side-view mirror.

He mentally saw that flash of light again. This time he recalled the way his headlights had momentarily outlined the gleaming chrome of the motorcycle.

He leaped into his car and backed out of the drive, quickly turning towards the other side of town. Ellroy raced through the city streets, trying to figure out what the hell Ryan might want at Leland's house.

When a possibility occurred to him, he leaned forward and hit the accelerator.

The unmarked car surged forward, racing back towards Leland's home.

'How was your evening?'

'Fine, Dad. Where's Ryan?'

'He went out,' Thomas said curtly. 'Did you reach an understanding with Councilman Lewis?'

'Yes.' Jane smiled. 'We worked everything out.'

'That's good. I appreciate your putting in the extra hours on this, Jane. I really do,' Howard said, then surprised both of them by reaching out to touch her shoulder.

Jane's glance traveled from his hand to her father's face.

He quickly looked way and withdrew his hand.

'Are you all right, Dad?'

'Fine, just fine, Jane. Everything is going according to plan.'

'What plan?'

'*The* plan.' Thomas smiled secretively, then, winking, turned and stepped back into his office.

Jane found Ricky in his bedroom.

'What's going on with Dad?' she asked, stepping inside.

Seated at his desk, Ricky shrugged. 'I don't know. He's really being weird, isn't he?'

'Yes.' Jane plopped down on his bed. 'You seen Ryan?'

'After he and Dad talked, he went out.'

'He and Dad were talking?' Jane leaned forward.

'Yeah.' Ricky shrugged, then, noticing her glance, asked, 'Why? What's wrong with that?'

'I don't know, it just doesn't sound right.'

'Why not?'

'Dad hates him.' Jane turned to look at her brother.

'No, he doesn't.' Ricky shook his head, smiling at his sister. 'You should've seen Dad, smiling and patting him on the back when they came out of his office.'

'Dad was doing that?' Jane asked incredulously.

'Yeah.'

'Ricky, don't you think that's a little strange? Dad doesn't act that way – ever.'

'Well, maybe he's changing.'

'Into what?'

'Into a nice guy.' Ricky smiled, then added. 'He was fine at the office today, except for those faxes.'

'What faxes?'

'Didn't he talk to you?'

'No, he didn't say anything to me.'

'Well, I don't think it's any big deal,' Ricky said dismissively, turning back to his desk.

'What isn't any big deal?' Jane demanded.

'Jees, sis, what're you so upset about?'

'Tell me about the faxes.'

'It wasn't anything. Somebody was just playing games.'

'What kind of games?'

'I don't know, Jane. That's what Dad said. He got these faxes telling him to sell the property.'

'The mall property?'

'Yeah, it was just some idiot out there trying to shake him up.' Ricky paused, then shook his head. 'I guess that – and that contract thing – had him going for a while. You should have seen—'

'What contract thing? What are you talking about?'

'The offer to sell. I found it in your computer.'

'Ricky.' Jane said patiently, stepping over to him. 'Tell me what happened today at the office.'

'Not much, just—'

'Richard,' Jane cautioned. 'Just tell me everything that happened today.' She reached out to touch his shoulder.

Ricky swiveled around to face her. 'Well, the first thing was the fax...'

Twenty-Three

'You were right.'

'He's there?' Christian smiled triumphantly. He shifted the receiver against his ear as he reached for his drink.

'No, he isn't, but that Ryan guy is.'

'Ryan?'

'Yeah, that guy's who's staying at Howard's house.'

'Where are you right now?'

'Just down the road at a convenience store.'

'What's Ryan doing?'

Caldwell glanced down the road towards the dead-end street. He turned back to the phone. 'He's inside.'

Christian leaned back in his chair, thoughtfully.

'You want me to talk to him?'

'No, leave it alone for now.'

'It wouldn't be any trouble.'

'No, John,' Christian said sternly. 'Maybe later. But right now I think we need to see where he fits into everything.'

'It seems pretty obvious to me: Howard must've asked him to talk to Leland.'

'But why would he trust him?' Christian wondered out loud. 'Howard doesn't trust anyone.'

'He doesn't have any choice.'

'You could be right,' Christian replied a moment later. 'What do you want me to do?'

'Just keep on him, and let me know what's going on.'

'What're you going to do?'

Christian smiled. 'I'm going to move things along,' he said, then hung up.

He replenished his drink before he returned to the phone.

'Charlie, how are you doing?' Christian said heartily, once he heard the other man's voice.

'Good, Christian. How about yourself?'

'Just fine. I saw the retraction in the paper yesterday.'

'Yes.' The mayor sighed. 'On page four, wasn't it?'

'Well, it doesn't matter where it was. All that matters was that it was there.'

'I suppose you're right,' the mayor grudgingly conceded.

'Have you talked to Howard?' Christian asked carefully.

'Why on earth would I want to talk to him?'

'Well, the way things are going, I would have assumed that you'd have wanted to hear his side of things.'

'What are you talking about, Christian?'

'It's obvious, isn't it, Charlie, that someone's playing both sides against some mysterious middle.' Christian paused, allowing a moment for the thought to take root. 'It would seem reasonable to me for you to talk to Howard, to find out what he knows.'

'I don't know if I agree with that. Howard doesn't

seem any better informed about what's happening than I do.'

'Howard always holds something back.'

'Even if he does, I doubt very much he's going to tell me what that might be.'

'I think you're underestimating yourself, Charlie. Howard, if nothing else, respects you. I'm sure he's aware of what's happening, and must know that you're also a piece of the puzzle.'

The mayor sighed wearily. 'I think there's still quite a few pieces missing.'

'Well.' Christian shrugged. 'It's up to you. It was just a thought.'

'When are you planning on that endorsement, Christian?'

'Thursday.'

'Four days before the election? You think that's going to leave enough time?'

'I think the timing will work out perfectly, Charlie.'

'I'd be more comfortable with something a little earlier.'

'Trust me on this, Charlie. I know my constituency. If I give them too much time to consider it, half of them will never even make it to the polls. I'll make the announcement Thursday, and follow it up over the weekend.'

'It's your choice, Christian, but I think you're cutting it a little close.'

'Don't worry about my district, Charlie. They'll be there when I need them.'

'I'm counting on it.'

'I know you are.' Christian laughed.

* * *

Jane hurried over to the window when she heard the sound of the engine. She peered down at the drive. A moment later she saw a single headlight illuminate the garage doors.

She turned and raced down the stairs. Coming around the second-floor landing, she saw her father already opening the front door. Ryan appeared a moment later in the doorway.

'Mr Ryan, please.'

Jane watched as her father gestured towards his office. She caught Ryan's eye as he stepped into the house. He shrugged helplessly, then stepped into her father's office.

Howard quickly followed him inside. A moment later Jane heard the sound of the lock engaging. She turned to see Ricky standing there. His bewildered gaze reflected her own.

'What did he say?' Thomas asked anxiously.

'Nothing. He wasn't there.'

'Was anyone?' Thomas asked quickly.

'No.' Ryan shook his head.

Howard began to pace.

Ryan pulled a cigarette. He leaned back in his chair and watched the older man nervously move across the room.

'You want to tell me what's going on?'

'I already did.' Thomas shrugged impatiently.

'No. You just told me what you wanted to tell me.'

'It's the same thing.' Howard paused. He leaned over his

desk to meet Ryan's eye. 'Was there anything ... strange about the house?'

'Like what?'

'Anything out of the ordinary.'

'You mean like a body?' Ryan eyed the other man speculatively.

Thomas quickly glanced away and resumed his pacing. 'Mr Ryan, I'm sure this must seem slightly unorthodox to you but, believe me, there is a reason for it.'

'Yeah, I already figured out that much.' Ryan leaned forward to ash his cigarette. 'But what I haven't figured out yet is just *how* unorthodox we're talking.'

'Nothing too extreme, I assure you,' Thomas said, gesturing dismissively.

Ryan nodded thoughtfully. He glanced over at a side table set against the wall. 'Those bottles just for looking at?'

'Of course not.' Thomas grinned nervously. 'What would you like?'

'Daniels.'

'Water or soda?' Howard asked, stepping over to the bar.

'Just straight.'

Thomas handed him the drink, then stepped back behind his desk. He sat down, then immediately rose and began pacing again.

'What's this Leland got on you?'

Thomas froze. He turned slowly to stare at Ryan.

'It's a pretty easy shot, Thomas. You're not being Mr Cool about this whole thing,' Ryan said.

He paused to examine the older man carefully, before he added. 'How bad is it?'

'Not too bad,' Thomas replied quietly.

'You want to tell me about it?' Ryan raised his glass.

'Why should I?'

Ryan shrugged. 'No reason.' He stubbed out his cigarette, then glanced over. 'It might help, though.'

'How?'

Ryan snorted sarcastically. 'Think of it this way, Thomas. What the hell's it going to hurt?'

Thomas broke away from his gaze and returned to his pacing.

Ryan watched him. Howard's clothes were wrinkled and soiled. One shirt tail hung out from the back of his pants.

Thomas suddenly paused in front of the window. He clasped his hands behind his back and peered out.

'Why would you help me?' he asked, without turning.

'Why not?' Ryan finished his drink, then rose and stepped over to the side bar. He refilled his glass, then, after glancing at the other man, poured out another drink. He carried it over and offered it to Howard.

Thomas turned to see the drink. His gaze traveled up to Ryan's face.

'Drink it. It'll do you good.' Ryan moved back to his chair. Behind him, he heard the glass rattle against the older man's teeth.

'I know why,' Thomas whispered.

Ryan glanced up at him.

Thomas smiled nervously. The smile kept slipping. He raised his glass and finished off his drink.

Ryan watched as he returned to the bar.

'Neal and Zella,' Howard said carefully. He turned to meet Ryan's eye.

Ryan locked his gaze on the other man. His absolute stillness seemed almost preternatural.

'You're still trying to save them, aren't you, Mr Ryan?' Thomas whispered.

Without breaking from the other man's gaze, Ryan stood up.

'Fuck you,' he said, then carefully put his empty glass on the desk and turned to the door.

'Please?'

Ryan paused.

'Please, Mr Ryan?' Thomas whispered. 'Please, help me?'

Ryan closed his eyes, then a moment later turned.

'You'd be helping the whole town,' Thomas added.

'And you, too.'

'That goes without saying. No one does anything without some personal gain. But what I stand to realize out of this project is nowhere near the benefits that it would offer to the rest of the community.'

'Philanthropy?' Ryan said sarcastically.

'No, I'm no philanthropist. I'm a businessman, but I'm also concerned about the future of this city. I love this city, Mr Ryan. It's my home. It's been my home for almost fifty-seven years. I don't want to see it destroyed.'

'And you think the mall's going to prevent that?'

'Yes, it will offer employment and a tax base the like of which this city has never seen before,' Thomas said fervently.

'The mayor doesn't seem to share your belief.'

'That's his opinion. I don't agree with it.'

'That's all there is to it?' Ryan asked pointedly.

'Of course, that's all there is to it. I'm not above skirting the law on occasion – everyone does it. It's the way business is done.' He broke away from the other man's gaze. 'It's the way I've always done it,' he added softly a moment later.

'What does this Leland guy have on you?'

'It's not Leland.' Thomas shook his head.

'Are you sure?'

'Yes.'

'Why?'

'Because the man who called me about the tapes wasn't Will.'

Ryan examined him carefully, before he asked, 'What else?'

'What do you mean?'

'Tell me the rest of it.'

Howard sighed. He glanced down at his hands. 'He was at Will's house when he called me.'

'How do you know?'

'When I called Will, it was the same man who answered the phone.'

Thomas refused to meet Ryan's eye.

'And that's when you sent me over there.'

'Yes,' Howard replied, still without raising his eyes.

Ryan snorted disgustedly. He stepped back over to the bar. Then he turned and leaned against the side bar, holding a drink. He looked over at Thomas.

'Tell me all of it. And, this time, don't leave anything out.'

'He was there. I damn well know it,' Ellroy said into the phone.

'You're sure?'

'Yeah. I know that was his cycle. How many bikes with California plates are there around town?'

'I thought you said you had someone on him?'

'The idiot clocked out at eight. He figured Ryan was in for the night.

'What would Ryan have to do with any of this?'

'He must be working with Howard.'

'For how long?' the mayor asked.

'That's something I plan on finding out real soon.'

'Can you pull him in?'

'I don't know yet. I've got a couple of men running prints on Leland's place, but this guy Ryan's been around. I doubt very much they'll come up with anything.'

'What about Leland?'

'Nothing. He never showed up at his office today, and no one's heard a thing from him since yesterday.'

'Keep me posted, Tom.'

'Will do.'

Ellroy hung up the phone and glanced impatiently at the computer screen in front of him. He was waiting for a response on his query on Edward Ryan.

Driving back to the station, it had occurred to him that his only information on the biker had been given to him by Leland.

Ellroy was beginning to wonder just how far Leland could be trusted. Losing sight of the man made him nervous.

Ellroy leaned back, waiting for further information on Ryan, wondering just what it was Leland expected to get out of the deal.

It was beginning to seem to Ellroy that Leland wanted far more than just reinstatement. How much more, Ellroy was planning on finding out just as soon as he could locate him.

Ryan turned from the window as he heard his door open.

Jane stepped over to his side. She reached out to touch his arm. 'What's going on, Ryan?'

'Nothing.' He shrugged.

'What are you doing with my father?'

'Helping.'

'Why?'

Ryan glanced out the window. 'I don't know.'

'Are you doing it because of me?'

'Maybe,' he said, catching and holding her gaze.

'I don't want you to.'

'Why not?'

'Because I don't know anymore if what he's doing is right.' Jane glanced away.

'Why not?'

She shrugged uncomfortably. 'Just things.'

'What things, Jane?' Ryan gently touched her cheek, forcing her to turn to him.

Her eyes came up to his. 'Tell me about her?'

'About who?' Ryan pulled his hand away.

'About Zella.' Jane whispered.

'She's dead,' Ryan said brutally, turning back to the window.

'How did she die?'

'Badly,' Ryan answered softly, turning to her again.

'I don't want you to get hurt anymore,' Jane said softly.

'I don't think I can,' he finally replied, then reached into his pocket and pulled a cigarette.

It was warm. She could feel the heat of the sun beating down on her back and shoulders. She could almost smell the scent of the sea. She turned to see Ryan lying full-length on the towel beside her.

He smiled and reached for her.

As she went into his arms, it seemed almost impossible to her that any two people could fit so well together.

She felt his hands on her back, and she closed her eyes, letting the sense of his body and the security it offered hold her.

His hand suddenly lashed out, catching her on the side of her hip.

She tried to roll away, but his other arm held her in place.

She heard him grunt, then felt him kick out with his feet.

Jane jerked awake.

Ryan groaned and twisted beside her. He lashed out with his hand.

She ducked, then threw herself at him. Her hands slipped on the perspiration covering his chest.

'Neal,' Ryan groaned.

'Ryan,' Jane cried, shaking him.

His eyes suddenly opened and stared up at her blankly. The shadows made deep crevices in the lines of his face.

'Zella,' Ryan whispered hoarsely, then reached up to touch her cheek.

A moment later he closed his eyes.

Jane watched him sleep.

After a while, she curled up beside him. She took his hand and pressed it against her stomach.

She fell asleep, feeling the heat from his palm burn its way through her body.

Twenty-Four

Jane dressed quickly, anxious to have some time alone with Ryan before the rest of the household woke up. She wanted to talk to him about what happened last night, and about her father.

She climbed the stairs and stopped in front of Ryan's room. She listened, then knocked softly. A moment later she quietly opened his door.

His bed was empty.

She hurried downstairs, hoping to catch him before anyone else awoke. She heard the sound of her father's voice coming from the kitchen. Biting back her disappointment, she stepped into the doorway.

Catching sight of her, her father abruptly stopped in mid-sentence. He smiled nervously and wished her a good morning.

Jane nodded to him, and glanced over at Ryan. He sat at the kitchen table with a cup of coffee before him.

Her father stood in front of the kitchen sink, his smile still held stiffly in place.

'I will need you at the office today, Jane,' Thomas said, glancing over at Ryan, then back at his daughter.

'Will you be coming down yourself?'

'No, not this morning. I have some business I need to take care of.'

'What business?'

'It's nothing important.' Her father shook his head dismissively.

'Then why don't you let me take care of it for you?'

'No, that's quite all right. I need to...' He froze at the sound of the phone from his office. His glance again darted over to Ryan.

Ryan nodded encouragingly, which seemed to galvanize the other man. Thomas turned and quickly left the room. Jane heard the sound of his voice as he picked up the phone.

'What's going on?' she said, turning to Ryan.

'Nothing.' Ryan shrugged, staring off behind her at the doorway of her father's office.

Jane turned to see her father crouched nervously over his desk, holding the receiver to his ear.

'Tell me?' she asked softly, stepping over to stand in front of Ryan, forcing him to meet her gaze.

Ryan raised his eyes to hers. He reached out and rested his hand on the curve of her hip.

She could feel the heat of his palm burn through the fabric of her skirt.

'It's okay, Jane, honest,' he promised.

She turned as she heard her father approach.

'That was Margaret,' he said to Ryan. 'C&H is a holding company based out of Cook County.'

'Any listing on the directors?'

'No, but Margaret's trying to track them down.'

'Who's C&H?' Jane asked, glancing at her father, then at Ryan.

'No one important, Jane. It's just something that Mr Ryan asked me to look into.' Her father glanced at his watch. 'You should really be getting down to the office, shouldn't you?' he said gently.

'Dad, what is going on here?'

'Nothing at all, Jane. Just a few things that Mr Ryan asked me to clear up for him.'

'What things?'

'Jane,' her father cautioned, 'I don't think this is any of your business.'

'Ryan?'

Ryan shrugged, then turned away.

For a moment she stood helplessly between the two of them. Then, shaking her head in frustration, she turned and stalked out of the room. A moment later the two men heard the sound of the front door slamming closed.

'You should tell her,' Ryan said quietly.

'No, I can't.'

'Why not?'

'I don't want her to think that I've . . .' Thomas faltered.

'That you've what?'

'That I've done anything wrong.'

'She's your daughter. It's not going to matter.'

'It would to me,' Thomas said softly, staring out the window.

The sound of the office phone startled both of them.

293

Catching the older man's glance, Ryan quickly stood and motioned to the office.

Thomas picked up the phone. Before he could speak, Ryan heard the sound of a voice at the other end. Thomas glanced up at him and nodded.

Ryan sat on the edge of the desk and listened to Thomas's end of the conversation, which consisted of three 'yes's.

He hung up the phone and glanced over at Ryan. 'He wants to meet me at the lake front in fifteen minutes,' Thomas told him.

'Okay.' Ryan nodded curtly. 'Let's do it.' He rose from the desk and started towards the door.

'Ryan,' Ricky greeted him as he stepped out of the office.

Before Ryan could speak, Thomas stepped around him and said, 'Not now, Richard. We're busy.'

Catching the boy's disappointed glance, Ryan nodded to him. 'It's okay, kid. I'll talk to you later.'

Ryan had just grabbed his coat and was at the front door when he heard the sound of a car pulling into the drive.

'Who is that?' Thomas said anxiously, rushing over to open the door. He peered out at the car parked in his drive.

A moment later the driver's door opened and Detective Ellroy stepped out.

'It's the detective,' Howard said, glancing worriedly over his shoulder.

'Don't worry about it. You haven't done anything,' Ryan assured him.

'Is everything all right, Dad?'

'Yes, Richard,' Thomas said impatiently. 'Everything's just fine.'

The detective stepped up to the side door.

'Mr Howard.' Ellroy nodded to Thomas, then turned his glance on Ryan. He examined him closely.

'Mr Ryan, I have a few questions, and I was hoping you might have some answers for me.'

Before Ryan could respond, Thomas said, 'Detective Ellroy, this is a very bad time right now. I wonder if it might not be possible to do this later this afternoon.'

'Well I'm sorry if I'm inconveniencing you, Mr Howard, but there really isn't any need for you to hang around. This is just between Mr Ryan and me.' Ellroy grinned.

'Actually, detective, Mr Ryan and I were just on our way out to complete an errand.

'Is that right?'

'Yes, it is.'

'Mr Ryan working for you now?'

'In a limited capacity.'

Ellroy nodded thoughtfully. 'I'm afraid I'll have to insist, Mr Howard. This won't take very long at all. An hour at most. That won't be a problem for you, will it?' He leveled his gaze at Howard.

'No,' Ryan quickly interjected. 'That's no problem at all.'

'Good, I'd hate to be any bother.'

'I'm sure you would.' Ryan returned the detective's grin.

Howard glanced nervously at his watch.

'Dad,' Ricky called, 'maybe I could help?'

Thomas whirled around.

Ricky stood at the foot of the stairs, looking at him expectantly.

'That's an excellent idea, Richard,' Howard said in relief.

'Maybe not, Thomas. It might be a better to just wait until I'm finished here. It's not going to take that long.' Ryan tried to catch his eye.

Thomas avoided his glance, and gestured impatiently to his son. 'We should get going, Richard. We don't have too much time.'

'Thomas!' Ryan grabbed the older man's arm. 'Why don't you just wait?' he said pointedly.

Howard shrugged away from his grip and stepped around him.

A moment later Ricky followed him.

'Thomas?' Ryan called out.

Howard ignored him and quickly walked to his car. He climbed in and started the engine.

'Is there a problem, Mr Ryan?' Ellroy asked.

Ryan turned and caught the detective's gaze.

'No.' Ryan said, turning back to watch Ricky and Thomas head up the drive.

A moment later they turned on to the highway and disappeared from sight.

'Mr Ryan?'

Ryan turned to the policeman.

'Can we?' The detective gestured toward the house.

After a moment, Ryan shrugged wearily and opened the door. He followed the detective into the kitchen.

'Do you know Will Leland?' Ellroy asked casually, as he pulled out a kitchen chair and straddled it.

'Who?' Ryan responded, as he reached for a cigarette.

Ellroy smiled, then shook his head. 'Will Leland, he's in real estate. He's also done some work for Mr Howard from time to time.'

'Can't say I've ever heard of him.' Ryan shrugged. He lit his cigarette. 'We done now?'

'No, I'm afraid I have a few more questions I want to ask you. Are you that pressed for time, Mr Ryan?'

'No.' Ryan sighed, then hunched forward over the table and stared out the window at the empty drive.

Twenty-Five

John Caldwell sat in his car at the far end of the public lot overlooking the lake. He leaned back in his seat and stared out at the water, contemplating his upcoming meeting with Howard. He hoped Howard would not be cooperative.

Caldwell had long ago realized that there were only two things in life he truly valued. One was power, and the other was pain. In truth there was really only one – and that was pain.

The infliction of it.

Power, he had come to realize, was merely the currency he needed to spend in order for him to pursue this goal.

He liked to watch the faces of his victims as they gradually began to realize that there was no end to their agony, and that it was he, John Caldwell, who was their judge, and ultimately their only god.

His first experience with this desire came when he was much too young to fully appreciate what had taken place. A boyhood friend had fallen from a tree, breaking his leg. It had been John who had quickly scrambled down to his friend's side.

Crying hysterically, the boy had screamed for his mother as he had writhed in agony beneath the branches of the tree.

Examining him, with an intensity that he had never before experienced, John had crouched beside the boy and watched intently. He had seen the boy's eyes slowly come to focus on his face. And in that instant, John had suddenly realized the god-like quality he held.

The boy's life was his to do with as he willed.

Crouched beside his friend, watching the pain grotesquely twist the boy's features, John had hesitantly reached out and jabbed his fist into the swollen break of his friend's leg.

The boy had thrown his head back and screamed, then a moment later had lost consciousness.

Disappointed by his friend's quick retreat, John had slowly stood, then reluctantly gone to get help.

It was years later before John had another opportunity to continue his study of pain.

After a long night of drinking and rambling around town with a group of his construction cronies, Caldwell had found himself in an alley, facing off with another man. Everything leading up to that moment was something of a blur. But the instant his fist crashed into the other man's lips, and the blood began to flow, was a memory so vivid that John could recreate it at will. He did this often, watching the man's face slowly break apart before him.

On that night, he had circled the other man, lashing out with a calculation that had silenced the crowd of onlookers who had come out to watch the fight. The silence had grown until the only sound was the ragged breath of his opponent as he staggered from the ripping blows.

It had taken the other man almost an hour before he fell into a heap in a corner of the alley. And during that hour his agony had fed John well.

Caldwell had gone home that night having learned two important lessons. One was the realization that other people didn't understand the power in pain. And the other was that the study of true pain could only be seen in the faces of those who'd never experienced it before.

Caldwell got little satisfaction out of the world-weary and embittered. They were much too accustomed to pain. They almost seemed to expect it. But those who had never before experienced the epiphany of suffering offered John his greatest pleasure.

The prostitute had been interesting, but not completely satisfying. By the time Caldwell had taught her his lessons, she'd been so far gone that there had been little left he could appreciate.

Howard offered him much more. It was possible, John conceded, that at some point in his life Howard must have known pain. But over the years he had long ago forgotten its lessons. He had probably convinced himself that he was far beyond it.

Caldwell enjoyed the thought of reintroducing him to it, but he wanted to do it slowly. He wanted to break him emotionally, until Howard felt that he had reached the absolute bottom. And only then would John introduce him to new depths of physical punishment.

Caldwell swiveled around as he heard the sound of a vehicle pulling into the parking lot. He spotted Howard's car, and smiled in anticipation as he reached for the door.

Thomas saw the car parked at the far end of the lot. He gripped the steering wheel tightly.

'Dad, you okay?'

'Fine,' Thomas said curtly, unable to take his eyes off the car ahead of him.

'Dad?'

Thomas turned to catch Ricky's worried glance.

'I'm fine, son,' Thomas said, then reached out to grip the boy's shoulder.

At his touch, Ricky smiled warmly at his father.

'I really appreciate your coming with me, Richard,' Howard said softly.

'That's all right.' Ricky shrugged, unable now to meet his father's gaze.

'No, really. I just want to let you know how much I appreciate your helping me out.' Thomas paused. 'It means a lot to me.'

'That's okay, Dad.' Ricky turned to his father, then hesitantly reached out to lightly touch his arm. 'I want to help.'

'Good.' Thomas smiled affectionately, then glanced again at the man climbing out of the car ahead of him. 'Now I just want you to listen. You don't have to do anything, okay?'

'Sure. Whatever you want me to do, Dad, you just tell me,' Ricky said eagerly.

Thomas nodded, then reached for the ignition. He took a deep breath and climbed out. Over the hood he caught sight of Richard's smile, then turned to the man waiting for him.

'Mr Howard,' The man acknowledged him, then slowly turned and stared at Ricky. His eyes riveted hungrily on the boy.

The intensity of his gaze made Ricky uneasy. He glanced inquisitively at his father, who still stood uncomfortably by the side of the car. There was a sense of hesitancy about his father's posture that Ricky had never seen before. It worried him. He remembered that brief moment earlier when his father had reached out to touch him. It gave him the strength to ignore the other man's stare and walk over to his father's side.

Thomas rested his hand on Ricky's shoulder. Ricky could feel the grip of his fingers digging into his flesh.

'Who are you?' Howard asked.

'You can call me Raymond.'

'Do you have them?'

'Are you ready to sign?' Raymond countered.

'First the tapes.'

The man suddenly smiled.

Ricky was amazed by the difference his smile made. There was a sense of warmth about it that almost negated the hard blue stare of his eyes.

'No, Mr Howard, I think your priorities are all fucked up here.'

Ricky glanced at him sharply. The man grinned at him knowingly.

'I take it this is your son.'

'Yes.'

Ricky felt his father's hand tighten on his shoulder.

Raymond's grin widened. 'Odd that you would bring him along for something like this.'

'Like what?' Ricky turned to his father.

'Nothing. It's just business,' Thomas said quickly.

The man laughed disdainfully.

'What's going on?' Ricky asked, looking at each of them.

'It's okay, Richard.'

'Right, *Richard*,' said Raymond, sarcastically emphasizing the boy's name. 'It's just business. Just your father's business.'

'The tapes.'

'First this,' the man said archly, pulling a pen from his breast pocket. He waved it at Thomas, then reached into his car. He pulled out a sheaf of papers. 'I need you to sign right here on this line.'

'I want the tapes.'

'Mr Howard.' Raymond sighed patiently. 'Do I have to remind you who's holding the C-A-R-D-S,' he spelled, looking insultingly at Ricky. His eyes picked away hungrily at the boy's face.

Meeting his gaze, Ricky shuddered and looked away, but not before he saw the glimpse of a smile twist the man's lips.

'Dad?' Ricky turned to his father. 'Let's just go.' He tugged on Thomas's arm.

'*Daddy, I'm scared*,' the man taunted.

Ricky glared at him. He felt his father's hand on his shoulder, pulling him back.

The man's gaze shifted to Thomas's face. 'Sign, Mr Howard. Save yourself some grief.'

'Why? Why are you doing this to me?'

The man laughed. 'God, you are an egotistical ass, aren't you.' He transferred his gaze back to Ricky. 'It must be hell having someone like this as a father.' The man gestured disparagingly at Thomas.

'Leave him alone.' Ricky glared.

'Only when I'm done with him.'

'Richard,' Thomas cautioned, as Ricky took a step forward.

The man smiled encouragingly at him.

'Richard, don't!' Thomas gripped his son's arm and pulled him back.

'Sign the fucking thing, Howard. Then go away,' the man said wearily. He held out the pen.

'What about the tapes?'

Raymond shrugged. 'I'll give them to you after you've signed.'

'Why would I believe you?'

'What choice do you have?'

'No.' Thomas shook his head, holding the other man's gaze. 'I want to see the tapes first.'

'Dad, let's just leave,' Ricky said softly. 'You don't have to do this now.'

'Oh yes, he does.' The man grinned. 'He has to do it right now. Don't you, Howard?'

'Dad, why? What's this all about?'

'*C'mon, Dad,*' the man taunted. 'Why don't you tell the boy what it's all about?'

'Dad?'

'Tell him, Tommy, tell him what's going on. Tell him about—'

'Shut up,' Thomas yelled and started forward.

Before Ricky fully understood what had happened, he heard the sound of a slap. A moment later he saw his father reeling back, with his hand held to his cheek. His father's gaze was locked in disbelief on the man standing before him.

Ricky whirled around to stare in astonishment at the other man.

Raymond smiled back at him happily.

'You son of a bitch,' Ricky cried, and threw himself at the man.

'Richard!'

'C'mon, kid, let's see what you got,' Caldwell said, taking a step back.

Ricky charged, winging a fist toward Raymond's face.

Caldwell easily ducked the blow, and using the kid's momentum, spun him around, pinning him against his chest.

'Sign, Howard. Now.'

'What about the tapes?' Thomas asked, his gaze traveling anxiously to his son's face.

'Sign, and then we'll talk about the tapes.'

'Dad.' Ricky struggled against the arm, pinning him in place.

Caldwell snorted disgustedly and dug a knuckle into the boy's rib.

Ricky groaned.

'Richard!'

'We having fun now.' Caldwell grinned at Howard.

'Let him go.'

'Sign.'

'Richard,' Thomas called sadly, taking a step back.

Caldwell examined the older man carefully.

'Dad?' Ricky said hesitantly.

'You fucker,' Caldwell said, with a trace of admiration in his tone. Shaking his head in amusement, Caldwell broke away from Howard's gaze. He turned to the boy.

'You ever break a bone, Richard?'

'Don't,' Thomas shouted.

'Hurts like a son of a bitch,' the man said conversationally.

'Leave him alone.'

Caldwell looked over at Howard. 'You going to sign?'

Thomas peered helplessly at his son.

'Make up your mind, Tommy, time's a-ticking.'

'Dad?' Ricky called.

Abruptly, Caldwell turned and threw Ricky across the hood of his car.

Before Ricky could react, the man grabbed his arm and bent it backward at the elbow, over the front fender.

'Please,' Thomas pleaded.

'Sign.' Caldwell glanced over his shoulder at Howard.

'I can't,' Thomas suddenly screamed. 'I can't do it.'

'Hell of a father you got there, kid,' Caldwell said. His eyes locked on the boy's face.

A moment later he grinned.

A moment after that he threw his weight against the boy's arm.

'Richard!' Thomas cried.

Ricky screamed as he heard the sharp crack of the bone giving way. The pain shot through his arm and convulsed his whole body.

He rolled off the hood of the car and fell limply to the pavement.

Caldwell smiled, then gently nudged the broken arm with his foot.

The boy remained motionless on the pavement.

'He seems to be sleeping,' Caldwell said disappointedly. 'You ready to sign now, or would you like a little time with your son first. Maybe some quality time.'

Caldwell grinned, then turned and climbed into his car. 'We'll be in touch real soon, Mr Howard,' he said through the window, then, glancing thoughtfully at the unconscious figure of the boy, added, 'I'd do something about your son, if I were you. That's a dangerous place to rest. No telling what could happen to him, is there, Howard?' Caldwell smiled, then backed out of the parking lot.

Stunned, Thomas turned to the broken figure of his son. After a moment, he knelt beside him and tentatively reached out to touch the boy's shoulder.

Ryan stood at the window, watching Ellroy pull out of the drive. The detective had questioned him for almost an hour before finally leaving.

Ryan turned away and paced impatiently across the room. He poured himself a cup of coffee and carried it over to the window overlooking the drive. He lit a cigarette and stared out at the garage.

When he heard the sound of the phone, he whirled around anxiously.

'Hello . . .'

'Jane, have you heard from you father?' Ryan interrupted sharply.

'No, isn't he there? I thought he—'

'Have you heard from Ricky?' Ryan cut through her question.

'No. I thought he was with you.'

'No, he isn't.' Ryan shook his head wearily.

'Ryan, I just talked to Margaret about this C&H Corporation. Did you know they made an offer to buy the mall property?'

'I know.'

'What else do you know about all of this? What's going on? Is my father in some kind of trouble?'

'Yes.'

'How bad?'

'Bad enough, Jane. Listen, I'll tell you everything I know later. But right now I want to keep the phone open, okay?'

'No, Ryan, it's not okay. I want some answers. What's happening with my father, and who is C&H Corporation?'

'Jane, I'll talk to you later,' Ryan said abruptly, then hung up the phone.

It rang an instant later.

'Who the hell do you think you are that—?'

'Jane, please believe me, this is important. I'll tell you everything I know – just not right now.'

'Promise?'

'I promise.'

'Okay, but I want to hear everything,' she said emphatically.

Ryan replaced the receiver and sat at Thomas's desk.

He pulled the ashtray over and leaned back in Thomas's chair.

He stared up at the ceiling thoughtfully.

He closed his eyes. He felt the drift taking him, and he let himself go with it until he had recreated the texture and feel of it. It drew him back to the heat, and the brackish smell of the bay.

'I don't want to,' Neal said, glancing over at his older brother.

Ryan sat across from him on the other side of the pier. 'It'll be okay,' he told him.

'Why can't you come, too?'

'I go to a different school. I'm older.' Ryan shrugged, shifting around to face his little brother.

'But I don't want to be there all alone.' Neal pouted. 'I won't know anyone.'

'You will. It'll just take some time, and then you'll have lots of friends.'

'You don't have any friends,' Neal challenged.

'Yeah, I do. What about Charlie?'

'Charlie's my friend, too,' Neal said earnestly.

'Yep.' Ryan nodded, smiling at his brother.

Neal leaned forward and peered thoughtfully into the calm waters of the bay.

'Will Charlie still be my friend if I get other friends?'

'Sure, you can have more than two friends. You can have lots of friends,' Ryan told him.

'Daddy says—'

'Don't listen to Daddy.'

'Why not?'

'Just don't.' Ryan sighed, then turned away from his brother's inquisitive glance.

'Daddy'd get mad if he knew you said that.'

'Probably,' Ryan agreed.

'Daddy's always mad, isn't he? How come he's always mad, Eddie?' Neal asked softly, dangling his foot over the edge of the pier.

'He's sick.' Ryan glanced out at the bay. In the distance he could see a dark bank of clouds beginning to form.

'Like when I was sick?'

'No, different sick.'

'When's he going to get better, Eddie?'

'I don't know, Neal,' Ryan answered quietly. 'Maybe someday.'

'Sunday?'

'No, someday.' Ryan turned to see his brother's confused glance.

'When is someday?'

'I don't know.'

'June?'

'Sure.' Ryan grinned. 'He's going to be better in June.'

Two weeks later, Ryan was abruptly reminded of the

conversation when he found his father waiting for him downstairs.

Neal stood on the porch, staring in fearfully through the screen door.

'What the fuck do you mean I'm sick, you little asshole,' his father raged.

'I don't know what you're talking about,' Ryan said quickly, backing away from his anger.

'And I'm going to get better in June,' his father taunted sarcastically.

'I didn't mean—'

His father lashed out, catching him across the mouth with his fist.

The blow spun Ryan to the floor.

'Don't be telling your little brother that kind of shit.' His father's foot crashed into his side.

'Eddie, I'm sorry,' Ryan heard Neal wail from outside. 'Daddy's still sick.'

'What the fuck are you talking about?' His father whirled around and started toward the screen door.

Ryan pushed himself to his feet and staggered to the door.

'Leave him alone,' he shouted, standing between the door and his father. Behind him he heard Neal's terrified cries.

'Get the fuck out of my way, you little pussy.'

'No!'

'You little prick,' his father spat, then cuffed him across the ear.

The blow deafened him and threw him to the floor.

When he raised his head, he saw his father's fist descending on Neal.

'Eddie?' Neal screamed, the sound suddenly pierced through the silence.

Ryan tried to rise. He got to his knees, then staggered and fell back to the floor.

He woke to the sound of his father's truck pulling out of the drive, and his brother's cries.

He crawled out to the front porch.

Neal was hiding beneath it, clinging to one of the support beams.

'It's okay, Neal,' Ryan said softly, crawling in beside him.

'Daddy's sick. And he's never going to get better,' Neal cried defiantly, whirling to face him.

And Ryan put his arms around his little brother, and tried to think of another lie to tell him.

The ringing of the phone startled him. For a moment Ryan gazed blankly around the office, as the bell pierced the silence of the house.

Ryan grabbed the receiver.

'It's Ricky. He's at Victory Hospital,' Jane said breathlessly.

'What?'

'He's in the hospital. It's six blocks south on Sheridan Road. I don't know what happened. Dad just called me. I'll meet you there.'

'Is he okay?' Ryan asked, and listened to silence at the other end. An instant later the disconnect tone sounded.

Ryan raced out of the house to his cycle.

He kicked into gear and wheeled out of the drive. Five minutes later he stepped through the emergency room doors.

Jane stood at the front desk.

Ryan hurried over to her.

At his touch, she turned, then a moment later wrapped her arms around him.

Ryan held her. His gaze traveled over her shoulder, to the sight of Thomas sitting on a bench against the wall.

Gently disengaging himself, Ryan strode over to stand before the older man.

'What the fuck happened?' he demanded hoarsely, glaring down at him.

'It was an accident, there wasn't anything I could do,' Thomas said helplessly.

'Fuck you, Howard. I'm tired of hearing that shit.' Ryan gripped the front of the older man's shirt and jerked him off the bench. 'What the hell have you done?'

'Ryan!'

He turned to catch Jane's bewildered glance.

Disgustedly shoving Thomas back against the wall, he turned and stepped over to her side.

'How is he?' he asked, ignoring her shocked glance.

Examining him closely, Jane nodded slowly. 'He's going to be okay.'

Ryan turned to look at Howard, aware of Jane doing the same.

Thomas's gaze shifted nervously between them.

'We need to talk,' Ryan said.

Thomas nodded meekly, then rose to his feet.

'Outside.' Ryan gestured to the door.

He gripped Howard's shoulder and led him through the doors.

Twenty-Six

'How bad?' Christian demanded, glaring across his desk at his brother-in-law.

Caldwell shrugged. 'Not too bad.' He picked up a pencil and began to twirl it. He glanced up and caught Christian's gaze.

'Hey, lighten up. I didn't hurt him all that much.'

'Goddamnit, John, I told you to just talk to him.'

'He wasn't listening.'

'Then you should have left it alone. He would have eventually come around.'

'I thought maybe I could help him along a little.' Caldwell grinned, remembering the sound of the bone breaking.

Christian, reading the smile, shook his head disgustedly. 'If you can't control yourself, then you're no use to me.'

Caldwell glanced over at him sharply. 'And what's that supposed to mean?'

'Exactly what I said.' Christian held his gaze. 'We don't want Howard doing anything rash. We back him too far into a corner and he's going to come out fighting.'

'The guy's a pussy.' Caldwell shrugged disparagingly. 'He's not going to do shit.'

'He will if he thinks he has nothing to lose,' Christian quickly countered.

Caldwell stepped around the desk to his brother-in-law's side.

Christian turned to face him.

'I'm sorry. You happy now?'

'No, but I guess it'll have to do.' Christian nodded, without glancing away.

Caldwell snorted disgustedly and turned aside.

'All we have on him are the tapes. And the only things the tapes can accomplish are a little embarrassment and some minor complications,' Christian explained patiently. 'We need to keep him off balance. We don't want to make him so mad that he just starts striking out.'

'I don't think there's any problem about that happening.'

'And why is that?'

Caldwell turned to face Christian. He grinned knowingly. 'Howard just stood there while I broke his kid's arm. He didn't do one goddamn thing to stop me.'

'Nothing?' Christian asked in disbelief.

'Nothing at all.'

Christian smiled. 'Then maybe you should've broken the other arm as well.'

'Next time,' Caldwell replied, returning his smile.

'Not a thing,' Ellroy said exasperatedly.

'You didn't expect to find anything.'

'I know.' Ellroy paused to glance across the mayor's desk. 'But I was hoping I was wrong.' He began to pace again.

The mayor leaned back. 'What happened with Howard's son?'

'He broke his arm. Supposedly,' Ellroy added sarcastically, 'by tripping over one of the lot dividers.'

'You don't believe that?'

'No way do I believe that. Howard met somebody down there – I know that. What happened then, I'm not sure. But I damn well know that when I went over to that house this morning, there was something going on.'

'What?'

'I don't know.' Ellroy paused thoughtfully by the window. 'Closest I can come to it is that Ryan was supposed to go down there with Howard.'

'Why didn't he?'

'Because I was talking to him. Howard ended up going down there alone with his son.'

'You seriously think that someone broke Howard's son's arm, and he's just going to let it go?'

'Yeah, I do,' Ellroy said, holding the mayor's eye.

Mayor Presley shook his head in disbelief. 'I can't believe that. I can't see any father allowing that to happen to his son.'

'Hell.' Ellroy snorted disgustedly. 'You know what Howard's like. He probably never believed it would come to that.'

'You going to talk to the son?'

'Eventually – but the kid's still out of it.' Ellroy shrugged

319

irritatedly. 'I don't think it's going to do me a damn bit of good.'

'Why not?'

'Kid's not going to say anything to mess up his father. He'll back him all the way.'

'Despite having his own father watch something like that happen?'

'Yeah, even despite that.'

'What the hell is going on around here?' Mayor Presley exclaimed.

He stood and stepped over to the window. 'That goddamn mall has turned the town inside-out.'

'And we've got another week or so before it ends.'

'I'm going to call Christian,' the mayor said decisively, 'and get him to come out with his endorsement. Once he's done that, it's a *fait accompli*.'

'Yeah.' Ellroy turned to the mayor. 'But it doesn't solve any of the rest of this.'

'No, but it might stop anything else from happening.'

The mayor returned to his chair. 'Did you get anything from Ryan?'

'Nothing. Guy's like a rock. He's not going to give up anything.'

'What if you pushed him?'

Ellroy turned to catch the mayor's eye. After a moment, he shook his head. 'I don't think that would be such a good idea.'

'Why not?'

'I think he's somebody who might just push back.'

* * *

Ricky's right arm was suspended in a brace over his bed. His left cheek was bruised and scraped from his fall to the pavement. He was still heavily sedated.

Ryan, Jane, and Thomas stood around his hospital bed. Jane gently held his left hand.

Ryan stood at the foot of the bed, staring down at the boy's face. He felt a sudden flash of memory and quickly turned away.

He stepped outside the room and leaned against a wall.

'He's okay,' Jane said, stepping through the doorway after him.

Ryan nodded, without taking his eyes off the wall.

'It's not your fault. There wasn't anything you could do.'

Ryan turned to look at her.

'It isn't, Ryan.' Jane reached out to touch his chest. 'If it's anyone's fault, it's . . .' She paused, then glanced into the room behind her.

Thomas stood beside the bed, staring down at his son.

'C'mon.' She took Ryan's arm and pulled him down the hallway. 'We'll get a cup of coffee.'

He allowed himself to be led to the elevator.

They entered the basement cafeteria, and carried their coffee over to a back table.

'Why didn't you tell me what was going on?' Jane asked.

'There wasn't anything to tell.' Ryan shrugged. He went on before she could respond, 'and if there was, it was up to your father, not me.'

'Who would do something like that? He's just a kid.'

321

'He's your father's son.' Ryan held her gaze.

Jane glanced away. She brushed back a dark strand of hair.

'It's just money,' she whispered, shaking her head in disbelief.

'That's all it takes.'

'Do you think...' She stopped.

'What?'

She cleared her throat, then, closing her eyes, asked, 'Do you think my father knew what was going to happen?'

Ryan sighed, then looked away. 'No. If he did, he probably never would have taken Ricky along with him.'

Jane raised her glance to his. Ryan forced himself to hold her gaze.

After a moment, she smiled. She reached across the table and put her hand over his. 'He's going to be okay. That's all that matters.'

'Yeah,' Ryan agreed a moment later. 'That's all that matters.'

Ryan stood beside his cycle, watching Jane and her father pull out of the parking lot. He threw his leg over the seat, then pulled and lit a cigarette. He reached for the starter, then suddenly paused. He leaned back thoughtfully.

A moment later he flipped his cigarette to the side and climbed off his bike. He strode across the parking lot to the emergency-room doors.

'I'm sorry, sir, but visiting hours are over,' the duty nurse informed him.

'I know. I forgot my coat,' Ryan said brusquely, stepping around her.

'I can get for that you. Why don't you wait here and I'll...'

Ryan ignored her and kept walking.

'Sir, I'm afraid that you're not allowed on this floor,' he heard the nurse call after him.

Ryan walked down to Ricky's room and stepped inside. The kid was in the same position he'd left him in thirty minutes before.

Ryan stepped over to the side of the bed and examined his face.

Almost involuntarily, he reached out and brushed back the boy's hair.

At his touch, Ricky groaned.

Ryan quickly withdrew his hand.

Ricky opened his eyes. For a moment he stared up blankly at Ryan.

'How you doing, kid?' Ryan asked gently.

'Ryan.' Ricky sighed. He started to smile, then suddenly winced.

'You okay?'

'Yeah, I'm okay. Where is...?' Ricky glanced around the room.

'You're in Victory Hospital.' Ryan nodded encouragingly. 'You remember?'

'Yeah, I...' Ricky suddenly stiffened. He glanced up fearfully at Ryan. 'He's not here, is he?'

'Who?'

'That man. That guy who ... Is Dad okay?'

'He's fine.'

Ricky sighed in relief, then sagged back against the bed. 'It hurts,' he said, glancing at his cast.

'It's supposed to.' Ryan smiled softly.

Ricky returned his smile.

Ryan stood over him until the boy's eyes closed. He stepped to the foot of the bed and examined him. He leaned against the railing, suddenly remembering being in the same position a long time ago. Only then it had been Neal lying in the hospital bed.

Two broken ribs and a dislocated finger, the nurse told him. Then, looking at him closely, she asked, 'What happened?'

'He fell,' Ryan responded, quickly glancing away.

The nurse crouched before him. She reached out to gently grip each of his shoulders, forcing him to face her.

'You can tell me the truth. I won't tell anyone,' she promised.

'He fell,' Ryan repeated, feeling her eyes searching his own.

Sighing wearily, she reluctantly released him and stood.

'You know,' she said softly. 'This isn't the way it's supposed to be.'

Ryan glanced up at her sharply.

'Your brother doesn't deserve this,' she said, nodding to the unconscious figure of Neal sprawled across the hospital bed.

Then, a moment later, she gently added, 'And neither do you, Eddie.'

Ryan turned away, unable to accept the sympathy he saw in her eyes.

'Visiting hours are over, sir,' the nurse said sternly.

Ryan turned to find her and an orderly standing in the doorway.

'I just wanted to get my coat,' Ryan said. Then, after a last glance at Ricky, he turned and left the room.

He stepped into the elevator. When the doors opened again, Ryan strode across the parking lot and climbed on to his cycle. A moment later he wheeled out of the lot. He hit the throttle and raced down the highway. He didn't slow until he hit the outskirts of downtown.

He parked on a side street and walked toward the City Center.

The middle-aged woman sitting at the desk rose as he stepped into the office.

'Can I help you?'

'Is he in?' Ryan jabbed a finger at the door behind her.

'Do you have an appointment, sir?'

Ryan snorted disdainfully and stepped around her.

'Sir, you can't go in there.'

Ryan ignored her and pushed his way through the door.

Startled, Mayor Presley glanced up sharply, then quickly rose to his feet.

'Sir, you can't—'

'I'm Ryan. I want to talk to you.'

'Mr Mayor, I'm sorry but he just—'

'That's okay, Jean. There's no problem,' Presley assured her.

He turned away from her astonished glance and examined the man before him.

'What can I do for you, Mr Ryan?'

Ryan snorted derisively, then stepped inside the room and hooked a chair with his foot. He pulled it over and sat in front of the mayor's desk.

'Question isn't what you can do, but if you'll do it,' Ryan said, leveling his gaze at the other man.

Glancing over Ryan's shoulder, Mayor Presley smiled. 'Jean, please. Everything is quite all right.'

A moment later Ryan heard the sound of the door closing behind him. He pulled out a cigarette.

'I'd rather you didn't smoke,' the mayor said, returning to his chair.

Ryan lit his cigarette and slouched back in the chair. 'Howard's son got his arm broken this morning.'

'I know.' The mayor nodded, studying the biker closely.

'I'll bet you do.' Ryan grinned. 'What else do you know?'

'About what?' Presley casually leaned back in his chair and steepled his fingers before him.

'About what's going on? About Leland, about Arnold—'

'Arnold?'

'The woman who got wasted in the condo,' Ryan explained.

'I don't know anything about any of that.'

'I don't believe you.'

'Your belief, one way or another, is not a concern of mine, Mr Ryan.'

'Maybe it should be.'

'Why is that?'

326

'Because, Mr Mayor, you're sitting right in the middle of it all.'

'I don't know what you're talking about.'

'Bullshit,' Ryan said softly. 'You and Howard are the targets, and neither of you seems to give a shit – one way or the other – who else gets in the way.'

'I certainly appreciate your concern for the public's welfare, Mr Ryan,' Mayor Presley said sarcastically, 'but I have trouble believing that this is your only motivation.'

'Ricky's my friend,' Ryan said bluntly. He held the mayor's gaze.

Presley was the first to glance away. 'I see,' he said thoughtfully.

'I don't like people fucking with my friends.'

'And what do you think you can do about it?'

'A hell of a lot more than you can.'

'What makes you think so?'

'Because I *want* to.' Ryan stood up and leaned over the mayor's desk. 'I'm not looking to get re-elected, or to put together some million-dollar deal. I'm just looking for some justice.'

'Justice, Mr Ryan? Isn't that a little naïve?'

'Where I come from, mayor, people pay their bills.'

The mayor swiveled his chair around to look out at the lake.

'What do want from me?' he said, without turning.

'Information.'

'And what do I get in return?' the mayor asked softly, still looking out the window.

Ryan snorted in disgust.

The mayor whirled around to face him.

'Always the trade-off, isn't it, mayor.'

'That's the way politics works, Mr Ryan. You must know that by now.' He paused to survey the man before him. 'You look like you've been around long enough to realize that fact.'

'Long enough to realize it – not long enough to like it.'

'I'm still waiting to hear what you have to offer.'

Ryan glanced around the desk. He grabbed a piece of paper from a tray and carefully folded it in half. He stubbed his cigarette out in the paper, then crumpled it and put it on a corner of the mayor's desk.

'I'll find out who did Ricky.'

'That doesn't help mu—'

'Same guy who did Ricky is probably behind everything else,' Ryan interrupted. 'He's playing you and Howard off against each other.' Ryan paused. His glance traveled disdainfully over the politician before him. 'He figures you're both too concerned with getting your own shit together to worry about the pedestrians.'

'Mr Ryan, you don't have the vaguest idea of what's at stake here.' Mayor Presley glared across his desk at the biker. 'You come storming into my office, accusing me of all sorts of things, without the faintest idea of what I'm doing about it. I have men working on this around the clock, and I resent the intimation that I'm simply trying to protect my political career.'

'How many?'

'What?' the mayor responded in confusion.

'How many men you got on this thing?'

'That's neither here nor there. It's not a matter of how many. It's a matter of how qualified those—'

'How many?' Ryan demanded.

The mayor glanced away without answering.

Ryan shook his head wearily. He pulled another cigarette, then sat on the edge of the mayor's desk.

'Why don't you tell me about Christian?'

'What are you talking about?' the mayor asked sharply.

'He's the only one who hasn't declared, isn't he?'

'Yes, but that doesn't mean anything. He's waiting for the proper time.'

'And when's that going to be?'

'A few days before the election. I just talked to him the other day about all of this.'

'And that's what he told you?'

'Yes. He has no reason to lie to me.'

'Maybe not, but he's the only one out there that hasn't made his play yet. It would seem to me, Mr Mayor,' Ryan said sarcastically, 'that he might be the *first* one you'd want to talk to.'

'Christian would never be a part of something like this. I've known Christian for almost twenty years,' Presley said defensively.

'I'm not saying he is.' Ryan shrugged. 'But he's certainly worth talking to.'

Mayor Presley leaned back in his chair. He stared thoughtfully across his desk at the man facing him.

'Why don't you take a chair, Mr Ryan.' The mayor nodded to the front of his desk.

Ryan lit another cigarette before he sat down.

'Jean,' the mayor said, hitting his intercom. 'Could you please bring in an ashtray for Mr Ryan.'

The mayor turned and smiled at Ryan. 'Would you like some coffee or something?'

'No, I'm fine, Mr Mayor,' Ryan said, then leaned back and waited for the other man to begin.

Twenty-Seven

'Dad?' Jane called softly.

Thomas Howard sat at his desk, staring blankly out the window. Evening had begun to shade the back yard. The office was dimly lit by a small lamp on Thomas's desk.

'Dad, are you all right?' She stepped over to his side.

Howard turned to her. For a moment he seemed unable to recognize her.

'Jane?' he said hesitantly.

'Yes, Dad.' She reached out to touch his arm.

'You looked so much like Mary that, for a minute there, I...' he paused, peering at her intently.

'It's okay.' Jane smiled encouragingly. 'Everything's going to be all right.'

Thomas sighed, then, after a decisive shake of his head, asked, 'Is it time?'

'No. Visiting hours don't start again until six.'

Her father nodded, and turned back to the window.

'He looked so small in that bed,' Thomas said quietly. 'He reminded me of when your mother was sick.' Thomas glanced up at his daughter. 'Do you remember that, Jane?'

'Yes, Dad.'

'She was so sick.' Thomas shook his head. 'I didn't know what to do then, either.'

'You did what you had to do,' Jane offered.

Thomas turned and held her eyes. After a moment he glanced away. 'It wasn't enough though, was it?'

Jane sat on the edge of his desk. She reached out to take his hand.

'He's going to be all right, Dad.'

'It should never have happened.'

'But it did, and it's over now. That's all that matters.'

'I wonder,' Thomas said reflectively. 'I wonder if Richard will ever be able to forgive me.'

'Oh, Dad, don't say that.' Jane threw her arms around her father. She held him tight, and it was only as he returned her embrace that she realized she couldn't remember the last time he had hugged her.

'No, I want to go alone,' Thomas said unequivocally. He stood at the front door, pulling on his coat.

'Are you sure?' Jane asked, reaching to help him.

'Yes, I want to talk privately to Richard.' Thomas paused in front of the hall mirror. He straightened his collar, then turned to her.

'I want to apologize to him.'

'Okay.' Jane nodded.

'I'll be back soon.' Howard turned and started for the door. As he opened it, he paused and looked back at her. 'Thank you.'

'For what?'

Thomas suddenly smiled. He reached out to touch her shoulder. 'For everything,' he said softly, then quickly turned and walked out the door.

Jane watched him climb into his car and pull out of the drive.

It was only as she stepped into the kitchen that she suddenly found her thoughts turning to Ryan.

Where was he – and what was he doing?

'Richard,' Howard whispered. He stood over his son. He held the boy's left hand in both of his own.

Ricky winced, then slowly opened his eyes. He saw his father staring down at him intently.

'Dad,' he sighed.

'Richard...' Thomas paused. He shook his head, then reached down to touch the boy's cheek. 'I'm so sorry, Richard. I didn't think...'

'It's okay, Dad, really it is.' Ricky tried to smile.

'No, it isn't.' Thomas shook his head. 'But it will be. I promise you it will,' he said, holding the boy's gaze.

'It's all right, Dad. You didn't know.' Ricky shifted against the pillow. He winced as the movement sent a sharp stab of pain through his arm.

'Are you okay?'

'Yeah.' Ricky glanced around the room. 'Where's Jane?'

'She's at home. She'll be down later.'

'Where's Ryan?'

'Why?'

Ricky started to shrug, then stopped. 'I don't know. I was just wondering where he was.'

'He's out,' Howard answered curtly, then took a step back. He clasped his hands behind his back and examined the boy before him.

'What is it, Dad?'

'Nothing, I was just thinking how proud I was of you this morning,' he said, meeting his son's eye.

Ricky blushed and glanced away. 'I didn't do anything.'

'You did more than I had any right to expect. I should never have asked you to come along.'

'You didn't know it would turn out that way.'

'No,' Thomas said quickly, glancing away. 'I didn't know.'

'What happened to that man?'

'I don't know.'

'Are they looking for him?'

Thomas turned back to the boy. 'That's something I wanted to talk to you about, Richard.'

'What?'

'This is a very complicated situation, and I don't want to confuse it any more than it already is.'

'What are you talking about, Dad?' Ricky asked, examining his father closely.

'Richard.' Thomas sighed. He reached out again to rest his hand on his son's shoulder. 'I know I asked a great deal of you today, but I need to ask one more thing from you.'

'What is it, Dad?'

'I want you to forget about that man.' Thomas went on quickly before Ricky could interrupt. 'It's important,

Richard. I would never ask you to do this if it wasn't. I'll take care of everything. I promise you,' Thomas vowed.

Ricky turned his head on the pillow, so that he looked out the window.

'It *is* important, Richard, believe me,' Thomas said softly, gripping the boy's shoulder.

'Okay.' Ricky nodded, without taking his gaze from the window.

'You'll say it was an accident?'

'If that's what you want, Dad.'

'It is, Richard.'

They both turned at the sound of footsteps entering the room.

Jane stepped over to the side of Ricky's bed.

Ricky reached out for her hand.

'How you doing, champ?' Jane grinned.

'Good.' Ricky smiled back at her.

Jane glanced over at her father.

'He's doing much better. I talked to the nurse and he'll be released first thing tomorrow morning,' Thomas said heartily, avoiding her gaze.

'Jane?'

'Yes, Ricky.'

'Where's Ryan?'

'I don't know,' Jane said thoughtfully. 'I don't know where he is.'

Howard stepped over to the window. Jane glanced at him curiously.

'I hope he's all right,' Ricky said softly.

Jane suddenly remembered her last sight of Ryan,

the bleak set of his features as he'd looked down at the unconscious figure of her brother.

She forced herself to smile.

'He'll be fine,' she said quietly.

Ryan parked half a block away from the house. He paused beside his bike and lit a cigarette. He flicked the match away as he examined the quiet residential street. The houses were all two to three stories high, and set on large well-maintained lots.

He tightened the collar of his coat and started down the block. As he walked, he went over his recent conversation with the mayor.

By the time he stepped up to the front door, he knew the questions he wanted to ask.

The woman who answered his knock peered out at him suspiciously from around the doorframe.

'Who are you?'

'Edward Ryan. I'd like to speak to your husband, please.'

Ryan heard the excited squeal of a child, and a moment later a small head peered up at him curiously from the bottom portion of the door.

'Casey, go back inside,' the woman said sharply.

The little boy glanced up at her, then turned back to look at Ryan, grinning up at him mischievously.

Ryan winked at him.

Startled, the boy stared up at him thoughtfully, then he suddenly smiled and tried to wink back.

'Casey!' the woman threatened. This time the boy quickly disappeared from sight.

'What is it you wish to speak to him about?' She demanded, fingering the door nervously.

'Business,' Ryan said.

He felt her eyes traveling over his clothes. Her gaze shifted up to his face, then over his shoulder to the street behind him.

'Listen, you have any questions, you can call the mayor. He'll vouch for me.'

'I might just do that,' the woman challenged, leveling her gaze on his.

'That's fine with me.' Ryan shrugged.

'Maureen, who is it?' a voice called from the interior of the house.

'An Edward Ryan,' the woman responded, without taking her eyes from the man in front of her.

'Who?'

Her eyes narrowed. 'Edward Ryan,' she said again, shifting her weight against the door.

'Who the hell is an Edward Ryan?'

Ryan heard footsteps approaching the doorway. A moment later the door itself swung open to reveal a man standing beside the woman.

'Who are you, and what do you want?' Jeffrey Lewis asked imperiously.

'I'm Edward Ryan.' Ryan paused to examine the man before him. He had the satisfied look of a well-fed cat. 'I wanted to ask you a few questions.'

Councilman Lewis snorted superciliously. 'You wanted to ask me some questions,' he repeated slowly. 'What on earth makes you think that I care what you want?'

After a last, disdainful glance, the councilman started to close the door.

'You might want to call either the mayor or Thomas Howard before you close that door,' Ryan said conversationally.

The man froze, staring out at Ryan.

'Just a few questions.' Ryan shrugged. 'And then I'm gone.'

Lewis eyed him speculatively. 'Wait here,' he ordered, then closed the door.

Ryan heard the sound of the lock clicking into place.

'Who is he, Jeffrey?' he heard the woman ask anxiously. The voice faded away.

Ryan turned and stepped over to the porch railing. He swung a leg over it and sat down as he pulled out his cigarette.

He lit up. In the distance he heard a dog barking.

'I just talked to the mayor,' Councilman Lewis said from the doorway.

Ryan remained seated on the railing.

'He said I should answer your questions,' Lewis said in disbelief.

Ryan shrugged. He flipped his cigarette off into the front yard and stood up.

'I think we'd be more comfortable out here,' Lewis said, quickly sliding through the doorway and firmly closing the door behind him.

Ryan went back to the railing. He glanced over at the window and saw the little boy peering out at him. He winked again.

Before the boy could respond, two pairs of hands whisked him away.

'What exactly is it that you wanted to ask me?'

Ryan turned to face him.

The councilman stood in front of the door. His hand still gripped the door knob.

'Nothing much, I was just interested in the upcoming vote.'

'Who are you?'

'A friend.'

'Of whom?' Lewis peered at him.

'Maybe yours.' Ryan raised his eyes to the other man's.

'I don't need any more friends, Mr Ryan. I have more than enough,' Lewis said pompously.

Ryan snorted.

'Is that supposed to mean something?' Lewis asked.

'Let's cut the shit, Lewis,' Ryan said in annoyance. 'Just tell me about your endorsement.'

'What's to tell?'

'Why?'

'Excuse me?'

'Why did you decide to endorse the mall? According to the mayor, up until six months ago you were backing him all the way.'

'I changed my mind,' Lewis said self-righteously, turning away from Ryan's glance. 'There were economical considerations that I hadn't fully taken into account.'

'Like what?'

'Well, for instance, the tax base the project would offer

the city. It was something I hadn't completely understood until I re-examined the issue.'

'You didn't think of that before?'

'Not in any cognizant manner,' Lewis said self-importantly.

Ryan eyed him speculatively.

Growing uncomfortable beneath the biker's gaze, Lewis said, 'There's nothing wrong with reconsidering a matter of this importance.'

'That's right.' Ryan nodded. 'Something like this could mean big bucks to everyone involved.'

'Is that supposed to mean something?' Lewis quickly responded.

'I don't know, Jeffrey. Does it?'

'I think I'm done speaking with you.'

'Fine with me.' Ryan shrugged.

After a last searching glance, Lewis turned for the door.

'The mayor seemed to think that someone might have changed your mind for you,' Ryan said conversationally.

'Well, that isn't the case. It was the facts and figures that ultimately dictated my change of mind,' Lewis said, opening the door.

'Nothing else?'

'No, Mr Ryan, nothing else.' Lewis grinned, then turned away.

'That your son, Lewis?' Ryan asked.

The councilman whirled around to face him.

'Looks like a nice kid,' Ryan continued, then let his gaze travel appreciatively over the house. 'Nice home you have here.' He could feel the councilman's eyes searching his own.

'The mayor said something else.' Ryan paused to pull another cigarette. He examined it carefully before he fitted it between his lips.

'Yes,' Lewis prompted. 'What did he say?'

'He said that, if it came to it, he didn't think you could be bought.' Ryan raised his gaze to the man before him.

Lewis smiled tightly. 'Well, he's absolutely right.'

'But he did say you seemed to have one weakness,' Ryan said. He pulled a match and lit his cigarette. He inhaled, looking at the other man intently.

'Women, Jeffrey. He seemed to think that you had a problem in that direction.'

'I don't know what the hell you're talking about,' Lewis whispered vehemently.

Ryan noticed he had closed the door again.

'I've got a home, a family, and a career. I wouldn't jeopardize any of that for some minor fling.'

'That's what the mayor said.'

'Well, he's right.'

'But you see, Jeffrey, that's where it kind of makes sense.'

'What makes sense?' Lewis demanded.

'The woman.'

'There isn't any woman,' the councilman insisted. He glanced nervously behind him, then turned back to Ryan.

'You want to tell me about her?'

'There's nothing to tell.'

341

'Then you wouldn't mind if I look into this a little deeper, would you?'

'Who the hell are you to think that you can come into my house and make these accusations? You have no authority here at all, and I'm going to make damn sure that you pay for this, regardless of the mayor or anyone else,' Lewis threatened.

Ryan smiled at him. He ashed his cigarette.

'I'll bet you,' he said casually, 'if I look into this, I could find out a whole lot about you in a pretty short time.'

Ryan paused to examine the other man. His gaze traveled disdainfully over the politician before him.

'You don't know what it is, Jeffrey, to have me in your life.'

'I'm not going to listen any more of this,' the councilman said, without making any further move toward the house.

'It's up to you.' Ryan stood and ground out his cigarette on the councilman's porch. 'But I'm going to tell you something, Councilman. A friend of mine got hurt today.'

Ryan leveled his gaze on the other man. He took a step towards him.

'And if I find out you had anything to do with it, your life is fucking bones, man. You understand me.'

'You can't—' Lewis sputtered.

'I can do whatever the fuck I want, Lewis. Because I don't have one goddamn thing to lose.' Then Ryan turned away.

He walked along the sidewalk, feeling the councilman's eyes on his back. It wasn't until he reached his bike that he heard the door close behind him.

Twenty-Eight

'What the hell do you mean, he's looking into it?' Ellroy exploded.

'It makes sense, Tom,' the mayor calmly responded.

'Bullshit. It doesn't make any sense.' Ellroy paused, staring incredulously at the man before him. 'What the hell were you thinking? This guy is trouble. And there's a damn good possibility he's involved in what's going on.'

'I don't think so.' Mayor Presley shook his head thoughtfully. He glanced over at the detective. They were standing beside the mayor's car in the city parking lot.

'I think he might be able to help us out.'

'How the hell is he going to do that?' Ellroy growled.

'Tom, the guy can help,' the mayor said patiently.

'Just how the hell do you figure that?'

'He knows Howard, and he's not involved with any of this. He doesn't have—'

'How do you *know* he's not involved?'

'He told me.' Mayor Presley shrugged.

'He told you,' Ellroy repeated in disbelief.

'Yes, and I believe him.'

'Jesus Christ.' Ellroy shook his head in disgust. He

turned away. 'Maybe I should just go over and deputize him. Make him an honorary policeman for the city.'

'Tom, will you please listen to me.'

'No.' Ellroy turned back, shaking his head. 'You haven't said anything worth listening to.'

'Did you know that Howard was being blackmailed?' the mayor asked abruptly.

Ellroy whirled around.

'Yes.' The mayor nodded. 'That's what Ryan told me. Someone's got some tapes on him that would make his life a little unpleasant. According to Ryan, there isn't anything on the tapes that's criminal, but it's close enough to be more than a little embarrassing for Howard, which is something he can't really afford right now.'

'Ryan told you this?'

'Yes, and he also told me that's what the meeting at the beach was all about. There was supposed to be an exchange.'

'The tapes for what?' Ellroy asked quickly.

'The tapes for the deed to all the mall property.'

'No way would Howard give that up.'

'That's why his son's in the hospital,' the mayor said dryly.

'What else did Ryan tell you?'

'He thinks Leland's dead.'

'What!'

'Howard told him that Leland was the only one who could have made the tapes. And the first time Howard got a call on it, the call was made from Leland's house.'

'That's why Ryan was there that night.'

'Right.'

Ellroy leaned back thoughtfully against the hood of his car. 'What about the woman?'

'A set-up against Howard.'

'And Sawyer?'

'Same thing against me,' the mayor said, then paused to let the detective digest this information. 'Ryan figures there's a third party working both sides against the middle. He thinks, once the dust clears, that this third party is planning on stepping in to pick everything up.' The mayor paused to examine the detective, then added, 'That sound familiar to you?'

Ellroy glanced at him sharply.

'That's almost exactly the same thing you told me this morning.' The mayor hurried on before the detective could respond. 'All he's doing is helping, Tom, and he has information that we don't. He's inside Howard's house.'

'But how do you know you can trust him?'

'There's no reason not to.' The mayor shrugged.

'How do you know that?'

The mayor glanced away. He sighed wearily, then turned back to the detective. 'I don't,' he said softly. 'But I don't see how I have anything to lose.'

'Where were you?'

'Around.' Ryan turned to see Jane step into his room.

'Where?'

'How's Ricky?' Ryan asked, avoiding her question.

'He's fine.' Jane moved closer. She hesitated, then reached out for him.

Ryan held her. He felt her body press against his. He closed his eyes – and for a moment saw the ghost of another face drift before him. He shrugged away from the image.

'Dad's been locked up in his office all night,' Jane said into his shoulder. She pulled back to examine him. 'Where were you?'

'Talking to some people.' Ryan stepped out of her embrace. He moved over to the window and pulled a cigarette.

'Who?'

'The mayor.'

'You talked to the mayor?'

'Yeah.' Ryan smiled.

'You're moving in some pretty fast circles,' she said wryly.

Ryan shrugged and lit his cigarette.

'What did he say?'

'Not much. He doesn't seem to know any more about this than your father does.'

'Maybe he knows more than he's saying.' Jane stepped over and sat on the edge of the bed. She leaned back and smiled.

Ryan went over and sat beside her. 'I don't think so. I think he's as confused as everyone else is.'

Jane shrugged. She rested her hand against the back of his neck.

'He gave me a couple of names.'

Jane shook her head in disbelief.

'What?' Ryan asked, turning to her.

'I just can't believe the mayor would talk to you.'

'He's worried.'

'Whose name did he give you?'

'Lewis and...' Ryan paused as Jane suddenly froze. He turned to look at her.

She quickly glanced away, then stood up and moved over to the window. Ryan examined her closely.

'What other names did he give you?' she asked quietly.

Ryan caught sight of her reflection in the dark glass.

'Jane?'

'What?'

Ryan started to speak, then stopped.

Jane slowly turned to face him. She held his eyes for only an instant before she looked away.

'Lewis?' Ryan said incredulously.

'It's not what you think,' Jane said softly, shaking her head as she walked across the room toward him.

Ryan rose to his feet.

Jane halted a step in front of him. Her glance rose to his, searching his face.

'That's why he endorsed your father.' Ryan sighed wearily.

'Ryan, please listen to me.' She reached out to grip his arms, forcing him to face her. 'It wasn't like that. It was—'

'What, Jane. Tell me what it *was* like?' Ryan said tiredly.

She shook her head in frustration. 'It didn't start out that way. It was just something to do, and then suddenly it got all involved in the endorsement.'

'Your father knew, didn't he?' Ryan asked quietly.

Jane turned to look at him, then glanced away as her eyes met his.

Ryan turned to the door.

'What are you going to do?'

'I want to talk to your father.'

'Don't, Ryan. Please, just leave him alone. Leave all of it alone. None of it has to matter,' she pleaded.

'All of it matters, Jane. Don't you know that by now.' Ryan said, then opened the door.

He found Howard sitting at his desk, staring out at the back yard. The office was dimly lit by a small lamp on the sideboard.

Ryan stepped over to the sidetable and poured himself a drink.

'Richard is going to be all right.' Thomas said quietly, without turning.

Ryan hit his drink. He refilled it, then stepped over to the edge of Howard's desk. He examined the man carefully before he raised his glass again.

'He's coming home tomorrow morning.'

'Good,' Ryan grunted. Then, pushing away a sheath of papers, he sat on the edge of the desk.

'I've got your word for the day, Thomas,' Ryan said harshly.

Howard turned to face him.

'It's pimp,' Ryan spat out.

'What are you—?'

'I talked to Lewis tonight,' Ryan interrupted.

Thomas looked away. He turned back to the window.

'So what?' he said, staring intently out at the darkness.

Ryan reached over and grabbed Thomas's chair. He twisted it around, forcing Thomas to face him.

'You've had quite a week, haven't you, Howard. You pimped off your daughter, then you stood by and watched your son get his arm broken. What's next? You planning on burning down the family home?' Ryan jeered.

'I don't know what you're talking about,' Howard said anxiously, struggling to get to his feet.

Disdainfully, Ryan shoved him back into his chair. He lifted his drink, eyeing the other man contemptuously.

'You know, riding up here, I listened to Ricky talk about you for better than a couple of hundred miles. You remember Ricky?' Ryan leaned over the older man. 'He's the kid with the broken arm. Your son – remember him?' Ryan snarled.

'I didn't know that was going to happen,' Thomas said helplessly. 'I didn't really think they would go that far.'

'Who the fuck are they, Thomas?' Ryan demanded.

'I don't know.' Thomas tried to edge away from the face before him, but Ryan pinned him to the chair and leaned into him.

'Listen, you worthless piece of shit. I don't give a fuck what happens to you, but I rode with Ricky, and he's got some justice coming. Now what the fuck is going on?' Ryan shouted.

'Ryan! That's enough.'

Ryan glanced over his shoulder to see Jane standing in the doorway.

Ignoring her, he turned back to Howard 'Tell me – *now*,' he demanded.

351

'Ryan!'

'I don't know,' Thomas whispered. 'I don't know who's doing this.'

'Bullshit,' Ryan shouted into the other man's face.

'Ryan, leave him be.' Jane rushed over and tried to pull him away from her father.

Ryan ignored her. He gripped each arm of Howard's chair and lifted it in the air. He slammed it back to the floor, then jammed his face inches away from Thomas's.

'Last time, Howard. Give me a name.'

'I don't know. I don't know who would do this,' Thomas cried.

'Ryan, please, just leave him alone.'

Ryan reached out and slapped Howard across the face.

Startled, Jane stepped back and stared at the two men before her.

Howard sobbed and raised both hands to his face.

'Who, goddamnit?' Ryan growled.

'I don't—'

Ryan hit him again.

'Ryan!' Jane screamed and launched herself at him. She fell on him, pounding his back and shoulders.

As Ryan turned to her, her nails raked the side of his face, leaving three bloody trails across his cheek.

Ryan pinned her arms to her side. He glanced down at Thomas, who sat slumped across his desk, sobbing.

Shaking his head, Ryan slowly released Jane and took a step back.

Her arm immediately rose and slapped him across the face.

'Get out,' she screamed. 'Get out of here, and don't you ever come back.' She darted to her father's side.

Ryan picked up his drink and finished it, then started for the door.

'Christian. Talk to Christian.'

Ryan turned to meet Jane's eyes.

'Go ahead, you son of bitch. Talk to him if you want, but just leave us alone from now on,' she said, glaring fiercely.

Ryan turned as she bent over her father and took him in her arms.

A moment later Jane heard the sound of Ryan's motorcycle firing up. She listened to it race up the drive and turn on to the highway. She heard it rapidly kick through the gears as it sped away into the night.

He was in a canoe on one of the canals leading back into the Everglades. Neal was in the bow, excited at the prospect of seeing his first alligator.

'Where are they all?' he complained, glancing back at Ryan in frustration.

'They're here.' Ryan smiled. 'You just have to look for them.'

'Where?'

'Over there,' Ryan suddenly said, spotting the tip of the snout and the two eyes, just barely breaking the water line.

Neal whirled around in excitement. His momentum upset the precarious balance of the canoe. For one moment, Ryan thought they might still be okay. But then, the next moment, Neal screamed, 'I see it,' and started to rise.

The canoe dipped to its side; water rushed over the edge. Neal made one frantic grab for the side of the canoe before he toppled into the brackish water. His terrified scream echoed in the torpid air.

Ryan quickly went after him.

'Where is it?' Neal yelled, twisting in horror in the water, trying to spot the alligator.

'It's okay, Neal. Hang on. I've got you,' Ryan said, grabbing his little brother's hand and hauling him back into the canoe.

Huddled in the boat, both arms wrapped around his knees and chest, Neal cried hysterically.

Ryan put an arm around his brother's shoulders and hugged him.

'It's okay,' he promised softly. 'I wouldn't ever let anything happen to you,' he said, feeling his younger brother's arm reach out and desperately cling to him...

For a moment the image was right there before him. It faded, and in its place was the sight of Ricky lying in his hospital bed.

The kid was curled up awkwardly on his side. His arm stretched painfully above him.

Ryan stood in the corner of the dark room, looking over toward him. He kept seeing that other face, that one that had eventually grown so cold and distant, and had left him with nothing but memories of what had once been. Or of what could have been, if he'd been able to keep his word.

Ryan turned and stepped out into the silent hallway. He moved quickly to the elevator and stepped inside. Turning to hit the lobby button, he caught sight of a nurse's startled glance.

Before the door's closed, he saw her hand dart for the telephone.

Ryan got off on the second floor and took the stairs down to the basement. He walked into the laundry room and found an exit door leading out to one side of the hospital.

Five minutes later he was standing beside his motorcycle. He lit a cigarette and stared up at the dark windows of the hospital.

He remembered Neal, and remembered all the promises he had made and never been able to keep.

Ryan suddenly flashed on the image of the kid's face as the two men had cornered him in his bunk. That hopeless expression of desperation that Ryan had once known so well.

He pushed the memories away. He flicked his cigarette off to the side, and swung his leg over the bike. He hit the starter and raced out of the lot.

By the time he hit the highway, he was topping fifth gear. He felt the cold lake wind cut through him, until its chill became as much a part of him as the bike he gripped in his hands.

'Let's give him a call.' Christian smiled across the room at his brother-in-law.

Caldwell grinned and reached for the phone. Christian leaned forward to hear the conversation.

'May I speak to Thomas Howard, please?' Caldwell politely requested.

Christian heard a murmured reply, but couldn't make out the words.

'Oh, I'm so sorry to hear that, but this is rather important,' Caldwell said, then listened for a moment longer.

Christian leaned forward to replenish John's drink. Caldwell winked at him.

'It's about a possible land transaction,' Caldwell said slyly, then a moment later looked over at Christian in surprise.

He held the phone out and replaced it.

'She hung up on me,' he said in astonishment.

'What did she say?'

'She said there had been a family emergency.' Caldwell hesitated, looking innocently at Christian. 'I wonder what *that* could have been?'

'Call her back?'

'Let's give her a moment to think about it.'

'Sometimes I think you enjoy this too much,' Christian said, eyeing his brother-in-law speculatively.

'And you don't?'

'No.' Christian shook his head. 'I only enjoy the results.'

'Well,' Caldwell grinned, 'that's what makes us such a perfect team.' He picked up his glass and strode over to the window.

Christian leaned back thoughtfully. He'd long been well aware of his brother-in-law's propensity for violence, but so far he'd always been able to control him. The incident this morning with Richard Howard worried him. He knew that losing control of John – at this point in the game – could cost them everything.

'How's Lynn?' Christian asked.

'Fine. I saw her just the other day.'

'She still the same?'

'Yes,' John said, turning to meet Christian's gaze.

Christian glanced away from the coldness he saw in his brother-in-law's eyes. It wasn't the first time, nor would it be the last, he knew.

'Try them again.' Christian gestured toward the phone.

A moment later he glanced over at John, who was still standing by the window. 'What is it?' he asked curiously.

John ignored him. He leaned forward and pulled back the curtain, staring intently out at the street.

'John?'

'I think we're going to have a visitor,' Caldwell said, glancing slyly over his shoulder.

'Who?'

'If I'm not mistaken, it's someone on a motorcycle.'

Christian suddenly became aware of the roar of a motorcycle coming down the block. He listened as the sound of the engine suddenly died in front of his house.

'Now, I wonder who that could be?' Caldwell smiled in anticipation as he turned to meet his brother-in-law's gaze.

Caldwell turned back to the window, and watched as Ryan climbed off his bike and started up the drive.

Christian stepped up beside him.

Caldwell turned to him. He smiled, then whispered happily, 'Let's kill him,' and waited impatiently for his brother-in-law to respond.

Twenty-Nine

'I'm—'

'Mr Ryan,' Councilman Christian Huntington completed, then, after an appraising glance, motioned Ryan inside.

Ryan stepped into a small hallway, then followed the councilman into the living room.

'Please, have a seat.' Christian waited for Ryan to be seated before he offered him a drink.

Ryan took the proffered glass of Daniels, then leaned back against the couch. He looked speculatively at the other man seated across from him.

'You're probably wondering how I knew who you were?' Christian said, toying with his brandy snifter.

'Thought had crossed my mind.'

'It's a small town, Mr Ryan. It's hard to keep anything a secret for very long.'

'You think so?' Ryan asked pointedly, then added, 'Seems as if there's quite a few secrets in your town, Mr Huntington.'

'Christian, please,' the councilman insisted.

Ryan nodded and lifted his drink. He glanced around the living room.

'Actually, I heard that you were staying with the Howards,' Christian said.

'Yeah, I've been there for a few days.'

'Some trouble down south with Howard's son, wasn't it?'

'Something like that.' Ryan shrugged. 'You seem to know a lot about me.'

'As I said, it is a small town.' Christian smiled dismissively. His gaze suddenly sobered. 'What exactly is it that you want, Mr Ryan?'

Ryan's gaze fixed on the other man. 'The mayor asked me to stop by.'

'Charlie?' Christian asked in surprise.

'Yes.' Ryan smiled. 'Charlie.' He paused, examining the other man closely. 'He was interested in your endorsement.'

'I've already talked to Charlie about this. We're in complete agreement.'

'That's one of the reasons I stopped by. Charlie,' Ryan said carefully, 'thought it might be better if you were to come out with your endorsement a little earlier than you had originally planned.'

'Why didn't he simply call me himself?' Christian asked.

Ryan shrugged. 'I don't know. That's something you'd have to ask him. I'm just a messenger boy.'

Christian smiled. 'I think you're underestimating yourself, Mr Ryan.'

'Think so?'

'Yes.' Christian nodded. 'I do.'

Ryan glanced away. His gaze traveled around the room and stopped at a partially opened door.

'Well, why don't you tell Charlie that I'll give him a call tomorrow morning about the endorsement.'

'You could call him now.'

'Much too late for that.' Christian rose and stepped over to the bar. He topped his drink, then glanced over at Ryan.

Ryan nodded and held up his glass.

As Christian measured out the drink, Ryan said, 'You hear about Howard's son?'

'No, what happened?' Christian said easily.

'Seems he broke his arm this morning.'

'I'm sorry to hear that.' Christian replaced the bottle of Jack Daniels and moved back to his chair.

'Was it bad?'

'No, not too bad. He'll be out of the hospital tomorrow morning.'

'That's good to hear.' Christian nodded. 'I don't really know him that well, but I hate to hear something like that.'

'Like what?'

'Accidents,' Christian said carefully. 'Sometimes they're so unnecessary.'

'Oh, I don't know,' Ryan responded thoughtfully. 'Sometimes they just can't be avoided.'

'Could Richard's have been avoided?'

Ryan glanced over to catch Christian's gaze. It was right there waiting for him.

'I don't know, but it's not one that's going to be forgotten.'

After a moment, Christian smiled and leaned back. He

rested one arm along the arm of the chair and looked over at Ryan.

'Was there anything else?'

'Yes, there was.'

'And what was that?'

Ryan crouched forward. 'It's about your endorsement.' Ryan smiled disarmingly.

Christian nodded for him to continue.

'Just exactly who are you planning on endorsing?'

Christian laughed. Then, shaking his head in amusement, he said, 'Why, Charlie, of course. Who else would I endorse?'

'I don't know. That's why I asked.'

'Dumb question, Mr Ryan,' Christian said softly.

'Maybe.' Ryan shrugged. He reached for a cigarette. He took his time lighting it.

Exhaling a stream of smoke, he looked across the room at the other man.

'You know, Christian...' Ryan hesitated. He glanced dismissively around the room, then brought his gaze back to Christian. He examined him disdainfully. 'I don't like you, and that's no big deal, because I don't much like too many people.'

Ryan stood. He stepped in front of the councilman and looked down at him. 'But I find out you fucked around with Ricky, and I'm going to make your life one miserable place to live.' Ryan crouched forward. 'You understand me?'

Christian met the biker's gaze. 'I think it's time you left, Mr Ryan. You've delivered your message,' Christian said coldly.

Ryan snorted. He finished his drink, then put the empty glass on the table. He dropped his cigarette into the glass, then turned and strode across the room to the door.

As the biker stepped out of the house, Caldwell pushed opened the partially opened door and stepped into the room.

'Touchy asshole, isn't he?' he commented casually, then walked over to the window and peered out.

Caldwell watched as Ryan swung a leg over his cycle. The biker paused for a moment to look back at the house, then turned and hit the starter. The engine roared to life.

Caldwell glanced over his shoulder at his brother-in-law.

'Kill him,' Christian said, meeting the other's eye.

Caldwell grinned and quickly started for the front door.

Christian moved over to the window. He saw Ryan's tail-lights disappear around the corner. A moment later he saw his brother-in-law's car pull away from mid-block and take off after him.

He stepped back to the couch and stood there thoughtfully, trying to understand the instant antipathy he had felt for the biker.

One glance at him, and Christian had immediately known that Mr Ryan was trouble. Ryan wasn't interested in the finer points of the evidential process. The only justice that concerned him would be the kind that he could dispense himself.

Christian suddenly smiled at the thought of how easily dispensable Ryan had become.

* * *

Caldwell kept a few blocks behind the motorcycle. He followed it through the residential streets, out to the main highway leading eastward. At this time of night there were few other cars on the road, which suited Caldwell just fine.

As they approached the first intersection leading off to the downtown area, Caldwell pulled up within half a block of the motorcycle.

He followed the bike through the blinking yellow lights to the last intersection before the lake.

As the biker approached the turn-off at the light, Caldwell hit the accelerator and rushed up to the left side of the cycle. He came up fast on Ryan's side, forcing him to swerve out of the way and continue towards the lake.

Caldwell grinned as he caught sight of Ryan's furious glance beneath the spray of his headlights.

Ryan jerked the bike out of the way of the oncoming car. The rear wheel slipped, then suddenly caught and shot the bike forward.

Ryan started to pull over to the side. He immediately hit the throttle when he heard the sound of the car racing towards him again.

He surged forward, hearing the sound of the engine behind him. He crouched over the steering wheel and threw a glance over his shoulder.

The car was only yards behind him and closing fast.

Ryan threw his weight to the side and swerved to the right. Ahead of him was the final turn-off to the lake. He accelerated and hit the turn with the car only inches behind.

Trailing his foot across the surface of the pavement,

Ryan leaned into the bike and came out of the turn, shooting toward the other side of the road.

He heard the blare of the car's horn behind him. He struggled with the bike, until he managed to regain his balance. Leaning forward, the bike shot down the small incline towards the foot of Lake Michigan.

The car raced after him.

Ryan glanced at the road ahead of him, desperately looking for a way out of the path of the oncoming car. There was nothing in front of him but a straight-away paralleling the lake. On the turns, he knew he could take the car. But on a straight run, the car would eat him alive.

Ryan hit the throttle and crouched forward until he was almost parallel to the bike.

The cycle shot along the straight-away.

The car edged up behind him.

Ryan glanced over his shoulder. The headlights blinded him. The horn suddenly blared, cutting through the silence of the night.

The car shot forward and nudged his rear fender.

The cycle wobbled dangerously toward the shoulder.

Frantically, Ryan tried to ease it back on to the road.

He heard the roar of the car, then a moment later the headlights washed over him again.

The car hit his rear wheel.

He felt the wheel lock beneath the fender of the car. There was the smell of burnt rubber, then an instant later the cycle jerked sideways.

Ryan felt it going.

He threw his weight to the side, trying to pull it back to

the road. For an instant he almost had it, and then the footstand kicked the pavement and threw the weight of the bike to the other side.

Ryan rode it down.

As the bike began to slide out, Ryan swung his leg over the tank. He crouched over the falling bike, hanging on to the handlebars and balancing himself on the gas tank.

The bike skidded across the pavement, leaving a trail of sparks in its wake.

It crashed into the shoulder and smashed against the embankment.

The momentum threw Ryan into the air. He twisted, trying to regain a semblance of balance. He was dimly aware of the road rising up to meet him. He tried to roll into the fall, but the ground thudded into his chest. It slammed into him and sent him skidding across its surface, and into the darkness waiting for him.

Caldwell pulled over and parked.

After a five-minute wait he climbed out of his car and cautiously approached the motorcycle.

It lay on its side on the shoulder of the road, in a tangle of twisted metal. The acrid stench of gasoline rose from the debris.

Caldwell nudged it thoughtfully with his foot, then stepped around it and walked over to Ryan.

The biker was spread out motionless across the ground.

Caldwell slowly approached him. He paused a step away from him, then lifted his foot and brought it down on the biker's outflung hand. He ground his heel into the back of Ryan's hand, examining him closely.

Satisfied that he wasn't going to be any trouble, Caldwell crouched on his heels beside the body and turned him over.

He was still alive.

One side of Ryan's face was scraped and bleeding. There was a deep cut above his right eye. A stream of blood dripped across his cheek.

Caldwell, almost gently, touched his forefinger to the eye. He pulled his hand back to examine the blood. He smeared it thoughtfully between his forefinger and thumb, trying to decide what to do next.

After a moment, Caldwell glanced over at the lake and smiled. It was only yards away from the road.

Caldwell stood up, then bent over and grabbed Ryan's arms. He began to drag him across the pavement towards the dark waters of Lake Michigan.

After the fire, after the death of their mother, and after Ryan had been released from jail, the three of them moved into an apartment in town.

His father quit drinking. He began attending AA meetings.

Neal no longer spoke to him. The few times Ryan tried to talk to him, Neal's face would once again twist into that same expression of horror and fear he had seen on the day of the fire. Only now, Ryan had come to understand where the horror was directed.

Ryan left home that same summer.

He packed a duffel bag with his few belongings, and took his life savings of seventy-six dollars and headed west.

He was fifteen years old.
No one ever came to look for him.
No one had ever found him until Zella.

Ryan heard the sound of the water. For a moment he thought he was somewhere else.

'Neal,' he gasped, then felt the water closing around his head.

He opened his eyes, but there was only the cold wet darkness before him.

He tried to move, but his arms and legs were stiff and unyielding.

His lungs heaved and, before he could stop himself he drew the water into his throat.

His chest spasmed, and he felt a bright burst of pain rip through the muscles of his chest.

Suddenly he was out of the water.

Coughing, feeling the water spraying out before him in huge painful gasps, he could dimly see the dark reflection of the lake before him.

'Drink some more,' the voice gently encouraged.

And it was then that Ryan felt the hand, forcing his head beneath the surface again.

He struggled against the grip, but his body felt lethargic and unresponsive.

The water rose around him. Its cold bit into the bones of his face. He felt its fiery lick on his eyes and cheeks.

He thrashed beneath the surface, trying to find air.

Caldwell grinned in anticipation and held him beneath the water.

As Ryan's movements slowed, Caldwell abruptly lifted him by the hair. He crouched to the side of him, with one knee set in the center of Ryan's back, pinning him to the sand. He listened to Ryan's sodden lungs, heaving against the frigid liquid, struggling to draw in oxygen.

The hand shoved him back beneath the surface. Ryan felt the darkness moving around him. It whispered to him, and for a moment he saw all of its promises: Neal, Zella, all of them waiting for him, calling to him. He wanted to reach out, to draw them to him, but suddenly the hand jerked him back into the cold night air.

His lungs convulsed, and he retched spastically.

'Just a little longer,' the voice cooed gently.

Ryan shook his head, trying to clear it.

He felt the hand shoving him back beneath the surface.

He felt the weight shift against his back. And for a moment, watching the water rise up to meet him, he wanted it. He wanted to let himself go into the darkness.

'Let it go,' the voice urged.

Ryan closed his eyes. A kaleidoscope of images flashed before him. Ricky, Neal, Zella, and finally Jane.

The water closed around him.

'No,' Ryan screamed, and shoved himself backwards.

The sudden movement dislodged Caldwell. He fell to the ground, then quickly scrambled to his feet.

Ryan struggled to his knees. His lungs heaving, he forced himself to rise. Shaking his head, he tried to focus on the man before him.

'You're awake,' the man said conversationally.

Ryan grunted and stumbled back. His knees threatened

to buckle. He locked them stiffly in place and looked at the man before him.

'Actually,' Caldwell said slyly. 'I was hoping you might be a little more fun. I was getting bored.'

Caldwell suddenly lashed out with his fist.

The blow caught Ryan on the lips. Staggering back, he felt blood begin to flow from his mouth.

Caldwell followed patiently, eyeing him hungrily.

Ryan felt the pavement beneath his boots. He tried to plant his feet, but Caldwell threw another punch.

The blow caught him on the cheek and whipped him to the side. He managed to just barely maintain his balance.

He turned to face the man in front of him, struggling to raise his hands.

'Time to play.' Caldwell smiled, then threw another fist at Ryan's head.

Ryan staggered, rather than moved, out of the way of the blow.

Caldwell shook his head in amusement. 'Let's see how many times I can hit you before you fall down.' He grinned, then lazily reached up and slapped Ryan across the face.

'One.'

Ryan shook his head and stepped backwards. He could smell the stench of gasoline behind him.

'Two.' Caldwell slapped him across the other side of the face.

Ryan threw a glance behind him and saw the ruins of his motorcycle.

'Three,' Caldwell said, connecting with a fist.

The blow threw Ryan backwards.

He fell against the bike. He felt something jab painfully into his back. Trying desperately to focus his thoughts, Ryan reached behind him and touched the warm chrome of the handlebars.

Caldwell stepped over and stood above him.

'This is hurting my hands. What do you say we go back to the water for a while?'

He crouched in front of the motorcycle. 'And if you're good,' he grinned excitedly, 'we can do this some more later.'

'Fuck you,' Ryan managed to spit out.

Caldwell drew back, feigning surprise. 'That's no way to talk. We're going to be good friends,' Caldwell told him.

Ryan carefully slipped his hand into his back pocket. He touched the familiar pack of cigarettes, and beside them felt the small cardboard rectangle

He locked his fingers around it, fighting against the pain.

Caldwell reached for him.

Ryan slapped the hand away, and quickly scrambled backwards over the wreckage of his motorcycle.

'Why are you making this so difficult,' Caldwell said sadly.

Ryan struggled to a sitting position and stared across the motorcycle at the other man.

Caldwell grinned back at him and took a step forward.

Ryan watched and waited.

Caldwell shrugged, then took another step toward Ryan. He paused at the side of the motorcycle.

'You're only hurting yourself,' Caldwell said, then, grinning, he began to step over the bike.

Fighting for concentration, knowing he'd only have one opportunity, Ryan whipped his hand around. He tore a cluster of matches loose, and grated them against the small, slightly damp strip of flint.

They sparked, fizzled, then suddenly burst into flame.

Ryan threw the match at the motorcycle as the man brought his foot down on the other side.

Ryan flung himself backwards as the gas ignited.

He heard a high-pitched scream, then an instant later heard the gas tank explode. Burning embers flew across his back and shoulders.

Ryan rolled in the dirt, and looked up to see the man's burning figure stumbling towards the lake.

Ryan knelt at the edge of the lake. Behind him, the charred handlebars of his motorcycle jutted up in grotesque silhouette from the dwindling flames.

He shook his head and glanced down at the figure sprawled before him. The man's face was blackened and blistered. His lips had peeled back so that his teeth gleamed palely in the darkness.

The man suddenly heaved convulsively. His hand rose and twisted at the front of Ryan's shirt.

'Kill me,' the man gasped hoarsely, struggling to rise.

Ryan crouched over him, until his face was only inches away. He could smell the greasy stench of the man's burns.

'Not a fucking chance,' Ryan snarled. 'You're going to look like the freak you are.'

Ryan pushed himself to his feet. He staggered down the

road until he came to the breakwater. At the foot of the concrete embankment, he found a pay phone.

Ryan sagged against the booth and dug out a coin. Taking a deep breath, he picked up the receiver and dialed.

'He's ruined everything,' Thomas said softly.

Jane turned to look at her father. She was standing beside him at the door to his room.

'He's trying to destroy us. Look at what he's done so far.' Her father's eyes sought hers.

'What? What has he done, Dad?'

'He's turned you all against me.'

'What are you talking about?' She reached out.

Thomas shrugged away from her hand. 'Look at what he did to Richard. He's just a boy. If he hadn't...'

'Hadn't what, Dad?' Jane said. She tried to hold his eyes, but her father looked away.

He shook his head without responding.

'Ryan didn't do anything,' Jane said softly.

'Then who did?' Thomas turned to face her.

This time it was Jane who glanced away.

'You're not blaming me, are you?' he said incredulously. 'It's all his fault. I've seen the way you look at him,' he accused.

Jane shook her head wearily and stepped away.

'See,' Thomas cried. 'You're *all* against me. He did that – Ryan. He's the one who turned you against your own flesh and blood.'

Jane paused. She felt the anger rising. She struggled against it.

'If he hadn't come around, none of this would have happened.'

'What wouldn't have happened, Dad?' Jane suddenly demanded. She whirled around to confront her father.

Startled, Howard took a step back.

'I wouldn't have had to sleep with Lewis to make sure you got your vote, or maybe Ricky wouldn't have had to have his arm broken. What about that, Dad?' Jane threw at him. 'You think Ryan did that? And what about when Ricky was in jail. Where were you then? It was Ryan who took care of him. You would have just left him there,' she finished, glaring at him across the hallway.

'It wasn't my fault. It was all his,' Thomas replied, shaking his head helplessly.

'No, it wasn't. It's all been your fault, Dad. Everything right from the start of this whole mess,' Jane said wearily, then abruptly turned and strode off down the hall.

'Jane?' she heard her father call out.

She slammed the door of her room and stalked over to the window. She leaned against the cold glass, staring out at the back yard.

'Ryan,' she whispered, then closed her eyes.

Thirty

Detective Ellroy pulled into the mayor's drive at eight forty-six. He parked in front of the garage and wearily leaned back against his seat, feeling exhausted. He'd been called out late last night when the burned remains of a motorcycle had been discovered on the lake front. A few yards away, at the edge of the water, a man had been found. With third-degree burns covering two thirds of his body, he had barely been alive. He'd been rushed to the hospital. Identification, at that point, had been impossible.

Arriving on the scene, Ellroy had taken one look at the motorcycle and felt sure that the burned man was Ryan. It had surprised him when he'd finally received news from the hospital that not only was the casualty alive, but that he had also been identified as John Caldwell.

Receiving this news, Ellroy had immediately put out an APB on Edward Ryan. So far no one had been able to locate the man.

Wanting nothing else than to crawl home and into bed, Ellroy had gotten a call from the mayor, asking him to stop by before he checked out. Reluctantly, Ellroy had agreed.

Sighing tiredly, Ellroy opened his eyes, then pushed himself out of his car. He shook his head, trying to clear it, then started up the drive to the mayor's front door.

'You look terrible,' the mayor greeted him.

Ellroy was too tired to be diplomatic. He grunted and followed the mayor into the dining room.

'Coffee?'

'Yeah, sounds good.' Ellroy settled back in his chair, thinking that if he closed his eyes he'd never be able to open them again.

'What'd you find out so far?' the mayor called from the kitchen.

Ellroy took a deep breath before he responded. 'We identified the guy. It was John Caldwell.'

'Of Caldwell Construction?'

'Yeah.'

'That's Christian's brother-in-law.'

'Right,' Ellroy agreed, turning as the mayor stepped into the room with two cups of coffee. He placed one in front of Ellroy.

Gratefully, Ellroy wrapped his hands around it.

'Can I get you something to eat?'

Ellroy shook his head and lifted his coffee cup.

'You sure, Tom?'

'No, I'm fine.' Ellroy sighed.

'Have you talked to Christian yet?'

'No, we haven't been able to find either him or Ryan.'

The mayor smiled – then hid his smile in his coffee cup.

Ellroy was too tired to wonder about it.

'How is Caldwell doing?'

'They don't know yet.' Ellroy shrugged. 'It's going to be touch and go for the next twenty-four hours.'

'Can he talk?'

'No.'

'So where's that leave you?' the mayor asked, leaning back in his chair to examine the detective.

'I don't know.' Ellroy ran a hand across his eyes. 'I'm too tired to think straight right now.'

'Well, just give me a quick run-down.'

'I think it looks like Caldwell and Ryan got together, and Ryan was the only one who walked away,' Ellroy said, then glanced over at the mayor.

The mayor smiled thoughtfully.

His smile mystified Ellroy. It didn't make any sense to him.

'What exactly is so amusing?' Ellroy looked across the table at the other man.

Before the mayor could respond, Ellroy heard the sound of footsteps coming from the living room. He glanced over his shoulder and suddenly froze.

Standing in the doorway to the dining room was Ryan himself. He wore a pair of ragged jeans and a white sweatshirt. The clean sweatshirt made a sharp contrast to the soiled jeans.

He had a line of dried blood over his right eye, and his lips and one cheek were bruised and swollen.

Ryan nodded casually to the detective and limped over to the table. He sat at the head of the table and glanced over at the mayor.

'Coffee looks pretty good, Charlie. Think you could spare another cup?'

Ellroy stared in astonishment as the mayor grinned back at the biker and answered, 'Sure can, Eddie. No problem.'

'How you doing?' Ryan turned to the detective.

'What the fuck is going on?' Ellroy gasped.

He wasn't at all pleased when his question was answered by the sound of the mayor's laughter.

Christian moved nervously around the room. He stepped over to the window and glanced out at the back yard, then moved over to the sidetable. He examined the bottles longingly, wondering if it was really too early for a drink.

He decided against one, realizing that it was important that he keep his thinking straight. It was still possible to come out of this on top. In truth, Christian now realized, he had always thought of his brother-in-law as an expendable part of this operation, though he would have liked to keep him around for a little while longer. But in the long run, Christian decided, the loss of John Caldwell shouldn't make that much of a difference. Christian still had the tapes, and Howard was still there for the taking. The only real change in his plans was that Christian would be forced to take a more active role. He hadn't wanted to do that. But, after carefully going over everything he'd accomplished so far, he still felt it was a viable plan. The tapes would ensure Howard's silence, and there was no connection, other than the familial one, between himself and Caldwell.

Of course there would be an investigation, but Christian had been very careful about his meetings with John. He was positive there wasn't anything that could publicly link the two of them together.

The thing to do now, Christian had realized an hour before, was to proceed with the plan as quickly as possible. Speed was essential. He needed to shore up all the loose ends before a full-scale investigation could be mounted.

Christian knew that, once that happened, there would be no way he could close the deal with Howard before the vote took place. And it was essential that Christian establish control of the mall property before the results of that vote were counted. Howard would have nothing to lose if he had the town behind him. Embarrassment, Christian realized, was not a deciding factor in anyone's quest for the million-dollar deal.

He stepped over and sat behind the desk, then leaned back and stared thoughtfully up at the ceiling. He went over various ways the conversation might go, until he felt sure he had every eventuality covered.

He smiled softly, then straightened his shoulders. He reached into his side pocket and pulled out the gun, then gently laid it on top of the desk.

Councilman Christian Huntington swiveled his chair around and looked out the back window, and waited.

Jane pushed Ricky's wheelchair along the hallway, while Thomas anxiously walked alongside of his son.

'I feel fine.' Ricky smiled, twisting to look at his sister.

'Well, you're still supposed to take it easy for a while,' she sternly reminded him.

Ricky rolled his eyes and glanced over at his father.

Thomas smiled hesitantly, and nodded his head in agreement.

'You okay, Dad?'

'Fine, fine, Richard. Just happy to get you out of here,' Howard quickly replied.

There was a nervous energy about him that worried Ricky.

'Here we are,' Jane said, stopping the wheelchair at the door.

Ricky started to rise.

Howard quickly moved to help him. Ricky felt his father's arm come around his shoulders. For a moment his glance met his sister's.

'You got him, Dad?'

'Yes, I've got him.' Howard smiled, then carefully helped his son down the front steps to the car.

Ricky felt the tension in his father's arm. He glanced over at him inquisitively. 'Dad?'

'Yes, Richard?'

'You sure you're all right?'

'I'm fine.' Thomas laughed shrilly. 'I'm just happy that you're coming home.'

'I am, too, Dad,' Ricky said softly, then blushed and glanced away.

His father eased him into the back seat, then raced around to the driver's side. Before Jane had completely closed her door, he'd already started to pull away from the curb.

'Things are going to be different from now on, Richard. Just you wait and see,' Thomas said enthusiastically, catching his son's eye in the mirror. He tapped his fingers on the top of the steering wheel.

Ricky tore his gaze away from his father. 'Where's Ryan?' he asked.

'Why do you want to know?' Howard abruptly demanded.

Ricky shrugged sheepishly. 'I was just wondering where he was, is all.'

'Well, he's not here. Does that answer your question?'

Ricky caught his father's glare in the rear-view mirror. 'Yeah, it's no big deal.' He shrugged.

'Good. Because it's about time we started acting like a family again. Don't you think so, Jane?'

'Yes, Father,' Jane replied noncommittally.

'*Yes, Father*,' Howard mimicked cruelly. 'Do you hear that, Richard? Your sister can be so cold sometimes. I don't know where that comes from. Maybe it's from your mother, because there certainly wasn't any of that on the Howard side of the family.

'Ahh, here we are.' He turned through the wrought-iron gates into the drive.

Thomas quickly jumped out of the car to help his son.

Jane walked a few feet behind as her father and brother made their way up to the house.

Inside, Howard abruptly hugged his son. He pulled back to examine the boy, then smiled and said, 'You just wait, Richard. Everything is going to be just fine from now on.' He broke away and turned to Jane.

'Jane, why don't you help your brother up the stairs. I want to make a few calls, and then I'll be right up to join you.'

'Sure, Dad.' Jane stepped over to her brother's side.

'It's okay, sis. I can make it on my own.'

'Don't be silly, Richard. We don't want to take any chances, do we?' Thomas chuckled.

Jane put her arm around Ricky's shoulders and they started up the stairs.

'I'll be up in a few moments,' Howard reminded them. Then, humming nervously, he turned and stepped into his office.

'What's going on?' Ricky asked softly.

'I don't know.'

'Where'd Ryan go?' Ricky asked a moment later.

Jane shook her head as she helped her brother into his room.

'Where'd he go?' Ricky asked again, once he was propped up on his bed.

'I don't know.' She turned and started for the door.

'Did something happen, Jane?'

'Yes, something happened,' Jane answered, then quickly glanced away. Without turning, she added, 'I'll tell you about it in a minute. Let me check on Dad first.'

'What *happened*?' she heard Ricky call, as she started down the stairs towards her father's office.

Without knocking, she stepped through the door.

Her father stood frozen in the center of the room, staring at his desk.

Seated behind the desk, smiling at her, was Christian Huntington.

His easy smile made the gun he pointed in her direction all the more difficult to comprehend.

'So nice of you to join us, Jane,' Christian said conversationally, and waved her inside. 'Close the door behind you, please?' he added politely.

Jane shut the door and turned.

'Now, why don't you step over here beside your father, and you can witness this little transaction we were just about to complete.' He turned his gaze back to Howard.

'Now where were we, Thomas?' Christian grinned.

'Tell me again.' Ellroy sighed wearily, rubbing a hand across his eyes, trying to focus his thoughts. He was still thrown slightly off balance by the discovery of Ryan in the mayor's house.

Ryan leaned back and lit another cigarette. 'Caldwell tried to do me.'

'And you think it was Christian that put him up to it?'

'Hell, I *know* it was Christian that put him up to it.'

'Why?'

'Christian was the last person I saw before Caldwell made his run at me.'

'That doesn't prove anything.' Ellroy shook his head. He glanced over to see the mayor eyeing him speculatively.

'What?' he asked.

'You're overlooking the obvious, Tom. Christian stood to make a great deal of money out of this project.'

'Yeah, I know,' Ellroy said patiently. 'You've already

pointed that out. But I don't see how Christian goes from being an upstanding city councilman to a stone psychopath in just a matter of weeks.'

'I don't think that's the way it worked out. I have a feeling that this is something that Christian's been planning for a long time.'

'Why do you think that?' Ellroy reached for his coffee. He took a sip, then winced at the taste of the cold liquid.

Noticing his expression, the mayor pushed the coffee pot over to him.

As Ellroy refilled his cup, Ryan held his own empty cup out. Ellroy glanced at him and caught an almost imperceptible smile. It only served to increase his irritation.

'C'mon, Tom, you're being purposely obtuse,' the mayor said in annoyance. 'Christian's brother-in-law already had the highway contract for the mall. He came in at a ridiculously low bid. I remember wondering at the time how he could possibly expect to make a profit. Well, now I know. He wasn't planning on making a profit. The profit wouldn't have happened until after he and Christian had a lock on the rest of the property. Then they could have set any price they wanted to, and the city would have to pay.'

'But how would that have helped them with Howard?'

'Because then they would have been *inside* the process. Once there, they could find out what everyone else was doing, or what they planned on doing. Once they had that, they had everything. They could take steps to counter anyone who tried to make a move on them.'

Ellroy nodded tiredly. He leaned back in his chair and looked over at Ryan. 'Tell me some more about last night.'

'C'mon.' Ryan groaned. 'How many times you want me to go through this?'

'Humor me,' Ellroy replied, holding his gaze.

After a moment, Ryan shrugged. 'Caldwell came at me with his car. By the time I knew what was happening, it was too late. Next thing I knew he had me in the water.'

'See, that's what I don't understand. Why the water?'

'He liked it,' Ryan said softly. 'It was a game with him.' He hit his cigarette, then carefully stubbed it out. He raised his eyes to the detective's. 'You remember the woman – what happened to her?'

After a moment, Ellroy nodded, flashing on the butchered body of the woman spread across the bed.

'He liked hurting people,' Ryan said quietly.

Ellroy shook away from the image. He reached for his coffee, then glanced speculatively at the mayor.

'Just what exactly do you expect me to do now?'

'Well . . .' Mayor Presley nodded to Ryan. 'Eddie's got a suggestion.'

'Eddie?'

'Yeah.' Ryan grinned. 'Eddie.'

Shaking his head in disgust, Ellroy stared at the biker. 'What?'

Ryan smiled wryly. 'I'd like you to give me a ride over to Howard's place, so I can get my stuff. And then, if it isn't too much trouble, I'd like you to take me down to the train station.'

'Hey, no trouble at all,' Ellroy said sarcastically. 'I'd love to do that for you. Maybe, while we're at it, you could hit a bank or two on the way out of town, just so you have some spending money on your way home.'

'Detective!' the mayor said sharply, halting Ellroy's mounting tirade.

Ellroy turned to him.

'It won't serve any purpose to keep Ryan in town. He'll only confuse an already complicated issue. I think it would be in everyone's best interests, Mr Ryan's included, to have him quietly disappear.'

'And what about Caldwell?'

'Write it off.'

'And Christian?'

'I don't think Christian's stupid enough to have left anything lying around, but if he has, I would certainly like you to find it.'

'And if he hasn't?'

'Well,' the mayor leaned back and smiled, 'I'm sure there's other ways we can make Christian's life extremely unpleasant.'

Ellroy glanced over as Ryan eased himself into the front seat. He caught the other's man wince as he closed the door.

'You okay?' Ellroy asked gruffly.

'Yeah,' Ryan grunted.

'You should get that checked out.' Ellroy nodded at Ryan's leg.

'Just a strain. It'll go away.' Ryan pulled out his cigarettes.

'You know, I don't like this one damn bit.'

'Yeah,' Ryan turned to look at him, 'I can understand that.'

Ellroy glanced over at him.

'It's pretty raw,' Ryan added, then lit his cigarette. He cracked open the window.

'What about Christian?' Ellroy asked a few moments later. He didn't have to explain what he meant.

Ryan shrugged. 'It's no big thing with me. Caldwell was the one who did Ricky.'

Eyeing him curiously, Ellroy said, 'You don't let much go, do you?'

Ryan turned to meet the detective's gaze. An instant later he nodded. 'Neither do you.'

Ellroy grunted and glanced back at the road. He turned into the Howards' drive and parked in front.

Ryan reached for the door, then paused to look inquisitively at the detective.

'Nah, I think I'll just sit this one out. I have a feeling I'll be seeing quite a bit of the Howards over the next few days.'

Ryan opened the door and stepped out. He limped over to the side door and opened it.

Ellroy watched him. He leaned back and closed his eyes, as Ryan stepped into the house. Within moments he was asleep.

Ryan started for the stairs, then stopped as he heard voices coming from Thomas's office. He hesitated a moment, then turned and stepped into the office.

He stopped abruptly as Christian smiled at him, and pointed a gun at his chest.

'Mr Ryan.' Christian nodded happily. 'Now we're all here. Isn't that nice.'

Ryan quickly glanced around the room. Howard and Jane were standing before the desk. Christian sat behind it with the gun now trained between the three of them.

'The door, please.' Christian gestured with the gun.

Ryan turned and closed the door.

'Now, why don't you step over this way and join your friends.'

Ryan moved to Jane's side. He caught Howard's glare as she reached out to touch his hand.

'Isn't that nice, Thomas? They make such a good-looking couple, don't you think?' Christian said, noticing the gesture of affection.

'What do you want?' Howard demanded angrily.

'Oh, Thomas, I thought we had already agreed on that, before Mr Ryan decided to join us,' Christian said conversationally.

He reached out with his left hand, and pushed the contract to the other side of the desk.

'Just sign right there where I made that little X, and everything will go away.'

'And if I don't?' Thomas challenged.

'Well.' Christian grinned. 'Then things could get a touch unpleasant.'

'Just sign the damn thing, Howard,' Ryan said disgustedly.

Thomas turned to glare fiercely at the biker. 'Why don't you just stay out of my business? You've been nothing but trouble since you arrived.'

Surprised by his outburst, Ryan simply stared at him.

'You've disrupted my whole family. If it weren't for you, none of this would have happened. I would be more than—'

'Now, now, Thomas. Let's not allow family squabbles to interfere with our business,' Christian admonished.

Howard turned to the councilman. 'I refuse to sign,' he said defiantly, glaring across his desk at him.

Christian's smile disappeared. He leveled his gaze first on the other man, then slowly turned to examine Jane.

After a thoughtful moment, he rose and moved around the desk. He gestured Ryan and Thomas back, and stepped in front of her. His smile returning, he ran the barrel of the gun along Jane's neck, down between her breasts.

'Christian.' Ryan warned.

Christian glanced at him curiously, then turned to Howard. 'How odd that it should be him rather than you that objects, don't you think, Thomas?'

'Leave her alone,' Howard said.

'A little late, I think, Thomas. Mr Ryan has much better timing. Don't you agree, Jane?' Christian taunted, slipping the barrel of the gun beneath the top button of her blouse. He jerked it towards him. The button came free and skittered across the floor.

'You fucking touch her and I'm going to hurt you.'

Christian paused to look at Ryan. He suddenly laughed, then shook his head in amusement. 'You know, I actually think you mean it.'

'Try me.' Ryan challenged.

'You forget, Mr Ryan, that I have the gun.'

'And you forget that I'll take that fucking thing away from you and jam it up your ass sideways.'

'Mr Ryan,' Christian said, feigning offense. 'There's a lady present.'

'Fuck you, Christian,' Jane spat out.

'Both of you?' He glanced at the two of them, then looked over at Howard. 'He seems to have had rather an unseemly influence on your daughter, Thomas. If I were you, I'd do something about that.' Christian suddenly became serious as he eyed the older man. 'Now sign the contract, Thomas.'

'No.'

'Thomas, sign it, or I'm going to put a bullet through your daughter's left kneecap.' Christian lowered the barrel of the gun until it was leveled at Jane's leg.

'Sign the fucking thing, Howard,' Ryan growled.

'No.' Howard glared back.

'Sign it, Thomas,' Christian warned.

'No! I won't do it. You understand, don't you, Jane?' Thomas pleaded.

Jane looked at her father in disbelief.

'I guess she doesn't.' Christian shrugged, then centered the gun on Jane's knee.

'Thomas?' Ryan snarled.

'No, I won't do it,' Howard screamed.

Christian glanced over at him. 'You really are something, Thomas.' He said, almost admiringly, then turned back to Jane.

Ryan looked back at Christian. He could see the determination in the other man's eyes.

Steeling himself, Ryan took a step forward.

'Don't,' Christian warned softly, noticing the biker's move. 'This doesn't concern you.'

'Let it go, Christian.'

'I'm afraid I can't do that.'

Ryan took another step.

'You'll never make it, Mr Ryan.'

Ryan shrugged. 'Neither will you.' He edged forward.

Christian snorted disdainfully, then quickly leveled the gun at Jane's head.

'Now what, Ryan?' he taunted.

Ryan took another step.

'Don't, I'm warning you. I'll shoot.'

'I'm coming for you, Christian.'

Christian turned the gun on Ryan.

'Ryan!' Jane cried, glancing desperately over her shoulder at her father.

Howard screamed and suddenly launched himself at Christian.

Before Christian could turn, Howard smashed into the other man. They toppled back against the desk.

Ryan threw himself at the two struggling men. As he charged passed Jane, he shoved her roughly to one side.

A shot exploded in the silence of the room.

Ryan fell on top of Howard, and tried to pull him away to get at Christian. The older man slid limply to the floor.

'Dad?' Jane cried, scrambling across the room to her father's side.

Christian crashed a knee into Ryan's ribs.

Ryan felt something splinter inside of him. He ignored it, and desperately gripped the hand that held the gun.

Christian slammed his knee up again, but Ryan twisted out of the way. His momentum flung both of them to the floor. They rolled across the room until they smashed against the sideboard.

Christian grunted as Ryan slammed the top of his head into his chin.

Ryan felt him weaken, and quickly jerked at the hand holding the gun. The gun flew out of Christian's grip and slid across the room.

Ryan heaved himself to his side and launched a fist at Christian's face.

The councilman ducked, avoiding most of the punch, but it still caught him on the shoulder and threw him back against the sideboard. For a moment the blow stunned him.

Ryan fell on him, crashing fists continually into his stomach and face.

He suddenly felt hands tearing at his back.

'Ryan, that's enough,' he dimly heard Jane's voice calling, and he slumped to the floor.

Ellroy jerked awake. For a moment he looked around in confusion. He yawned, then stretched and glanced at his watch. He had no idea how long he'd been out. He looked up at the house, then back at his watch. He figured he'd give Ryan another five minutes, and then he'd go inside to fetch him.

Satisfied with this plan, Ellroy cracked open the window

to let some air inside the car, then slumped back in his seat and closed his eyes again.

Ricky heard the sound of the shot. He quickly scrambled out of bed and down the stairs.

Rounding the office door, he froze as he saw Ryan standing beside the desk with his sister kneeling in front of him.

Ricky's gaze traveled to his sister.

Sprawled out on the floor beside her, was his father.

Ricky slowly raised his eyes to Ryan's.

Ryan shrugged, then shook his head sadly.

'What happened?' Ricky screamed.

'He's dead,' Jane cried, then turned back to her father.

Ricky's gaze shifted to Ryan. Beside him, on the top of the desk, was a gun. He glanced at it, then back at Ryan.

'What did you do?' Ricky gasped.

He took a step into the room. 'How could you...?'

Ryan's gaze locked on the boy's. He was unable to break away from the kid's stare.

Ricky took another step toward the desk. His gaze held a combination of horror and fear.

'How could you do that? How could you do that to my father?' Ricky asked helplessly.

He stepped over beside the desk, glaring at Ryan.

Ryan saw the boy's glance dart towards the gun.

For a moment Ryan started to reach for it. Then, sighing wearily, he stepped away from the desk.

Ricky grabbed the gun and turned to Ryan.

'You shouldn't have done that. You shouldn't have ever . . .' Ricky hesitated.

He raised the gun and pointed it at Ryan.

'Ricky!' Jane screamed.

'Neal?' Ryan whispered softly, then, raising his arms, took a step towards the boy.

Ricky shot him.

Ryan felt himself spinning backwards. The floor rushed up to meet him. He felt the blackness moving around him, calling to him.

'Ryan,' he heard Jane's cry, and suddenly saw her bending over him. 'Ryan, please,' she sobbed.

Neal, Ryan thought, and saw the boy turn and run out of the office.

'Ryan, please hang on,' Jane cried, scrambling for the phone.

'Jane,' Ryan grunted.

'Ryan, what – what is it?' She turned back to him frantically.

'The gun.' Ryan nodded weakly towards the gun.

Jane shook her head in confusion.

'Give me,' Ryan grunted, feeling the weakness moving through him, carrying with it a tide of darkness that was slowly easing him away.

'What do you . . . ?

'Give it to me,' Ryan demanded hoarsely. 'Put it in my hand.'

Wiping at the sudden flood of tears, Jane grabbed the gun and put it in Ryan's hand.

Ryan forced his fingers to close around the handle.

'This is what...' Ryan coughed. He felt something tear inside his chest. 'Happened,' he gasped.

And Jane bent over him to listen.

Ellroy scrambled out of the car and ran up the drive. He charged across the lawn towards the front door, pulling out his revolver.

As he reached the door, it suddenly burst open and the kid came running out. Ellroy shoved him out of the way, and raced through the entrance.

He paused in the hallway and glanced around. He saw a body sprawled across the front of the office floor.

Crouching to one side of the door, Ellroy took a deep breath, then threw himself through the doorway with his revolver stretched out before him.

He slowly lowered the gun as he saw the three bodies splayed across the room.

In the corner was Christian, his face battered to a pulp.

Alongside of the desk was Howard. The back of his head seeped blood on to the oak flooring.

Beside him was Jane, sobbing, as she crouched over the limp body of Edward Ryan.

Thirty-One

Two weeks later, Detective Ellroy disgustedly slammed a newspaper across his desk. The headline read: MAYOR WINS MALL DENIAL.

The story went on to describe the two-to-one margin that turned back the vote for the mall. Pictured above the article was the mayor shaking hands with the city's newest councilman, Donald Alder.

Ellroy snorted in disbelief. He pushed the paper aside and glanced at the police report below it.

It was a report of the shooting that had taken place at Howard's. Of the four people in the room, only one was left to give testimony.

Jane Howard was the name signed at the bottom of the report.

The report stated simply that Howard had been confronted with a gun by Councilman Christian Huntington. In the ensuing struggle for the weapon, both Edward Ryan and Thomas Howard had been shot. Before being shot, Edward Ryan had been able to subdue the councilman.

A broken jaw and twenty-five stitches seemed like a hell of a lot of subduing to Ellroy. But there was no one around who seemed at all interested in hearing Ellroy's objections.

In Jane's version of the incident there was no mention of her brother's involvement. Ellroy knew that there was more to it all, but no one seemed willing to pursue things further.

The mayor had been perfectly happy with the way everything had worked out. Christian was out on bail and awaiting trial. His brother-in-law, John Caldwell, had died two days after being admitted to hospital. He had never regained consciousness.

Ellroy snorted in irritation. He picked up the report and carried it over to his file cabinet. He filed the report, then returned to his desk.

He leaned back and stared up thoughtfully at the ceiling. He figured he had another year to go before he could pop the pin. He wouldn't be eligible for full benefits, but it would be more than enough to keep him going, he thought wearily, glancing down at the front page of the newspaper.

A moment later, Ellroy crumpled it up and threw it in the wastebasket.

Thirty-Two

Three weeks after the shooting, Ricky stood nervously on the front steps of the hospital. He glanced up as he saw the wheelchair come through the elevator doors.

He quickly stepped up to the front doors and held them open as the wheelchair approached.

'You're on you're own now.' The nurse smiled.

Ryan grinned back at her, then pushed himself out of the chair.

He stretched, trying to ease the stiffness, then turned to look at the kid.

'Ryan, I'm really . . .' Ricky started hesitantly.

'Hey, it's no big thing.' Ryan reached into his pocket for a cigarette.

'But—'

'Here,' Ryan gently interrupted, handing him the pack.

Gratefully, Ricky took the cigarettes and pulled one out.

'How's the arm?'

'It's okay. I get the cast off in two weeks,' Ricky responded, pulling a pack of matches from his back pocket.

Aware of Ryan's eyes, Ricky used one hand to bend a match out and light it. He casually offered it to Ryan.

Ryan grinned and bent over the light.

'C'mon. The car's right over there.' Ricky gestured to the parking lot.

Ryan followed, limping slightly.

'The leg okay?' Ricky asked anxiously, as they approached the car.

'Yeah, it's still a little stiff, but it'll be all right once I start moving around.'

'What about ... ?' Ricky paused, then nodded at Ryan's chest.

'It's fine, kid, just let it go.' Ryan glanced away and hit his cigarette.

Ricky nodded and ducked around to the driver's door. Ryan climbed in and watched as he easily started the car with one hand and pulled out of the lot.

'You're getting pretty good at that,' Ryan said admiringly.

'It's easy.' Ricky shrugged modestly.

Ryan hid his smile behind his cigarette. He glanced out the window, then turned back to the kid. 'Where we going?'

'I want to stop by the house first,' Ricky said quickly.

Ryan sighed.

'It'll just be for a minute,' Ricky promised, then pulled into the drive. He parked in front of the garage and stepped out.

He moved around to the front of the car, and waited impatiently for Ryan to climb out.

'What's going on, kid?' Ryan asked, looking at the boy closely.

'Well, you know, I wanted to thank you for everything.'

'Hey, it was no big deal, kid. Forget it.' Ryan waved him off.

Ricky met his gaze, then, smiling, turned and opened the garage door.

Parked in the center of the garage, was a Harley Davidson Sportster.

Ryan stared appreciatively at the bike. 'Nice one,' he said, turning to the kid. 'But you'd better wait until you get both arms working, before you take it out.'

Ricky grinned and shook his head. 'It's not mine.'

'Jane?' Ryan said incredulously.

Ricky shook his head again and looked at him pointedly. 'Hey, kid, you didn't . . . ?'

'It's yours, Ryan.' Ricky paused. He glanced away, and added. 'The key's in it, and the papers are all in back.'

'Kid, you shouldn't have done this,' Ryan said, stepping over to the bike.

He ran his hands lightly along the gleaming chrome. He crouched before it, eyeing it admiringly.

'It's no big thing,' Ricky said.

Ryan turned to look at him.

'Ride hard, Ryan.' Ricky smiled, then turned and started up the drive.

At the doorway he paused to look back.

Grinning widely, Ryan nodded to him.

Ricky waved and stepped into the house.

Ryan turned back to the bike. He was just reaching for the key when he turned to see Jane leaning against the doorframe of the garage.

'Do you like it?' She nodded toward the bike.

'It's too much. You shouldn't have done this,' Ryan said, noticing that she was wearing the same outfit she had worn the last time they had ridden together.

'It wasn't up to me. It was Ricky who decided. He wanted to get you something to let you know how much he appreciates everything you've done.'

'It wasn't that much, Jane,' Ryan said, then a moment later softly added, 'And ultimately it wasn't enough.'

Jane stepped over to him. She reached out to touch his shoulder.

'It was more than enough, Ryan,' she said quietly. She raised her hand to his face.

After a moment, she turned away.

Smiling brightly, she turned back to him and nodded at the bike. 'Do I get a ride, or are you just going to take off on me?'

'No.' Ryan smiled. 'You get the first.'

'What about the last?' Jane asked softly, raising her eyes to his.

Ryan glanced away, then turned back to her. 'You're going to be cold.' He nodded to her clothes.

'No, I won't.' Jane shook her head, but kept her eyes fixed on his.

A moment later she turned away and climbed on the back of the bike.

Ryan slid into the seat and felt her hands lock tightly around his waist. He started it up and slowly wheeled out of the drive. He eased up through the gears, and they rode out towards the northern edge of town.

Fall had stripped the trees of all their leaves, and the branches stretched darkly into the blue sky. The fields had been turned and were waiting patiently for the first snowfall.

Jane pressed her face against his back, and held on tightly as Ryan slowed and turned back towards the house. He wheeled in and circled the drive. Without cutting the engine, he pulled up and stopped at the side door.

Reluctantly, Jane climbed off and stood beside him.

Ryan glanced up at the side of the house. He saw Ricky standing at a window, looking down at him.

The kid slowly raised his hand and waved.

For a moment, Ryan flashed on the face of his brother. He saw Neal smiling down at him – then, after a brief nod, saw him turn away and disappear from sight.

Shaking his head, he turned back to Jane.

'You know, you don't have to go,' she said softly.

'Yeah, I do.'

'Why?'

'There's just too much, Jane.'

'Too much what?'

Ryan shrugged helplessly. He held her gaze, feeling her eyes move inside of him.

'Just too much,' he said sadly, then turned and reached for the clutch.

Jane leaned against the doorframe. She heard the pitch of the engine change, and closed her eyes.

When she opened them again, he was gone.

Thirty-Three

Eleven hours later, and six hundred miles south, Ryan stood over the grave site.

With snow dusting his head and shoulders, he crouched stiffly before the gravestone and stared down at it.

For a moment, another face threatened to intrude on his memories.

Shaken, he pushed it away, then reached out and gently traced the name etched into the face of the granite.

'Zella,' he whispered, and closed his eyes.

More Thrilling Fiction from Headline Feature

DANGEROUS ATTACHMENTS

A silent watcher in the dark . . .

Sarah Lovett

Psychologist Sylvia Strange is called to New Mexico's male prison to evaluate a convicted murderer seeking parole. But, after deciding that Lucas Watson is seriously disturbed, she cannot recommend his release.

That's where her nightmare begins . . .

Watson is the son of an influential politician, and soon Sylvia finds herself exposed to personal harassment. At first she reckons that Lucas himself is somehow responsible – so when he is dramatically removed from the scene, surely her life will return to normal?

Except it doesn't.

All around her, events spin out of control. Her good friend Rosie, prison investigator, has to cope with a mythical inmate called 'the jackal' who hideously amputates body parts from other human beings – both dead and alive . . . A professional associate is bludgeoned to death in his bath tub . . . And Sylvia finds herself reluctantly attracted to a brash police officer.

As she struggles with her investigations through the bitter cold of a desert winter, a shocking tale of family secrets, obscene murder and diabolic obsession unfolds.

FICTION / THRILLER 0 7472 4616 5

More Compelling Fiction from Headline Feature

JOHN T. LESCROART

HARD EVIDENCE

'A GRIPPING COURTROOM DRAMA . . .
COMPELLING, CREDIBLE' *Publishers Weekly*

'Compulsively readable, a dense and involving saga of big-city crime and punishment' *San Francisco Chronicle*

Assistant D.A. Dismas Hardy has seen too much of life outside a courtroom to know that the truth isn't always as simple as it should be. Which is why some of his ultra-ambitious colleagues don't rate his prosecuting instincts as highly as their own. So when he finds himself on the trail of a murdered Silicon Valley billionaire he seizes the opportunity to emerge from beneath a mountain of minor cases and make the case his own. Before long he is prosecuting San Francisco's biggest murder trial, the accused a quiet, self-contained Japanese call girl with an impressive list of prominent clients. A woman Hardy has a sneaking, sinking suspicion might just be innocent . . .

'Turowesque, with the plot bouncing effortlessly between the courtroom and the intraoffice battle among prosecutors . . . The writing is excellent and the dialogue crackles' *Booklist*

'A blockbuster courtroom drama . . . As in *Presumed Innocent*, the courtroom battles are so keen that you almost forget there's a mystery, too. But Lescroart's laid-back, soft-shoe approach to legal intrigue is all his own' *Kirkus*

'John Lescroart is a terrific writer and this is one terrific book' Jonathan Kellerman

'An intricate plot, a great locale, wonderfully colourful characters and taut courtroom drama . . . Highly recommended' *Library Journal*

'Breathtaking' *Los Angeles Times*

FICTION / THRILLER 0 7472 4332 8

More Thrilling Fiction from Headline Feature

ABOVE THE EARTH,
BELOW THE EARTH,
THERE'S NO DEATH MORE HORRIFYING

Gary Gottesfeld

ILL WIND

When a massive earthquake uncovers a large
Indian graveyard in Beverly Hills, forensic expert
Wilhelm Van Deer – known as 'the Dutchman' –
is confronted by more bones than he can cope
with. But he soon realises that some of the remains
are not as old as they should be, nor the manner of
death as straightforward as first appears.

Digging deeper, he comes across weird
underground passages and strange paintings of
giant centipedes. Somehow these discoveries are
linked to mysterious deaths that occurred over
twenty years earlier, but there are powerful
anonymous people now determined to keep their
dark secrets buried for ever.

When the chilling murders begin anew, the
Dutchman sets out to catch a maniac – an elusive
psychopath obsessed with a grotesquely unusual
method of killing . . .

FICTION / THRILLER 0 7472 4168 6

More Thrilling Fiction from Headline Feature

John Peyton Cooke

TORSO

'AMONG THE BEST NOVELS EVER WRITTEN ABOUT A TRUE CRIME'
Colin Wilson

A BREATHTAKING PSYCHO-CHILLER OF MURDER AND PERVERSION

There are a lot of people who might want to kill a punk like Eddie Andrassy. He could be the target of just about anybody – rival pimps, gangsters, narcotics suppliers or even a jealous spouse. Which still does not explain why his once-handsome body has been reduced to a headless and sickeningly mutilated stump.

Eddie is the first victim of the Cleveland Torso Slayer – at least as far as homicide detective Hank 'Lucky' Lambert can tell. However, he's certainly not the last. As the number of grotesquely dismembered corpses increases Hank, under mounting political and personal pressure, knows with horrible certainty that his luck has finally begun to run out . . .

'A powerful and atmospheric recreation of one of the most gruesome serial murders in American criminal history' Colin Wilson

'A slick, pungent reconstruction of the true case of the Cleveland Killer' *Time Out*

FICTION / THRILLER 0 7472 4193 7

A selection of bestsellers from Headline

BODY OF A CRIME	Michael C. Eberhardt	£5.99	☐
TESTIMONY	Craig A. Lewis	£5.99	☐
LIFE PENALTY	Joy Fielding	£5.99	☐
SLAYGROUND	Philip Caveney	£5.99	☐
BURN OUT	Alan Scholefield	£4.99	☐
SPECIAL VICTIMS	Nick Gaitano	£4.99	☐
DESPERATE MEASURES	David Morrell	£5.99	☐
JUDGMENT HOUR	Stephen Smoke	£5.99	☐
DEEP PURSUIT	Geoffrey Norman	£4.99	☐
THE CHIMNEY SWEEPER	John Peyton Cooke	£4.99	☐
TRAP DOOR	Deanie Francis Mills	£5.99	☐
VANISHING ACT	Thomas Perry	£4.99	☐

All Headline books are available at your local bookshop or newsagent, or can be ordered direct from the publisher. Just tick the titles you want and fill in the form below. Prices and availability subject to change without notice.

Headline Book Publishing, Cash Sales Department, Bookpoint, 39 Milton Park, Abingdon, OXON, OX14 4TD, UK. If you have a credit card you may order by telephone – 01235 400400.

Please enclose a cheque or postal order made payable to Bookpoint Ltd to the value of the cover price and allow the following for postage and packing:

UK & BFPO: £1.00 for the first book, 50p for the second book and 30p for each additional book ordered up to a maximum charge of £3.00.

OVERSEAS & EIRE: £2.00 for the first book, £1.00 for the second book and 50p for each additional book.

Name ....

Address ....

....

....

If you would prefer to pay by credit card, please complete:
Please debit my Visa/Access/Diner's Card/American Express (delete as applicable) card no:

Signature .... Expiry Date ....